PUNISHED IN PINK

Pain was very much in the nature of Dr Tarquin Rodd's fast-track course for lazy girls, as each one knew, when she signed for a term of rigorous tuition, to propel her to university. Rigorous tuition meant traditional English discipline: the cane, whose absence led to the modern generation of slobs and slackers, according to Dr Rodd. Yet he never administered punishment himself, indeed was rarely seen at all, preferring to remain a shadowy and menacing background presence. Prefects ruled, with the cane-loving, but ineffectual Miss Persephone Hurt as vice-principal. Knowledge, taught Dr Rodd, must be beaten into young English ladies, by a stern mistress, who knew how smutty, lazy and defiant modern girls really were.

By the same author:

BELLE SUBMISSION
BELINDA BARES UP
CAGED!
CHERRI CHASTISED
CONFESSIONS OF AN ENGLISH SLAVE
THE CORRECTION OF AN ESSEX MAID
THE GOVERNESS ABROAD
THE GOVERNESS OF ST AGATHA'S
THE HOUSE OF MALDONA
THE ISLAND OF MALDONA
THE CASTLE OF MALDONA
THE DISCIPLINE OF NURSE RIDING
GIRL GOVERNESS
LACING LISBETH
LICKED CLEAN
MISS RATAN'S LESSON
NURSES ENSLAVED!
PEEPING AT PAMELA
POLICE LADIES
PRIVATE MEMOIRS OF A KENTISH HEAD-
MISTRESS
SANDRA'S NEW SCHOOL
SKIN SLAVE
SOLDIER GIRLS
SCHOOL FOR STINGERS
THE SCHOOLING OF STELLA
THE SMARTING OF SELINA
THE SUBMISSION OF STELLA
THE TAMING OF TRUDI
THE ENGLISH VICE

PUNISHED IN PINK

Yolanda Celbridge

This book is a work of fiction.
In real life, make sure you practise safe, sane and
consensual sex.

First published in 2005 by
Nexus
Thames Wharf Studios
Rainville Road
London W6 9HA

www.nexus-books.co.uk

Typeset by TW Typesetting, Plymouth, Devon

Printed and bound in Great Britain by Clays Ltd, St Ives PLC

ISBN 0 352 34003 7

The Random House Group Limited supports The Forest Stewardship
Council (FSC®), the leading international forest certification organisation.
Our books carrying the FSC label are printed on FSC® certified paper.
FSC is the only forest certification scheme endorsed by the leading
environmental organisations, including Greenpeace. Our
paper procurement policy can be found at
www.randomhouse.co.uk/environment

Contents

You'll notice that we have introduced a set of symbols onto our book jackets, so that you can tell at a glance what fetishes each of our brand new novels contains. Here's the key – enjoy!

 cp (traditional)

 cp (modern)

 spanking

 restraint/bondage

 rope bondage/hojojutsu

 latex/rubber/leather/enclosure

 fem dom

 willing captivity

 medical

 period setting

 uniforms

 sex rituals

1

Upper Crust

Caning on the buttocks is a punishment as old as crime. It's quick, clean, more shocking than painful, and a girl hasn't the right stuff, unless she has a few dainty bum weals to show for it. That is what Candace Crupper assured herself, as she sat, heart thumping, in the tiny wooden cubicle, waiting for the door of the prefects' punishment room to open, and a summons for her beating. She was due the stiff end, for slacking. At Rodd's Academy, everything a pupil did, it seemed, was a crime. It wasn't as if you even had to be caught smoking, swearing or stealing; if a weekly report contained only two C's, then she was automatically a slacker, and caned for it. A Rodd's mot could never hope to avoid thrashings, for that was the whole point of the place.

Rodd's – of venerable Victorian provenance – was the foremost Anglo-Brazilian academy. Its Gothic pile, on the lush southern grasslands outside Porto Alegre, formed for the world generations of girls who, though resoundingly English, had often never visited their homeland. Victorian was the aspect of Rodd's: the turrets and gables, the playing fields, the arbours, the ponds and the rose beds; and Victorian were its values: the awful girly uniforms, the petty rules, the dreadful punishments, the grinding academic study and, for lowly mots, the ghastly food. Some girls were actually sent from England, their parents considering that, these days, a girl's strict education was only obtainable abroad. Girls were virgins, of course – at least, they left Rodd's no less virgin than they arrived, a fact ensured by Miss Simm's monthly 'twat peeks' – but besides, were divided into good girls and mots. How Candace hated being called a mot.

She had never been caned before, for youthful spankings and strappings didn't really count, so the penalty itself was frightening enough, but taking it from a another *girl*, no older than her own eighteen years, was added shame. At least a mere girl couldn't swish very hard, which was some consolation. She probably wouldn't want to, either; she would go easy, for girls were soft, soppy creatures, and inflicting pain wasn't in their nature. Candace desperately wanted to believe that, but the chill in the pit of her stomach said otherwise. The terrifying majesty of the cane was quite different from the intimacy of spanking, even on the bare. The cane was shaming, scornful, and designed to inflict a pain more gut-wrenching than any palm or slipper. Presenting her arse in the 'up' position, to be reddened under the panties, like some pink baboon's – what could be more humiliating to a girl?

Pain was very much in the nature of Dr Tarquin Rodd's fast-track course for lazy girls, as each one knew, when she signed for a term of rigorous tuition, to propel her to university. Rigorous tuition meant traditional English discipline: the cane, whose absence led to the modern generation of slobs and slackers, according to Dr Rodd. Yet he never administered punishment himself, indeed was rarely seen at all, preferring to remain a shadowy and menacing background presence. Prefects ruled, with the cane-loving, but ineffectual Miss Persephone Hurt as vice-principal. Knowledge, taught Dr Rodd, must be beaten into young English ladies, by a stern mistress, who knew how smutty, lazy and defiant modern girls really were.

There were petty humiliations: mature girls having to wear short skirts, and go bare-thighed, with girly fluffy white socks and buckled shoes; bowing to the prefects – senior girls, who corrected girls' bottoms. The other girls sneered knowingly at caned mots, and giggled when one walked stiffly. They *knew* she had received the 'stiff end': the awful ceremony of lifting those pleated school skirts, the peep of white knickers, all shiny and stretched over luscious full bums, and the swish, as the cane lacerated the panties cloth, with the caned girl dribbling and squeaking, her buttocks squirming, and face twisted in agony – as if she was on the receiving end of a good hard fuck. Serve the snotty bitch right. However, any schoolgirl whose bottom *had* been caned, even to crust, was obliged by pride to maintain a haughty Rodd's strut.

Study was a girl's only escape from the harshness of the prefects. Those were not just any girls, but drawling aristos, from the topmost of top drawers, who treated the young mots no better than horses, and a lot more spitefully. Candace Crupper, without a tortured toff drawl, was just a 'beastly nouveau' to these snobs. Because it was impossible to know such haughty goddesses, unless on the receiving end of their canes, they were infinitely jealous-making.

Their superb physical poise, their uncanny, mouthwatering grace, showed their superiority, especially at play. It was not unusual for a mot to burn with an undeclared 'pash' for some cruel prefect, and even commit offences on purpose, for the privilege of stretching her panties under the desired girl's cane. Of course, Candace played body games, as all girls did, but that was only natural, when there were no boys around. Wanking off, mock cat spats in the nude and hot kissing was all harmless fun – certainly not the same as a pash, or . . . or being a *lezzie*.

3

Rodd's swimming pool was reserved for the prefects' use at certain times, and it was possible, though a caning offence, to peek from the skylight. The girls goggled at the tall young prefects, as long-legged as gazelles, in one-piece swimsuits, whose contours flowed in shimmering, iridescent, pastel hues. The swimsuits swooped backless, cleaving deep and low between jiggling, half-bared breasts. The wet cloth hugged bottoms of impossibly ripe firmness, like a second skin, clinging to the coolly swaying buttock pears, their clefts perfectly outlined, arrogant in their snaking perfection. In front, their swollen quim hillocks bulged, the slit lips perfectly visible, pouting and winking beneath the thin fabric, as the girls glided on their long bare feet.

And their thighs. Candace had never glimpsed such beauty as those rippling, smooth thighs, the creamy skin of the long flanks quivering with muscle, slightly curving from the narrow waist. The tight elastic of the swimsuits bit into the bare thigh flesh, to make it swell a little, before swooping in a delicate quivering arc towards the smooth, muscled shanks, and dainty bare feet. The thighs glowed pale and powerful, beneath the tender slabs of buttock meat, both inviting and threatening any intruder to the mysteries of the quim bulges, rippling at the crotches. No accident that a lustful boy's hand strayed under a girl's skirt, to her thigh: the gateway to paradise, yet also to his enchanted submission. Candace worked hard in the gym to pump her own thighs up to rippling, luscious firmness.

Sometimes, Candace had naughty, lustful dreams, from which she awoke with her quim sopping, and aching for a wank. She felt guilty when she tweaked her clit to orgasm. In her fantasy, those girls' thighs, soft, fragrant and creamy smooth, with a dew of girl sweat, sat on her face, crushing and engulfing her in their sweet warmth. Her nose was pressed in their cleft, as they rode her, pumping up and down, squashing her in perfumed pain and pleasure. It wasn't as if she was a lezzie, or anything – how *infra dig*! – but in admiring another girl's flesh, she was really admiring her own, and girls were allowed to be narcissistic.

She trembled at the thought of touching a prefect's thigh, kissing the naked flesh, or her gorgeous, shimmering nylons, so shiny and tight, and of kneeling to worship the creamy flanks, rippling in coltish beauty. The firm bare arse globes and titties, the cooze, wet and warm and succulent: those were the treasures to which a girl's thighs were the gatekeepers, sneering in their sultry ripeness: *you must worship us, or we will crush you.* A girl's thighs were the symbol of her power. They could open, promising bliss of quim or buttock, yet snap shut, trapping her enthralled prey. How Candace wanted thighs to crush any boy who dared desire her. Kneading his trapped balls, until he whimpered for mercy.

Visions of glorious naked girl thigh milking stiff cocks faded to Candace's glum present reality. She had no gap year to hitch-hike round the world or to party on a Greek island. To come into the money from her trust fund, she *had* to get to university and *had* to get an honours law degree, in order to follow the Crupper family tradition. St Ursula's, at Belo Horizonte, and St Cecilia's, at Curitiba, had failed her, with their relaxed Brazilian discipline. Now she had to submit to the fearful, last-chance discipline of Rodd's. Torts, trusts and probates: what a bore. But a girl couldn't live without money, could she?

Candace shivered in the cubicle, wishing she had a smoke. She did not shiver from cold, although she sat, by decree, in only her frilly gym skimpies, which, she imagined, would provide modesty, if not much protection, from a cane. She wished she had company, but a miscreant had to take punishment alone, after parading in skimpies through the gloomy corridors, to the smirks and giggles of the other girls. Schoolgirls could be so cruel and punishment parade was deliberately humiliating. It came after an awful, compulsory full-body shaving by Miss Simm, the matron, after she had supervised her under a blistering cold shower. Candace shifted uncomfortably in her seat as she recalled what had happened in Matron's office.

Matron was well-tittied and full-arsed, a Scots wench, not yet thirty. She knew her allure, seductively wiggling her buttocks, unpantied, in their crisp tight skirt, slithering her sheer black nylons together, to allow a peep of firm bare thigh, frilly stocking top, and garter strap, while leaving her first two blouse buttons undone, so that her victim could see all the way to her crimson bra. Blushing, Candace stripped, revealing her bulging mons, and its jungle of pubic fronds, snaking up over her belly and dangling well below her full red cunt lips. As the matron shaved her mound, clean and powdered from the shower, it was impossible for Candace's quim not to moisten, even knowing the full-body shave was intended to be shameful and girly. Candace had to be certified fit to receive corporal punishment, after an examination, during which Matron ran her soft fingers up and down her bottom, and into her arse cleft, tickling her anus, and caressing the backs of her thighs. Licking her lips, Matron murmured that some of the crueller prefects liked caning mots there, on the thighs, since underswipes were very painful indeed.

'Ooh, that tickles,' Candace squealed, as Miss Simm's finger poked in and out of her anus. Her finger was wet with Candace's arse grease, and she put it to her lips to suck.

'I think you've been well tickled there, miss,' said Miss Simm with a chuckle. 'Most girls have. English virgins here, as is proper –' she tapped Candace's long, clamlike gash '– but party girls in their bumholes. It's the Brazilian way, isn't it?'

Candace blushed hotly. The matron's bottom waggled before Candace's eyes, smooth, without panty line, and the white cotton stretched as tight as a drum against the firm, fleshy globes. At Miss Simm's touch to her quim lips, Candace's gash was sopping wet – to her blushing mortification – but the matron pretended not to notice, except that an occasional wink, or pursed lip, gave her teasing game away. She soaped Candace's clam, as she called it, slowly and sensuously, sometimes brushing her stiffening clitty, and holding her gash flaps tight for the razor. She remarked how long and sumptuous her clam was, and opined that it would be an achievement to retain the virginity of such a tempting slit. At the strokes of the blade on her bare flesh, Candace's cunt spurted juice, and she felt a hair's breadth from coming. It was said that some bold mots did come when Matron wanked them on purpose, and sprayed cunt juice all over her hand, for her to lick up.

Miss Simm sprayed her all over with some sickly cologne, which made her quim sting, for the prefects were insistent that smelly mots for caning should offend their nostrils as little as possible. Then, her body wet and dripping, she had to don her gym skimpies, her shaven pubes and excited erect nipples quite visible through the damp fabric, and tramp through the school, with a grim, cane-wielding sub-prefect clamping her arm, all the way to the prefects' caning room. Even knowing that the giggling girls were leering at her with utter scorn, her cunt seeped juice. Maybe, she thought uneasily, it was their very cruelty which excited her.

After the humiliating punishment parade, the victim was shown by the sneering sub-prefect into one of a row of tiny cubicles, with no way of knowing if the others were occupied, and forbidden to make any sound. Locked in, she had to sit on the hard wooden slat, to wait for the door at the other end of the cubicle to open, and the summons to punishment.

* * *

7

While Candace waited, she twice heard steps, a cubicle door open, a girl's bare feet padding, and the door of the punishment room thump shut.

Girls who had been caned were forbidden to speak of their experiences, and all that Candace knew was that after two whole weeks at Rodd's, she was well due a whopping. The mots showered communally, and a caned girl, though forbidden to swank and flaunt her weals, could not stop the others gaping. The cane weals were sometimes awesome – an intricate web of bruises, all over the naked buttocks; dark, scabbed and jagged, even several days after the beating. When a girl limped back through school, after caning to crust, her white gym skirt was often wet, especially after a beating for 'vile crimes'.

Would caning be so painful that she would weep, or, despite Miss Simm's warning, just a tickling, from which she could walk away with a smile? The clock ticked ominously towards the dreaded hour. If only she could burst in and get it over with. She heard shrill laughter from the prefects' room, and the normally enticing sound chilled rather than enchanted her. For there *were* rumours. How could there not be, in a school where imperious girl prefects wore crook-handled canes strapped to their pleated skirts, swirling around their shiny nyloned thighs? Ogling mots sometimes caught a glimpse of stocking top and frilly garter strap, even a prefect's powder-blue panties, if a strong breeze twirled the girls' skirts. This feminine touch made the prefects no less terrifying.

The prefects were rumoured to be as cruel as possible to their victims, humiliating them utterly, and joking how soon it would be before a mot's caned bottom would be 'up' again, with old welts scarcely healed. They licked their lips, above her tear-stained face, assuring her what fun it was, to flog a bottom still crusted in last week's weals, and break open the lovely

8

purple bruises one by one, until the mot screamed, as her welted buttocks threshed under the cane; screaming, unless cruelly gagged with a nylon stocking, stinky with foot sweat. Candace shuddered at those vile rumours.

This first caning would be her first beating as a . . . as a big girl, and, most shamefully, it would be from some snobbish, sneering girl no older than herself. Spanking, or even the strap, from a favourite uncle led to hugs, but there were no hugs here at Rodd's. Vain, superbly icy girls – those rumours again – when brandishing their canes, became beasts of prey, and spine-chillingly cruel. Their mocking laughter, as a mot's buttocks squirmed under lashes, was the mirth of little girls picking the wings from butterflies. And the *cane* . . . the hard wood of the cane, ripping her helpless squirming panties. It was so awful and shiver-making.

Whap! Candace cringed, *sure* she had heard the whistle and smack of a cane; then girls' laughter. Whap! There it was again, or was it just the creaking of her seat? A muffled whimper . . . or the summer breeze in the palm treetops? She began to sweat, wishing *they* would get the business over with. Waiting was almost the worst pain. It was all so damned unfair. *What if they split my panties with their cane?* Candace thought, shuddering. That would be the greatest shame of all. She would have to go into town to buy new panties, while the other mots laughed at her.

Candace heard more taps and whimpers, and the sound of a mot actually crying, which she hoped was a trick of her ears. Suddenly, her exit door was unlocked, and her sub-prefect escort, hair bobbing in a ponytail, summoned her with a flick of her cane handle, her lips twisted in a sneer, as she announced her name and offence. She remembered Miss Simm's advice, to be humble, with lowered head, and hands behind the back, and never to argue or defy, or the prefects would make her punishment harder. The sub-prefect took up position at the door, presumably in case she tried to bolt.

'Poo! The mot hums like a horrid smelly boy,' drawled a girl's voice, cutting the air like a knife.

How shaming! Yet the sudden, outrageous thought made her nipples tingle.

'Shall we flog her for it?' said a second, provoking peals of mirth.

'What a super idea,' said a third. 'The thought never crossed my mind.'

'Ha! Ha!'

Candace took the opportunity of their musical, girlish laughter to look up. She saw three prefects, all waggling their yellow crook-handled canes, with their breasts heaving under their tight white blouses, as they laughed. She recognised three of the haughtiest princesses in Rodd's: Cindi Cadwallader, Fiona Dondelay and Arabella Straipe. They preened and simpered, ignoring their victim.

'Please, miss,' she blurted. 'Permission to speak?'

'Very well, worm,' said Fiona, scornfully tossing her long blonde mane.

Even for Rodd's, which admitted only girls over 180 centimetres in height, she was tall; an imperious girl, high-cheekboned, with wide, cruel lips, glossed scarlet. Her long legs were carelessly crossed beneath firm, swelling buttocks, and her pleated navy skirt draped well above her shiny, white-nyloned thighs, showing the tops of her stockings, and her frilly, powder-blue garter straps. Even a glimpse of blue prefects' panties, a bulging triangle at her cooze mound, was disdainfully granted, as if Candace's gaze was of no importance. Yet seeing those powder-blue panties and white lacy trim, against the girl's golden thigh, made Candace's clitty and nipples throb.

'Please, miss,' she said, addressing Fiona, 'I know I'm due the stiff end, and accept my punishment, so I would respectfully ask to get it over with quickly.'

The girls' laughter turned to mocking frowns.

'The horrid little trollop accepts it.'

'She respectfully asks.'

'The beastly lez.'

Once more, tinkling laughter filled the room, the amusement of girls born to command. Candace blushed deep crimson, horribly aware of their swishing nyloned legs under impeccably pleated, swirling skirts, blouses rising and falling with quivering teats, and their perfume of superior breeding, against her own sweating, scarcely dressed shame. Her twat oozed come. She could smell, in those gorgeous fragrances, the superiority bred into their long, cool bodies and graceful limbs, the ripely jutting teats and buttocks, equally fit for the saddle, bed or caning stool, to wield or receive an aristocratic whip.

Candace knew that she *was* a worm, compared to these superb beauties, and *did* deserve to be beaten by them. If her bottom smarted, and she took the pain, perhaps these arrogant, superior girls would not be so cruel. Her quim juiced, wetting her knickers and seeping into the front of her gym skirtlet, for all to see. It was so cruel to call her a lez – yet how to explain that the fearful prospect of a girl caning her bottom, on the panties, caused her to moisten? She could not explain it to herself.

'Well, get your pants orff,' drawled Fiona, 'we haven't got all day.'

'We have, if she squirms well,' cried Cindi, and Arabella giggled.

'I . . . I beg your pardon, miss?' Candace gasped.

Fiona frowned: 'Are you deaf? Skirt, top and panties off, you cringing worm. That's *off*, not down.'

Candace stood, frozen and gaping; to her horror, her skirt was drenched in a powerful spurt of quim juice, and she knew it was shamefully visible. The girls did seem to be staring quite openly at her groin, and Arabella licked her wide pink lips. Candace hung her head, looking down at the polished mirrors of their black shoes, and fancied she could see a blurred reflection of their panties.

'All canings are on the bare bottom,' said Arabella, with a cruel smirk. 'There are no exceptions.'

Candace gaped.

'You shall take your flogging in the nude,' snapped Fiona.

Candace stared, seeking a sympathetic face, but not finding one. The three girls, smiling tight little smiles, shared joy at her anguish. Taking a deep breath, she turned, pulled her top off, unzipped and discarded her skirtlet, and then began to slide her panties down. The panties were a very thin and high bikini cut, which revealed most of her soaking mound, with the gusset nipping her pink wet pouch, between her swollen cunt lips. The rear scarcely covered her croup, so even those panties would afford little protection from the cane. But *bare bum* – the cane slicing her *completely naked buttocks*? Candace's heart raced, as come spumed from her lips. Fiona struck the table with her cane.

'Nobody ordered you to turn round,' she rapped. 'Face your superiors, mot.'

Scarlet, Candace faced the prefects, who were staring at her with wide eyes and pursed lips; she continued to pull down her panties. Juice glistened, dripping from the shaven, alabaster smoothness of her cunt hillock, and the older girls purred. In a rush, half-closing her eyes, she ripped down the sopping knickers, and stepped out of them.

'Hands behind your back, and feet apart,' Fiona commanded.

She obeyed, blushing with the shame of exhibiting herself like a zoo animal. The girls licked their lips, and caressed their canes, as they scrutinised her dripping cunt mound. Did Fiona blush? She seemed the least cruel, with the loveliest face, high cheekbones and wide, sensuous lips. Once more, she was ordered to turn, now to show her bare bottom. She did so, and heard them whisper amongst themselves, with little giggles.

'You seem to be wet between your legs, mot,' drawled Fiona. 'Can you explain it?'

'I . . . I . . .'

'Struck dumb? Have you peed yourself in fear? Disgusting.'

'No, miss, it's . . . it's girl's stuff. I'm sorry, miss, honestly,' Candace blurted. 'I can't help it.'

'She doesn't *try* to help it,' Arabella snorted.

'Did you become excited at the idea of a caning on the bare?' demanded Fiona.

'Why, no, miss,' Candace said with a gulp, 'I was already . . that way.'

'A big clitty like that should be ringed,' Cindi said giggling. 'It's so *taming*.'

'Beating excites the slut,' sneered Arabella. 'She is a pervert. Look at that slice. I've never seen a mot with such a long deep gash, like a bally whipthong stuck to her belly. It's positively obscene – a sure sign of depravity.'

Trembling, Candace blushed deep red. 'That's unfair, miss,' she blurted. 'It's sometimes exciting to imagine being lashed on your bottom, you know, being really helpless and submissive, and everything. Surely the other girls you cane are no different?'

'You're not to know how others behave,' drawled Fiona. 'Each bum to be thrashed is a unique case. In yours, we detect a perverted craving to be thrashed.'

Candace shivered. Could such a thing be true? Fiona's lovely, regal voice brooked no opposition. The girl *knew*.

'Since you seem one of those filthy sluts who take pleasure in bare-bottom chastisement,' Fiona commanded, 'you must beg for what you evidently find a privilege. Down on your knees, and crouch, mot.'

13

Numbly, Candace crouched on the floor, like a puppy.
'Beg,' Fiona spat. 'Tell us your sins.'

Fiona towered over Candace, her shiny court shoes inches from Candace's nose; the ripe aroma of her feet, in their white nylons, filled Candace's lungs, and made her quim wetter. She gazed into the prefect's polished shoes and, sure enough, they were mirrors, showing the bulge of her mons, encased in the skimpiest powder-blue thong, a mere triangle, adorably fringed with a white frilly trim, amid her creamy bare belly and hips. Candace gasped, when the image dissolved, and Fiona lifted her leg, to place her sole on the nape of Candace's neck.

'Please, miss, I beg you to cane me,' she stammered.

'Not enough. Bum up a bit more. That's better. You *do* look pathetic. Go on, confess – your filthiest, smuttiest sins. It's for your own good.'

'I . . . I request the hardest kiss of your cane, on my naked bum,' she blurted, scarlet with shame. 'I am a smutty worm, and crave punishment for my filthy thoughts. I have imagined each of you nude, with your bottoms and titties for me to feel, and your lovely, cruel thighs for me to kiss, as they crush me, and your twats all wet, for me to suck. I have wanked off, watching you nude in the swimming pool. Please beat my insolent bottom for it. Cane my bare bottom till I scream. Please, miss . . .'

Candace trembled, sweating. Her tongue darted to Fiona's shoes, and began to lick the upper, then the heel and sole. Changing posture, Fiona presented her with her other shoe, which she licked clean. The pressure of her foot on Candace's nape increased, and the harder she crushed, the more Candace's nipples and clitty throbbed, and the more eagerly she licked. Come spurted from Candace's cunt, as she breathed the perfume of nylon, leather and sweaty toes. Her lips and tongue caressed the fabric of the shoe as if it were

14

Fiona's dress, her damp, smelly panties or stockings, or her skin itself.

'Unless you ladies need a shoe shine too, I suggest we proceed to satisfy her request,' Fiona said, smirking, 'and thrash the living daylights out of her. She's an insolent hussy, so palms-and-tiptoe will shame her properly.'

So casual, the cruelty in her haughty voice cut the air like a razor.

'Agreed,' they sang.

Fiona ordered Candace to rise, and assume position for the cane. She stood with legs well apart, four feet from the rosewood table, then stretched forwards, arms splayed, to place the backs of her hands, palms up, on the table. This made her trunk lean at an angle, and naked buttocks rise, presenting themselves for the cane. Finally, she had to stand on tiptoe, a poise which must be maintained throughout the beating, which would start again from scratch if she ever slackened. Palms up, Fiona explained delicately, was especially cruel, as she had no grip to absorb the impact of a cane stroke. Tiptoes tightened and spread the bottom, making it difficult to squirm, in order to disperse the pain.

She heard a rustling of skirts and blouses behind her, and smelled a fragrance of sweat, as the prefects raised their caning arms. Candace stood, trembling with fear and shame, awaiting the first cane stroke on her bare buttocks from the trio of divinely scented, utterly scornful schoolgirls, and with her twat gushing, as Fiona's cool fingertips stroked her bare melons, caressing her cleft, and tickling the anus bud.

'Quite the prettiest bum I've seen for ages,' Fiona purred. 'I shall enjoy caning it to pink. I suggest each of us strokes her in turn, with you first, Cindi, then Arabella, and I'll, um, take up the rear.'

They laughed, a tinkle of bells. Fiona reminded Candace that any undue whimpering, any cries or bleats

15

or 'girly noises', and she would take the cut over again. She must on no account turn her head to look round at her caners. Candace nodded that she understood, and Fiona murmured that the punishment could begin.

There was a swishing, whistling whir, slicing the still air. Whap! Liquid fire streaked across Candace's bare mid-fesses. She tried to squirm, but found herself dancing on tiptoes, legs rigid and trembling, and fingers clenching helplessly, while the smarting agony of the weal seeped up her spine and belly.

Whap! Tears leaped to her eyes, and her gorge rose, as a second cut thrashed her higher, on top buttock, where the skin was tender, and the pain was a thousand times worse than that of the first stroke. Whap! The third stroke was worse than both of the others, stinging the haunch, and making her gasp out loud. She felt her smarting cheeks clench tightly, as if to squeeze away the pain.

'Keep still, mot,' Fiona rapped.

Whap! The fourth cut lashed the back of the thighs, just under Candace's wriggling bottom, and a white-hot lance of agony pierced her. Her breasts bounced, flapping against her ribs.

'Ooh!' she gasped, through tears.

'A noise,' said Cindi gleefully.

'Cut repeated,' said Fiona.

'Please, miss,' she blurted, 'may I know how many strokes I'm due?'

'Impudent wretch,' snarled Arabella.

'Two dozen ought to do it, with an extra stroke for asking,' replied Fiona.

'Oh, miss,' the caned girl said with a sob. 'I can't take two dozen of those. You cane so fearfully tight.'

'And another cut for *that* outburst.'

Candace began to whimper; her seared croup was already crimson with jagged welts.

'You *did* ask to be flogged till you scream,' Fiona said coolly. 'If luncheon doesn't interrupt, we may oblige you. It's so lovely to watch a mot's welts weep and harden into gorgeous dark blisters. We call it the upper crust.'

'There's nothing lovelier than a mot's stiff end caned to a nice crust,' said Cindi thoughtfully.

Whap! Candace's hoarse panting drowned the peals of their cruel laughter. She sobbed, buttocks wriggling, as the stroke to mid-fesse spread flames of smarting pain through her whole dancing croup. *What must my melons look like?* She could see the prefects, reflected in the window glass: blurred shapes, skirts swirling, and raised canes glinting. *I wish I could cane their bare bottoms, and make their twats juice like mine.*

Their skirts were up, white stockings gleaming, and each prefect had a hand between her legs, frotting her panties . . . or so it seemed. While every girl wanked off, and that was accepted, it was unthinkable that English girls should play with themselves, watching another caned on the bare. Whap! Whap!

'Ohh,' she panted, her breath labouring in hoarse gasps.

The girls flogged Candace without mercy, until she thought she should collapse. Her wealed buttocks were a lake of fire, her legs jerked rigid and her croup squirmed at each cane stroke, yet, after twelve strokes, her agony became a fierce, almost friendly glow, and she began to take the cuts without whimpering. Whap! Whap!

'Uhh . . . uhh . . .'

Behind her, reflected in the glass, the caners' skirts swirled, with a glimpse of powder-blue panties, and fingers nimbly frigging stained wet crotch cloth. There was no doubt. *They are masturbating as they beat me!* Candace's quim swam with pride that she could excite them so. She heard them pant, sigh and sweetly whimper, with their legs and bellies trembling, as they masturbated their wet cunts. The caning went on, her

17

clitty throbbing, as she imagined how her bottom looked: a brutal tapestry of welts, yet enough to thrill them to a wank. Whap! Whap!

'*Ahh!*' she screamed.

Squirming and sobbing at the shock of two vicious cuts at once, Candace felt crusts rub together on her buttocks.

'*Yes!*' cried Arabella.

'Beautiful,' Cindi panted.

The girls' coos of pleasure became louder; looking in the glass, Candace saw them openly frotting their twats, as they licked their lips, staring at her crusted bum. Their skirts were up, and fingers stuck in panties, stained dark with come. Whap! Whap! The cane strokes became erratic, as fingers frigged pantied quims, beneath skirts carelessly swept back, exposing bare thighs and nylons wet with oozing gash juice. Candace heard Arabella and Cindi wank themselves off to panting orgasms.

'What a squirmer! Oh . . . oh . . . *yes!*'

'Pretty mot's bum crusts! Ahh! *Ahh* . . .'

Whap! Whap! The pain of the cuts became pure agony. Fiona's voice was loveliest, coolest and most shivery in its cruelty, yet she too gave way, gasping hoarsely, with breasts and belly heaving – 'Mm . . . mm . . . *ohh!*' – and nyloned thighs rippling, as she masturbated to spasm. The girls withdrew their wet fingers from between their thighs with little sucking sounds.

'I count twenty-seven strokes, and her arse is nice and ridged, but it seems the disgusting slut's twat is still juicing,' said Arabella, panting. 'I've never seen such a monstrous clit. What's to be done? It's nearly time for luncheon, and there's goose liver pâté today.'

'I could eat her bum,' purred Cindi, drooling a little. 'And her clitty.'

The girls cooed, rubbing their wet panties, with squishy sounds.

'Let me . . .' murmured Fiona.

Leaning back on the table, she raised her quivering, coltish thigh, letting her skirt spill all the way back to her waist, and exposing her full sussies, the lacy garter straps and suspenders, and the tiny blue thong stained wet, its swelling triangle at her pubis prettily adorned by the lacy trim, snow white against tanned thigh skin. Her naked belly and upper thighs were silkily bare-shaven on each side, the smooth, clinging panties gusset unmarred by any pubic hairs beneath.

She kicked Candace's clitty with the tip of her shoe, and Candace gasped, the impact of the cool leather sending shock waves of pleasure through her cunt. Fiona kicked again, then brought her other leg up, sandwiching the swollen clitty helmet between the sole and upper, and her shoes began to slap Candace's lips, with dainty, disdainful taps to the clit. Her long legs rippled, smooth and firm as a gazelle's, and Candace wanted to lick her naked thighs, inhale their perfume, worship them, as they shamed and excited her.

Gracefully, Fiona slipped off her shoes, and continued to rub Candace's cunt with her stockinged toes. The sweaty nylon felt hot and wet, and Candace whimpered, panting, as electric pleasure throbbed in her belly. Licking her lips, Fiona kept up her delicate frottage, rubbing the clit with one stockinged foot, while the other slapped the dripping quim lips, with the silky nylon slithering over her bare-shaven pubis. She poked her toecap inside Candace's pouch, and reamed hard. Candace groaned, as orgasm flooded her, and a fierce spurt of come splashed onto Fiona's white-nyloned ankle. The whipped girl's twat dampened Fiona's stockinged feet, come seeping into the moist, fragrant leather of her shoes.

The luncheon bell rang. Panting, the girls smoothed down their skirts, affording Candace a last glimpse of bare, wet thighs, and bulging cooze hillocks, in damp blue panties.

'Naughty stuff, all over my stockings,' sneered Fiona, her lip curled, and eyes flashing. 'This outrage puts the mot quite beyond normal school discipline. I shall advise Dr Rodd to expel her.'

'No, please, miss,' Candace begged. 'Not that. I'll do anything, take any beating, serve you . . . be your slave.'

'A juicy lez,' purred Cindi. 'I'll have her, Fi, if you won't.'

Fiona gave a quizzical look, her eyebrows arched. 'Just look at my wet stockings,' she murmured. 'I've never seen a mot with so much come. Thank goodness she didn't pee herself. My knickers are in a state, too, all wet and sticky. Everything needs special laundering. You will report to my room, in your pyjamas, at nine this evening, mot.'

She drew a deep breath, through flared nostrils, and smiled icily, with her thoroughbred's thighs quivering.

'I've always wanted a slave,' Fiona purred.

2

Spankable Bum

'Which godemiché, miss?' murmured Candi, crouching before her mistress.

'The leather one, I think,' Fiona drawled. 'I feel like a little pain this evening. After all, I have to watch a poor girl suffer, miscreant though she may be, and it makes me feel better if I hurt in sympathy. Girls really shouldn't have such gorgeous, tempting bots, Candi, and *you* are the worst offender, you luscious trollop. They shouldn't squirm so prettily, and go such a tasty pink, when spanked. As for the cane on bare bum – why, at those gorgeous stripes, it becomes almost my duty to wank off.'

She stroked her crotch, over her pleated blue skirtlet, drooping lazily on her nyloned thighs.

'I wish you'd permit me to diddle, miss,' said Candi, blushing. 'I hate being spanked myself, as you well know I can't stand pain, but somehow I don't mind helping you discipline some naughty girl. It makes me all hot and all wet afterwards, and I'm longing to masturbate.'

Fiona, reclining on her bed, wagged a reproving finger.

'You know the rules, mot. You masturbate when I say so, and at no other time. Why, you enjoy plenty of show wanks for the boys, don't you?'

Candi bowed her head, blushing. 'Not exactly enjoy it's my duty – but, yes, miss.'

'You *can* stand pain, for you do, when you are naughty.'

'I suppose so, miss. I wish I wasn't quite so naughty. It's all right when you discipline me, for I know I deserve it, and you're my mistress, but I get so ashamed when boys do it. It is the pink panties that get them so excited.'

'It's supposed to be shameful.'

'Well, I suppose I can't complain, miss.'

'Can't you, indeed? Then I must do you harder. A slave who's not sullen isn't suffering enough. The boys pay well to watch a girl suffer – lustful swine, the lot of them.'

Fiona stroked her four-foot rattan cane, its oiled brown wood gleaming sensuously in the lamplight. Winking impishly at her slave, she licked the splayed snake's tongue at its tip. Candi shivered. She knew what that cane felt like on her bare bum, and hated the thought of the dreadful smarting on her naked skin. It wasn't so bad, once the beating got started – say, after eight or nine cuts – for a girl got used to the stinging wood, and it wasn't as if she didn't deserve it. Fiona was always careful to explain just why Candi had earned her thrashing. Somehow, from another girl, the cane seemed normal, and the punishment almost kind; it was boys whose touch she loathed, spanking for their own horrid perverted pleasure.

'Please, miss,' Candi blurted, 'I don't think I could possibly suffer more.'

She handed the gnarled leather dildo to her mistress, who sighed, licked her lips, and slid her skirt up over her thighs. Her stocking tops and lacy pink sussies were revealed, the bare tan flesh quivering firm, up to the minuscule silken barrier of her thong, moist with sweat, and threatening to burst under the massive swelling of

22

her shaven cunt hillock. She pulled aside the panties gusset, revealing her gash – moist, pink and swollen, like eager lover's lips. Then she opened her thighs, and parted the quim lips with her thumb and forefinger for Candi to insert the monstrous leather pleasure tool. As Candi plunged the dildo to its hilt, a good fourteen inches, wrenching Fiona's cunt lips to a pale circle, Fiona winced, gasped, and swallowed hard. Only the leather tassle of the dildo dangled from her cooze flaps, now that the entire engine filled her. Fiona's gasps stilled, until her lips creased in a smile.

'Wow!' she exclaimed. 'I'd forgotten . . . it really is a monster. The hardest tulipwood from Paraiba, wrapped in the toughest pampas leather.'

She pulled her panties over her cunt, and smoothed her skirt over her panties, making sure that her sussie straps were straight.

'Noblesse oblige,' she murmured. 'I don't suppose you'd understand. Spanking and caning are aristocratic pursuits, the perfect way to subdue an inferior; yet a true aristo must not impose pain, without knowing it herself. The pain of a Paraiba dildo, like that of a tulipwood cane on a girl's bare skin, is never far from the most gorgeous pleasure. This new bitch waiting outside, Nipringa Vere-Clissitt, is a tough mot, saucy and bold, with a bum like leather, so I hear. *Lady* Nipringa, her title is. Hmph. Arabella's thrashed her, Cindi's thrashed her, and she walked away whistling, jaunty as you please. We can't have *that*. She's been passed to me, on Dr Rodd's instruction. I'll have to hurt her ladyship's bottom very badly indeed.'

Obediently, Candi nodded. She stood nude, head bowed, and hands at her crotch, awaiting her mistress's pleasure.

Candi was in her sixth week of slavery to Fiona Dondelay. It wasn't called slavery at Rodd's, but voluntary servitude, although Candi suspected that that meant much the same thing. It was recognised that senior girls might employ one or more mots as slaves, in return for their services helping them with their schoolwork, or giving sisterly advice, perhaps with any emotional problems they might face, in preparing for the world beyond school. The mots knew this was all 'superbollocks', as they called it in their rude schoolgirls' parlance.

Fiona made Candi tell her everything about her sex experience with boys, not that there was much to tell. At first, Candi was reluctant, not understanding the full duties and submission of a slave, and when Fiona rewarded her insolence with quite a ferocious barebottom caning – over thirty cuts, with Candi bent over, touching her toes, and almost toppled by the whistling force of her mistress's stingers – she wept floods of tears, but couldn't talk. At that early stage, Candi still did not quite grasp that her mistress masturbated every time she caned or spanked the hapless girl's naked fesses. Mollified by her wank, Fiona rubbed Candi's striped bottom with zinc ointment, while caressing her shaven cunt quite sweetly, then made Candi serve them both a lovely pot of tea, with lots of milk and sugar.

Before Candi knelt to lap her tea from her feeding bowl, Fiona infibulated her twat with an adorable golden locket. She said merrily that it was a chastity device, used by the rollicking Brazilian *bandeirantes* of old on their lustful womenfolk. The locket clamped Candi's cooze lips tightly shut, so that she couldn't pee, although, after several cups of tea, she was desperate to do so. Fiona promised to unlock her clasp when she told all, and so, with her tummy bursting, Candi blurted the story of her romance with Darren Thrush, the rich young scion of an old Anglo-Brazilian family.

Right from their first snog, in the back of his Mercedes, he had spanked her – she admitted it – and

24

she hated the pain, although relished the love-making which seemed impossible without spanking. At first, he spanked her on the panties, then very hard on the bare bottom. She even consented to take the strap, enduring brutal floggings with his studded gaucho belt folded in two. She genuinely believed she was naughty, and must be chastised. Only later did it dawn on her that Darren was a beastly pervert, who could not pleasure a girl without a crimson bottom.

Worse, she learned that she was not the only girl he spanked. That was the worst insult, and she vowed never to see him again, and never to be forced into spanking by any brutal boy. Fiona laughed, and undid her infibulator. While Candi squatted, with pee hissing from her aching twat, and overflowing the porcelain pisspot, Fiona informed her that there were few relationships where spanking played no part, especially with boys, and that love without spanking was like beef without mustard. A girl's buttocks were designed to be spanked – that was the form, beauty and function of those firm, succulent orbs of flesh – and a Rodd's girl must get used to it.

Candi did not tell Fiona of her private fantasy, one that often fuelled her masturbation. An overgrown schoolboy – not Darren, but somebody quite like him – fell madly in love with Candi. He was putty in her hands, and she treated him with fabulous cruelty, making him beg for each kiss. One day, she opened her white school blouse and undid her bra, to show him her bare breasts, and he went all soppy, goggling with calf's eyes, and his cock bulging ramrod stiff in his grey flannel trousers. If he wanted to see any more, he'd have to be punished for that horrid erection. That meant the cane. 'The cane, miss?' 'Don't act silly. Of course, the cane. And on your bare bottom. Pants off, now.' 'Oh, miss, you are cruel.' 'All girls are cruel.' Candi's fount seeped come, as she watched the pants come off, revealing the firm, smooth orbs of his unscarred bare buttocks. Her cane would change that.

He bent over a chair for his licking, and she raised her cane, a lovely long whippy tulipwood, with a crook school handle. Vip! Vip! His bum streaked pink, and he began to squirm and gasp, his knuckles white as he gripped the chair. Vip! Vip! On and on she caned, as his naked buttocks squirmed, flogged to crimson; tears gushed from his eyes, and his face, red as his whipped bum, twisted in agony. Lovely vengeance, on all cruel, selfish boys, to watch this virgin squirm in agony. Furiously, Candi lashed the bare nates, until they were a tapestry of pink and crimson crusts, squirming violently to the music of the boy's sobs. Yet his cock trembled rigid, swaying, as his buttocks jerked under the cane. After thirty stingers on the bare, the boy knelt, and licked Candi's feet, sucking her toes, while she wanked off to orgasm. That's all she would allow him, until he reported for another thrashing.

Lust made a puppy of even the nastiest boy. She would thrash him hard, then show him her breasts, make him lick her boots, even her bum, on her smelliest soiled panties, and make him wank off into his hand, for shame. How thrilling, to watch the copious cream spurt high in the air from his peehole! She forbade him, of course, to do that at any other time. Sometimes she would vary the game, and have another boy (also in love with her) to administer the bare-bum caning, and witness the boot-licking, to sneer, as her slave wanked off in front of them both, his balls, filled to burst, shooting huge jets of spunk. The boy slave would crave her cane, plead for a thrashing on the bare, and the more his bottom smarted, the more he would worship her, and humiliate himself before her.

A girl slave was known, in schoolgirl slang, as a 'spank 'n' wank', for those were her principal duties: to pleasure her mistress in girly fun – heaven forfend a lezzie way! – and bare her spankable bum for her superior's cane, slipper or palm. In addition, a slave acted as assistant whenever her mistress was obliged to administer corporal punishment to the bottom of some recalcitrant mot. Candi would pinion the victim, subdue her, hold her in position for her caning, even sit on her face, if necessary, while the girl's bare bum threshed and wriggled under Fiona's whistling rod.

The mots hated girl slaves for their complicity in their pain, yet envied them, for a girl slave had a life far more luxurious than any Rodd's mot, with super food, passes to accompany her mistress shopping, and nice bras, knickers and underthings from her mistress's cast-offs. Not that Candi had much chance of wearing them for her mistress, for Fiona mostly kept her nude, with a bulky copper slave bracelet around her ankle, affixed to a chain leash, whose end Candi held in her mouth when unoccupied.

Fiona, with entrepreneurial flair, perceived Candi's tolerance of flagellant pain, and extended her slave's duties, so that spoiled boys of good family, bored with spanking their submissive maidservants, might part with silver coins for the privilege of recreationally thrashing a proper English lady on the naked buttocks: Candi. While a Brazilian maidservant traditionally took her lashes with sighs, rolling eyes, and no more than a snuffle, Candi was encouraged to snivel and weep, shriek and curse and protest and plead, as she knelt quivering and sobbing over a wooden stool, while her bare bottom squirmed under hearty drubbings from tulipwood or tamarind rod. That was after she had knelt, begging for mercy, only to have her dress, underthings and stockings shamefully ripped from her body by drooling aristocratic boys.

One after the other, the smirking boys, crotches bulging, would adminster six hard cuts to her bare, criss-crossing her naked girl flesh with cruel stripes, until her buttocks were a morass of crusted welts and bruises, the whole skin mottled dark and glowing, like coals in a fire. Afterwards, with her naked fesses glowing red and puce, she would masturbate to orgasm in front of her tormentors, to complete their haughty pleasure. Fiona required her slave to caress herself throroughly, rubbing her naked body, and flogged buttocks, with scented oil, and tweaking her nipples hard, while penetrating her slit with full fingers, till it plopped with loud squelchy noises, and come trickled down her quivering thighs.

She played her part to perfection, although Fiona knew she was not acting, and really did hate the cane; yet, as an English girl, her prime desire was to obey and do her duty. The boys were not allowed to approach, or touch her, and this delicious frustration increased her appeal; that, and her golden skin, blonde tresses and bulging, shaven English twat, the quim lips swelling and pink, under the hairless hillock. The aristocratic Brazilian boys, of the southern cattle country, marvelled at Candi's long, fine gash, much rangier than the pert little twats of Brazilian girls. It was like a slash in her belly, carved by some machete, and with a clitoris so big, it was never truly covered by the lush quim flaps, but always peeped pink and wet from the vulval folds.

But it was the arse, Candi's firm, quivering peach, that the boys truly loved. Fiona told her that all boys were like that. Although they might affect a preference for bouncing big titties, or ripe thigh-slabs, ready to crush a boy's balls between their scented bare muscle, or dainty feet, or a stem-thin waist – all of which Candi had – it was really the bulging, trembling arse flans that really turned a male on. Candi's bum plums were absolutely fabulous (Fiona drawled), like two eggs in a hanky – which Candi suspected was a tiny bit vulgar. Nevertheless, her mistress had been to England, and she had not.

28

Sometimes, for an extra fee, Candi would be intructed to turn around and show her whipped buttocks, while wanking herself off. As she manipulated her outsize, throbbing clitty, bursting from her gash folds, she would insert one, two or even three fingers into her own anus, right to the knuckle, poking herself in the bumhole, as she wanked to a climax. Fiona knew that Candi hated the anal stimulation, and said her discomfort made the show that much more special. In this way, Fiona acquired the money for as many stiletto shoes, silk stockings and frilly garter belts as she wanted.

There was almost no limit to the freedom of a senior girl, save one very small cloud on her sensuous horizon: the prospect, fainter than a snowflake, of a punishment from Dr Tarquin Rodd himself, the only personage at the school empowered to cane a senior girl. It had to be on Miss Hurt's recommendation, and the vice-principal, normally docile, had a fiery temper that blazed on unexpectedly; a girl's punishment had to be endorsed by the full circle of her peers, the prefects, which was an absolutely awful thought, like sneaking, or bullying. Nevertheless, the possibility was there.

It was, of course, up to Dr Rodd to decide the severity of a girl's thrashing, but, once the verdict from the 'Prefects' Court' was in, a thrashing there must be. Dr Rodd wore a gown and a black mask as he thrashed a girl's bare bottom. Sometimes, Candi dreamed of Fiona's bum bared and caned, of her proud mistress squealing and writhing under a bare-arse thrashing, as she surely must have suffered sometime in the past. She suppressed the thought, consoling herself that Fiona would probably take it with her usual aplomb; once the hurdle of a girl's first naked caning had been crossed, it seemed quite natural. The shame and pain, though frightful on each new beating, soon faded into the grim warmth of memory.

* * *

29

Nipringa Vere-Clissitt entered, her mouth twisted in a sullen leer. She was as tall as Candi, her figure svelte, with her breasts straining like massive pointed cannon-balls at her skimpy top, her waist a mere hand's breadth of taut flesh, her legs as long and powerful as a gazelle's. She wore the most humiliating of girly uniforms: a frilly white blouse, open to her bosom, and daringly tied below her ribs, to bare her sleek tummy; a short, pleated pink skirt, in shiny cotton, and showing her pink bikini panties beneath; her legs bare, with fluffy pink ankle socks, and rubber-soled shoes of scuffed pink canvas. Yet her clothing was embellished by a dazzling slave bracelet at her ankle, in gold and diamonds, with its thinner sister looped insolently at her waist, across her navel; a gold necklace, sparkling on her creamy bare breast skin; gold bracelets at each wrist, and a silver garter, clinging to the rippling muscle of her left thigh, just below her skirtlet. True aristocracy was always in the accessories.

Candi gasped, not only at the girl's lissome beauty, but at her skin, which was gorgeous, creamy and jet black. Long dark tresses framed her slender, Nilotic face, with flashing eyes, and full, sensuous lips, under high, haughty cheekbones. The girl stood with legs apart, powerful bare thighs quivering, and her hands behind her back, while staring defiantly at Fiona, and disdainfully at her naked slave. Her eyes danced over Candi's bare thighs, and Candi flushed, for she was surely comparing them to her own. Nipringa smiled faintly at Candi's slave bracelet, and the chain held obediently between her teeth. Fiona pursed her lips, stood up, and walked around the black girl, on a tour of inspection, tapping her lips with the snake's tongue of her cane.

'So, you are Nipringa Vere-Clissitt,' she said slowly.

'*Lady* Nipringa, miss,' said the black girl, pouting. 'Father is Baron Archbold Vere-Clissitt. You may have heard of him. He owns a bit of grassland hereabouts. Mother, of course, is Princess Grace of Bakwanda.'

'Oh, of course. But in my study, you're nothing but a cheeky mot, who's going to have her beastly bum tanned,' snapped Fiona.

With her cane, she flicked up Nipringa's skirt, revealing twin buttocks jutting superbly, as they swelled to bursting under the thin cotton panties, which scarcely seemed able to contain the orbs of rippling black arse meat. Nipringa trembled, glowering, her full, conic breasts quivering under the thin cotton, and skimpy pink bra, with the massive nipples visibly stiffening to big chocolate domes. Fiona poked her cane tip into the waistband of Nipringa's panties, and twanged it, slapping the elastic on the naked skin. Deliberately, she stretched the knickers, and slowly pulled them down Nipringa's thighs, until they dangled from her garter. With a moue of disdain, Nipringa flicked the panties to the floor, and asked, in her cool, contemptuous contralto, if she was now required to bare up.

'Just strip the skirt, I think,' replied Fiona. 'Your caning will be on the bare buttocks.'

The black girl gasped. 'On the bare?' she murmured, her eyelashes fluttering. 'I thought . . . on my skirt, pulled tight . . . but silly me. On the bare.'

'Of course.'

'Yes . . . of course . . . well then. I mean, you are stating the obvious, miss.'

'It's never obvious. Every punishment is decided on its merits. You were caught chewing gum, a vile, unladylike habit, and I shall take great delight in slicing your naked bottom with twenty – yes, twenty – strokes of my cane. Now, *orff* with your skirt, mot.'

Trembling, Nipringa twisted off her skirt, dropping it, and stood with her buttocks and shaven cunt mound gleaming bare. Her quim lips hung low beneath the cunt basin, moist and succulent, with the gleam of pink slit

31

flesh within the pouch. Candi pressed her thighs together, feeling come seep from her pulsing twat at the gorgeous spectacle of the black girl's belly, bum and crevice, nude for punishment. She wanted that arrogant bottom to sizzle under the cane, those titties to bounce in agony.

'Well, then,' said Fiona, flexing her cane, 'let's to business, miss. Over the horse with you, legs apart, and bum up.'

Tears moistened Nipringa's eyes, as her bravado seemed to desert her. Her upper body was drenched with sweat, wetting her clinging blouse to transparency, and revealing her chocolate breasts trembling in their full nudity, with the giant nipples as stiff as chimneys.

'Ooh,' she moaned, 'I didn't think you really meant it, miss. I've never been caned before, you see. Only for chewing gum. Please have mercy.'

'Twenty strokes *is* mercy, you slut. But now it's an extra five for lying. I know Cindi and Arabella have both caned you, and that you are a leather-arsed trollop.'

Nipringa's fingers flew to her lips, and her eyes widened. 'They said that?' she gasped. 'Oh, how could they?'

'You are suggesting my colleagues are lying?'

'No, miss. I just know I've never been caned, that's all. It must be a misunderstanding.'

'Then this shall be your first caning,' purred Fiona, 'and afterwards, you shall be a real Rodd's girl. Be brave, my dear Nipringa. I shall hurt you dreadfully, but you'll feel better afterwards. Why, my slave here thinks nothing of a cool twenty.'

'But she's a mere wank 'n' spank,' sneered Nipringa, with something of her old haughtiness.

'Then show yourself superior. Bare up like a lady, with heart and arse high.'

Fiona nodded at the high wooden punishment horse. Slinky with gold, Nipringa draped herself, snuffling, over the saddle. Her buttocks thrust up, glinting like black moons, with her legs stretched straight and wide, allowing Candi to peek at her glistening pink slit meat, well displayed by her parted black quim slice. Before gripping the front legs of the horse, she slapped herself on the bare bum, with a dry crack, that made the meaty arse flesh ripple slightly. She gave a little wriggle of her fesses to show that she was ready for punishment. Candi was gasping, her cunt seeping come, as she licked her lips, longing for the crack of the cane on those gorgeous, insolent fesses. Fiona lifted her cane, with her thighs parted, straining against her skirt, and her face flushed. The dildo, Candi knew, must be working inside her filled slit.

The cane hovered above Nipringa's ebony buttocks, stretched tight, with the skin of the cleft like a drumskin around the wide brown wrinkle of her anus pucker. Fiona's arm swung, and the cane whistled; Nipringa's buttocks trembled, clenching just a little, even before the cane struck, but then, with a frown from the black girl, her teeth drawn tightly in a fierce gleaming rictus, the buttocks relaxed, as if by an effort of will, to present no evidence of cowardice. She would take her first cane stroke unclenched. The cane suddenly sprang back, an inch from Nipringa's taut bum skin. Panting, breasts heaving, Fiona pressed the rod to her side. Her thighs were pumping, and tummy heaving, working on the dildo inside her; Candi could see a damp patch at Fiona's crotch where the dildo was making her ooze come.

'Wait,' drawled Fiona. 'No ... I think I'm going to spank you.'

Nipringa's nostrils flared. 'Spanking, miss?' she hissed. 'Is that all?'

'I thought you'd be relieved. You have a rather spankable bum.'

'I know that, miss. Must the slave watch?'

'Absolutely. You see, she is going to do the spanking.'

Fiona flicked Candi's leash, as her girl slave primly perched on the sofa, ready to accept Nipringa's upthrust buttocks.

'I've . . . I've never spanked anyone before, mistress,' mumbled Candi.

'You've been spanked,' sneered Fiona.

'Of course.'

'Well, then.'

Glowering, the black girl lowered herself onto Candi's thighs. Candi felt her naked belly and twat, warm and moist, slither on her own bare skin, with Nipringa's hips brushing the hillock of Candi's fount. Nipringa's finger-tips and toes gingerly touched the floor, as she wriggled into spanking position, thrusting her buttocks up, so that they almost touched Candi's streaked nipples. Come spurted in Candi's twat, as she gazed at the satin orbs, the fine, muscled skin rippling with tender power, and the lusciously crinkled bud of the anal pucker, writhing like a little sea anemone, in the girl's taut bum cleft.

'How many slaps, mistress?'

Fiona flicked her cane, smacking Candi across her nipples.

'Ooh!' Candi shrieked.

A thin pink stripe glared on her bare breasts.

'Till I tell you to stop, dolt. You'll start with the bare hand. After a hundred or so, I dare say you'll want to use the slipper.'

'A hundred! Ooh!'

Candi winced, as another cut took her across the breasts. Eyes moist with tears, she lifted her arm over the black girl's juicy rump. Smack! Smack! The flesh felt wonderfully tight and elastic under her cracking palm, with a pleasing mauve flush rising almost at once, as Nipringa grunted sofly under her hard spanking. Smack! Smack! Candi's titties heaved, as she put all her effort into the spanks, determined to tease more than

34

gasps and grunts from her sullen, haughty victim. As the spanked fesses began to writhe and clench ever so slightly, Candi panted at the flow of come wetting her cunt and thighs. She gasped, thrilling, as she felt trickling into her thigh cleft, a drip of come from the spanked girl's own cooze.

'She is pretty spankable, I'd say,' gasped Fiona hoarsely.

Candi looked up, and saw her mistress with face flushed crimson, skirtlet raised, and her hand inside her panties. She was vigorously masturbating, with her eyes fixed on the spanked girl's naked buttocks, gently pumping up and down under Candi's hard slaps. Smack! Smack! Nipringa's buttocks were unmistakably squirming in an undulating rhythm, with a fluting unbroken whine deep in her throat. At each spank, her dangling breasts twitched in their cotton sheath, slapping the firm tit meat against Candi's thighs. As she spanked on, past three dozen, then five dozen, Candi's hand burned with pain.

The black girl's wriggling buttocks were spanked mauve, the big nates now jerking and clenching quite unashamedly, as Nipringa moaned and gasped, with the trickle of come now a flood from her cooze, squelching against Candi's thigh flesh. Nipringa's head hung low, her long raven tresses trailing on the floor. Fiona's wanked cunt made powerful slurping noises, as she poked herself with the huge dildo, drawing it out of her slit by the tassle, then thrusting it deep inside her with the heel of her hand.

'Uh ... uh ... yes ...' Fiona gasped. 'Slipper the bitch, Candi.' She handed Candi a gym shoe.

Candi grasped the gym shoe, with its ribbed rubber sole, and lashed the naked bottom of her squirming victim. Vap!

'Ooh!' Nipringa squealed, suddenly throwing her head up, with her eyes screwed tight, and her teeth bared in a rictus of pain.

Vap!

'Ooh!'

Vap!

'Ooh! Don't!'

Vap!

'Ahh! Please stop.'

The dark bare buttocks, beaded with droplets of sweat, swayed furiously under the crack of the rubber slipper, as the black girl squirmed, clenching the nates until the bum cleft was a narrow line obscuring the writhing anus bud, and slamming against Candi's thigh, as if trying to burrow into her, for safety, to escape the furious spanks. Her blouse was completely undone, the tails swishing on Candi's ankles, and her flapping breasts slapped Candi's thigh. Candi felt the nipples, hard as bullets, jerk frenziedly at each thwack from the heavy slipper, and a sluice of cunt juice spurt from Nipringa's wriggling bare twat. Her own cooze was awash with come, squelching and slurping, at each motion of her spanking arm.

Pausing only to wipe the sweat from her brow, Candi slippered the girl to a hundred, then two hundred slaps. Her belly pulsed with electric pleasure, as her cunt spurted come, and she squeezed her thighs tight, to massage her massively swollen clitty, which throbbed between her sopping wet cooze folds. At each jerk of Nipringa's belly, she felt the black girl's own clit, stiff as a board, slap the bare skin of her thigh, and felt the gush of hot come from the flogged girl's twat. Candi's own moaning was as loud as her victim's, with Fiona gasping in counterpoint, as, soaked panties at her ankles, she wanked her cunt with the giant, come-soaked leather dildo. Fiona's powerful golden thighs rippled, clenching her spurting twat, with the swollen clitty waggling between the cooze lips like a big pink tongue.

'Ooh!' Fiona gasped.

'Ahh . . . ahh . . . yes,' Nipringa squealed.

Candi could hold back no longer. She relaxed her belly and twat, and groaned, as a lovely long orgasm washed over her, blurring her sweat-drenched eyes, until she saw only the bobbing bare buttocks flaming beneath her, winking and wriggling, while Candi felt ecstasy.

'Ooh! Ooh! I'm coming!' panted Fiona. 'Yes . . .'

The prefect's tummy convulsed and, with a plop, the dildo shot from her drooling cunt, to smack onto Nipringa's bottom, landing right in her bum cleft, where the firm fesses clutched it, waggling it up and down on the anus bud. There was a loud hiss, and a cloud of steam, as a jet of hot piss spurted from Nipringa's cunt, soaking Candi's thighs.

'Yes . . .' gasped the spanked black girl, as her piss was followed by an immense gush of hot come. 'Yes! Ooh . . . I'm coming . . .'

With the dildo, slopped with Fiona's come and caressed by her massive bare fesses, slithering up and down the bum cleft, to tickle her arse pucker, Nipringa's jerking under punishment became a writhing, lustful dance, as her belly heaved in climax, showering Candi's wet body with piss and come.

'You fucking slut,' hissed Fiona. 'Now you've really earned a caning.'

3

Bare Caning

'Oh, please, miss, no!' Nipringa wailed. 'Your slave is such a cruel spanker, and my bum hurts so. Haven't I been punished enough?'

'Not half enough,' Fiona hissed. 'You'll take a bare caning, miss.'

'Why, you've had your wank,' protested Nipringa, eyeing Fiona's bared cunt basin. 'Your twat's all wet, miss.'

'Insolence upon insolence!' cried the prefect, seizing her cane, and wrenching Nipringa by her hair. 'I decreed twenty, but you shall have twice that.'

She forced the sobbing black girl onto the sofa, her face pressed to the cushion, and her belly wedged on the arm, with her long bare legs splayed behind her.

'Pinion the bitch, Candi. Sit on her, keep her face down and her bum up.'

Candi squatted on Nipringa's head, suppressing a simper of pleasure, as the girl's hair tickled her sopping twat. She clasped Nipringa's face tightly between her thighs, feeling the crown of the skull poking her stiff clitty, and began to roil the black girl in an undulating motion of her fesses and cooze. Fiona stretched out her graceful fingers, and stroked the bare skin of her victim's buttocks. Her thumb playfully tickled Nipringa's outsized anal pucker, getting the nail inside the anal elastic, and reaming the shaft. Nipringa shivered at the prefect's penetration.

'Such a lovely peach,' cooed Fiona. 'Made for stripes. And that bumhole – I'll bet it's no stranger to a stiff cock. You must pay for your lovely bottom, bitch.'

She lifted her cane, and dealt a savage cut to the girl's outstretched buttocks. Vip! Nipringa jerked, moaning into the seat cushion, and her buttocks squirmed heavily, as Fiona lashed the bare black flesh, again and again, her breasts bouncing, and come spraying from her juicing quim. Candi swivelled, to watch the beating, and felt her own cooze seep with juice, wetting Nipringa's silky black tresses to a pudding of come. Vip! Vip! Nipringa's sobs and squeals vibrated through Candi's cunt, increasing her flow of come and the tingling in her hard clit. Vip! Vip! The flogged black arse danced, purple with deep bruises, as Fiona's teeth bared in a snarl of hatred. Whistling, the cane rose and fell, to streak the girl's helpless bare bottom. Vip! Vip!

'Can't take it like a lady, slut?' Fiona panted. 'I'll teach you to keep that arse still.'

Taking the come-soaked godemiché, Fiona moistened it further, with fresh juice from her twat, then she parted Nipringa's fesses and rammed it into her anus bud.

'Mm! Mm!' squealed Nipringa, as the gnarled leather dildo penetrated her anus, and filled her rectum.

Fiona slammed the dildo home, until only the tassle indicated its presence inside Nipringa's bumhole. Nipringa groaned, sobbing and writhing, with her buttocks splayed taut, both unable and unwilling to clench, at the cuts from Fiona's cane, for any squeezing of her buttocks would increase the dreadful pain of the dildo filling her tripes. Vip! Vip!

'Ooh . . . ooh . . .' the black girl moaned.

Her head jerked at each cane cut and, as Fiona took the flogging past the thirtieth stroke, Candi masturbated her clit quite unashamedly, while riding the black girl's come-slopped mane. Nipringa's face was washed in Candi's flowing come, and Candi heard slurping noises from her lips; she was swallowing Candi's cunt juice. Candi slipped her hands beneath Nipringa's ribcage, and felt her titties. She grasped the big meaty mounds, and squashed and kneaded the engorged stiff nips. Nipringa moaned in pleasure, panting, as she rubbed her skull against Candi's gaping wet cooze, slamming her head against Candi's clitty. Candi squeezed the big firm breasts quite violently, raking and scratching the soft flesh with her fingernails, and this seemed to increase the pleasure of Nipringa's squealing.

Nipringa's buttocks, lashed by the cane, began to perform a sensuous dance, and, to Candi's astonishment, she saw the dildo poke from the black girl's anus, extending to half its length, before a squeeze from the sphincter sucked it all the way inside. Fiona, eyes glazed and face crimson, masturbated her sluicing cooze, as she flogged the bare, squirming arse beneath her bouncing titties. Vip! Vip! The cane lashed faster, and the thrusting squelching of the dildo, in the black girl's self-buggery, grew faster in turn. Plop! Plop! Its oily leather shaft snaked in and out of the girl's anal lips. Candi's cunt poured come; she could no longer restrain her orgasm. Clutching Nipringa's head in her thighs, and mashing her clitty onto the drenched locks, her belly heaving, and throat gurgling in yelps of pleasure, she spurted a torrent of juice over Nipringa's face.

'Ahh ...' groaned Fiona, panting hard, after her fiftieth cane stroke, and spurting a stream of come over Nipringa's buttocks, as she wanked herself to orgasm.

'Ooh! Ooh!' groaned Nipringa. 'Yes ... ooh!'

Her whole body shook, and the dildo squelched frantically, sucked in and out of her rectum, as the black girl erupted in her own spasm, with come spraying from her twitching cunt, all over Fiona's stockinged feet.

'Mm! Mm! Mm!'

The black girl yelped long and shrilly, and at her last, tortured shriek of pleasure, the dildo plopped from her anus, and clattered to the floor, followed by a stream of golden steaming piss from her cunt, splattering Fiona's stockings and belly.

'You fucking bitch!' Fiona squealed.

The door opened, and Miss Hurt popped her nose in. She wore a slinky pink suit, with a short skirt hugging her powerful thighs, and a frilly pink blouse open to generous display of bare breast flesh, topped by a pink nylon bra.

'Is everything all right, Fiona dear?' she said mildly. 'I heard rather a lot of noise . . .' Her jaw dropped, as she surveyed the scene. 'My gosh!' she exclaimed. 'What's this? Have you been pissing? Are you . . . are these gels *lezzies*?'

'Yes, miss,' panted Fiona, 'these sluts are, and I was giving them a jolly good dusting for it.'

Miss Hurt nodded her approval, murmured that Dr Rodd disapproved strongly of tribadism, and must be informed, then withdrew. Fiona ordered Candi to bind Nipringa's wrists behind her back, then lash her ankles together, and draw her legs up, so that wrists and ankles were joined by their cords. Awkwardly kneeling, Nipringa was obliged to lick Fiona's body clean. Her tongue caressed Fiona's anus, cunt and belly. That done, Fiona drawled that the slut was due a tit caning.

'Please, no,' moaned Nipringa.

'You get what you're due bitch,' snarled Fiona.

Vip! Her cane landed right across Nipringa's bare breasts, lashing her nipples hard.

'Ahh!' Nipringa screamed.

For several minutes, Fiona caned Nipringa viciously across the breasts, while the black girl, sobbing, rocked backwards and forwards on her knees. Her teats were streaked livid purple with cane weals.

'Give the bitch a body drubbing,' Fiona drawled to Candi. 'Fists, feet, head butts, anything you please.'

41

Candi gulped, and set to work, pinching the groaning Nipringa in her cunt and belly, kicking the open lips of her twat, and slamming her flogged breasts with cruel blows, that smashed the massive tit flesh right against her shuddering ribcage. Nipringa sank to the floor, wriggling and squealing, and Candi began to kick her in the anus. Fiona arrogantly masturbated, poking herself with the godemiché, as she watched the beating, and from time to time gave Candi an encouraging spank on her bobbing bare bottom. Candi felt awful about hurting the helpless girl, but could not help come dripping from her cooze, as she relished her tiger's power over the battered nude body.

Fiona concluded Nipringa's punishment by caning her on her thighs, wrenched apart by her bonds, and on the soles of her feet, with several uppercuts between the spread lips of her cunt, making the whipped girl howl in agony. Candi could not resist wanking off, as the cruel wood lashed the defenceless bare girl meat. The cane made a dreadful sizzling, squishy noise, as it lashed the girl's juicy pink pouch and her massively swollen clitty. *That could be my twat. Oh, how awful.* Nipringa fixed her with baleful eyes, as her nimble fingers brought her twat to spurt, at the spectacle of the black girl's shame.

The next day, after classes, Candi caught up with the haughty figure of Nipringa, still arrayed in the pink frills of her girly uniform. She blurted her apologies, said she hated having to drub the girl, but Nipringa had no idea of a slave's obedience.

'Oh, but I do,' said Nipringa. 'Anyway, I always pee when I'm beaten. A lady pees where she pleases. Miss Simm gave me a lovely wank, afterwards, when she was rubbing my bum with ointment. She *so* likes a well-caned croup, as do we all, I suppose. What else is a girl's bum for? Are you one of Simm's wank set?'

Candi admitted she was not.

'I'm surprised. You've quite a bum and twat, what we call the apparatus. Still, no hard feelings, girl.'

'Thank you,' Candi said.

'Except you realise I'll want my revenge? Pride demands that I give *you* a thrashing, same as I got.'

Candi bit her lip. Thrashing: her worst nightmare, yet daily endured from the cruel Fiona. Suddenly, a thrill electrified her cunt, and she felt a gush of come wet her panties, as she imagined herself whipped and drubbed by this magnificent ebony girl.

'I see that,' she said. 'I couldn't object, Miss Nipringa.'

'Call me Nip,' drawled the black girl. 'Now, before I thrash you, I'm going to stitch up your mistress Fiona. In the school rules, it says a mot has the right to denounce a prefect to the Prefects' Court, and that's just what we are going to do – denounce Fiona for being a filthy lezzie.'

'We?' Candi's voice quavered.

'You are with me, aren't you?' said Nip, piercing Candi with her big dark eyes. 'You do *want* me to thrash you, don't you, and purge your guilt? String you up, cane you naked, no holds barred? I so want to see that bum wriggle, and your luscious twat spurt juice under my caning, so that I can drink your cunt juice up, while you dangle all helpless. What a magnificent gash you have. Almost as deep as my own. And those thighs . . . a real pair of nutcrackers you've got, Candi.'

'Why, yes,' stammered Candi. 'I am. I mean, I do.'

Fiona was duly summoned to appear before a court of her peers. The complaint was from Nipringa, accusing Fiona of monstrous misuse of her power and lesbian perversions in the guise of normal corporal punishment. Fiona glared at Candi, and bare-caned her fiercely on each of the three days before the hearing, giving her naked arse some really frightful stingers with a double

43

rattan, so that Candi was glad she had to remain standing to give her evidence. Candi followed Nipringa into court, where Fiona sat sullenly in the dock, in her blue school uniform. Cindi and Arabella, also uniformed, sat at the bench, presided over by Miss Hurt, in a black judicial robe over her frilly pink costume and pink silk stockings. The alcove behind the bench was closed off by a curtain.

'Well, Cindi – Arabella – this is a rum do,' Fiona said with a laugh. 'I expect we can see off these beastly snivellers, and get back to work.'

Cindi and Arabella frowned at Fiona, while Miss Hurt called the court to order. She told Fiona that it was no joking matter, that while Dr Rodd refused to appear in public, he himself took an interest in this case, and that proven miscreance would, by his order, earn the most severe punishment. Fiona paled and bit her lip. When Miss Hurt read the charges, Candi shot an anguished glance at Nip, who scowled, for they were named as accomplices to Fiona's miscreance. Their testimony would convict themselves. Fiona guessed as much, and grinned saucily at Candi. Yet her grin faded as Nipringa testified, in a clear, cold voice, to Fiona's drubbing of her, the penetration of her person with a dildo and the enforced masturbation of her clit. She called Candi to support her statement. Candi's eyes flitted fearfully between her mistress and her friend and, faltering, she confirmed everything Nip said. Fiona's strictness as a slave mistress was really a guise for her sapphism. A prefect was supposed to administer corporal punishment in a disinterested, even regretful manner, but her floggings from Fiona indicated that the slave mistress took pleasure. There were murmurs in court when Candi affirmed that Fiona routinely masturbated while bare-caning her, and encouraged her to wank off when her bum was red.

Arabella asked sternly if Fiona penetrated Candi, and Candi said yes, with her fingers, and sometimes her tongue. There were tuts of disapproval.

'But did *you* take pleasure?' snapped Fiona.

'It would be hard not to,' Candi mumbled.

The case of Nipringa versus Fiona seemed to broaden into Fiona's treatment of her slave. Candi found herself blurting the story of her spankings by arrogant, well-heeled Brazilian boys, so that Fiona could buy herself silk knickers and things.

'That's not lesbianism,' snorted Fiona.

'But did you wank off, watching the boys spanking your girl slave?' asked Cindi acidly.

Fiona blushed. 'I ... I may have done,' she stammered. 'I mean, she has such a lovely peach, a girl would find it very hard not to masturbate, watching those bare buttocks spanked. Especially *you*, Cindi, you lustful wanker.'

'You fucking slut,' hissed Cindi. 'I'll have you.'

'Order!' cried Miss Hurt, banging her gavel. 'The judges will consider their verdict.'

'Guilty, all three,' said Arabella.

'Guilty, all three,' echoed Cindi.

The curtain at the rear of the podium fell open, and Dr Rodd appeared, majestic in cap and gown, his face masked in black, and flexing a fearful rattan cane in his fingers. Fully five-feet long and springy, the cane was more of a whip.

'It is not often I interfere in judicial proceedings,' he purred, 'but what I have heard has so shocked and dismayed me – the supreme sentence shall be pronounced, Miss Hurt, and I shall execute it myself.'

Cindi and Arabella had their hands between their thighs, and Miss Hurt's fingers slipped to her crotch, her thighs wriggling, as she condemned Fiona to be flogged and hanged, while Nipringa and Candi were to be flogged and buried alive, the sentences to be carried out consecutively, with Fiona punished first. Blatantly caressing themselves under their skirts, Arabella and Cindi, bright eyed, licked their lips. Fiona's face was ashes. She did not resist, as her friends pinioned her and ripped off her uniform, until she stood shivering and nude. Candi and Nip were shackled, wrists behind their backs, and had their ankles locked in wooden hobble bars. They watched, as Fiona's wrists were roped above her head, the rope, curled slack, affixed to a beam in the ceiling, and her bound feet, weighted with bricks, positioned on a trapdoor in the floor. Miss Hurt covered her head in a black rubber hood, eyeless, but with a nose hole.

The masked Dr Rodd pulled a lever, the trapdoor opened, and Fiona fell, until the rope stretched taut, and she dangled, arms wrenched in their sockets, and only her torso visible, above her navel. A squeal emerged from under the girl's rubber hood, followed by wailing, choking sobs. The stretching of her arms forced Fiona's massive breasts to jut high. Flexing his cane, and carrying a black tulipwood dildo – even more massive and gnarled than the one Fiona had used on Nipringa – Dr Rodd descended to the cellar, where Fiona's naked legs and buttocks dangled helplessly, weighted by the heavy bricks. Cindi and Arabella took the shorter, whippy canes from their waistbands, and then stripped to bra, knickers and stockings, to stand in readiness, with sopping dark patches at the crotches of their panties.

'*Ugh*,' Fiona groaned suddenly, her waist writhing. 'Oh, it hurts, sir. My bumhole. Not my bumhole, I beg you. *Ooh*. Not all the way up me . . . oh please.'

Then, the first stroke of the masked doctor's cane echoed from the cellar, accompanied by a scream from the hanged, hooded girl. Vap!

'Urggh!'

Vap!

'Ooh!'

Vap!'

'*Ahh!*'

At Miss Hurt's signal, Cindi and Arabella positioned themselves on either side of Fiona's writhing bare torso, and lifted their canes.

Vip!

'Ooh!'

Vip!

'*Oh! Ahh!*'

Viciously, they began to whip Fiona's bare back and breasts, while the cruel flogging of her naked buttocks and thighs was accomplished by Dr Rodd below. Fiona's trussed body jerked frantically in her ropes, yet she was helpless to evade the threefold whipping of her naked girl flesh. Her breasts darkened to crimson, with livid welts streaking the bouncing teats, while a criss-cross of angry weals glowed on her twitching back. Candi glanced fearfully at Nipringa, whose eyes glowed with a strange fire, and whose thighs twitched together, mashing her cooze, as she watched the girl's flogging.

'Buried alive,' Candi whispered. 'It sounds awful. I'm so frightened.'

'Don't be,' replied Nipringa. 'It's nothing. Aren't you bored with Rodd's? After they flog us, let's escape from these blasted lezzies – to Rio, where we can wear pink thongs, and have some real fun, with lovely sleek boys.'

'But . . . but, my exams . . .' Candi blurted.

'Pah!' Nip snorted. 'Exams are for little people. I've got money. That's all a girl needs.'

'Oh . . . I don't know,' Candi wailed.

'I do,' hissed Nip.

As the whippers' arms flailed, first Cindi's, then Arabella's titties popped from their pink bras; their bright-pink, clinging, thong panties were soaked crimson, with come spuming from their cunts. Below, the dreadful thwack of Dr Rodd's rattan lashed the

47

squirming, hidden hinderparts of the victim. Fiona groaned, squealed and wept, until her head slumped in a faint. Miss Hurt revived her with a bucket of cold water, drenching her head and trunk, and the whipping continued, the canes now making an ugly hissing noise as they lashed her wet breasts and back. Candi's heart pounded, and her twat and belly tingled, as come filled her slit, wetting her panties.

The canes lashed Fiona's stretched armpits, her breasts, belly and shoulders, until her upper body was a mass of crusting crimson ridges. Miss Hurt's face was flushed, her hand moving more and more blatantly under her skirt, as she masturbated. Candi wished her wrists were not shackled, for she longed to touch her throbbing clitty, and bring herself off. Both Arabella and Cindi had their free hands groping inside their panties, wanking off, as they whipped the helpless bare girl. After a full fifteen minutes' chastisement, Fiona's flogged body glowed crimson with savage crusted welts. Miss Hurt said that it was the turn of Nip and Candi. The shackled girls hobbled into the courtyard, where a freshly dug grave awaited them.

They were pushed into the hole, and a gang of Rodd's mots in punishment fatigues began to shovel the vermilion earth on top of them. Cindi stuck a painful drinking straw into Candi's nose, for breathing, while Arabella attended to Nipringa. As the earth closed over them, hot and moist and dreadfully heavy, Nip whispered that they could dig their way out. If they dug their way out, they could escape, and be in Rio before anyone knew they'd gone. Candi agreed; there seemed little choice.

When the girls emerged, slimed with muck, into the warm night air, two hours later, Candi knew that she had exchanged Fiona's slavery for that of Nipringa Vere-Clissitt, and thrilled. Silently, they padded, nude, away from Rodd's Academy.

Candi felt a bit silly, hitching a ride in the hot darkness, wearing nothing but a seashell clamped on each nipple, and a slightly bigger one covering her cooze, but Nip assured her that it was quite normal girls' attire in Rio, especially with Carnival not far away. Candi needn't be worried about her belongings, for the scrupulously honest Dr Rodd would keep them bundled to await her. Nipringa preferred the challenge of nudity, and freedom from belongings: a girl surviving by sheer style. First, they needed money: a taxi ride into Porto Alegre, even though the banks were closed. After a few minutes, a taxi screeched to a halt, and the girls clambered in. Nipringa coolly stated that they had no money, and would pay in kind. Her hand swooped to the goggling driver's groin and, quickly and efficiently, she masturbated his cock, until he grunted, and spermed in her hand. Nipringa removed her fingers, licking them dry.

'That's the first instalment,' she murmured.

As the cab sped towards the city, Nipringa explained the theory and practice of 'quick wank', the bolder the better, and a certain way for a girl to get what she wanted from any male: 'Don't be a blushing violet, a shy witch, a reluctant virgin. Boys don't like it. They like a bitch, who knows what she wants. They say men like to conquer, but it's a myth. Who are the hottest club girls? The exhibitionists, the sluts. Men like dirty girls. By the time a chap has got a coy maid's knickers off, and she's all red and panting and wet, it's already been so much effort, he's lost interest. She's stupefied by her own juices, and hasn't really decided she wants seeing to, her body has decided it for her. Not much of a conquest. The best way to let him ravish you is to ravish *him*. Above all, be brash. If you want to feel his bum, or his balls, or his cock, feel them. He gropes you, doesn't he? We know that all girls relish bare-bottom spanking. The popular girl doesn't wait, but demands

49

up front whether he is man enough to spank her till she squeals. Or fuck her, if she prefers that sort of thing.'

Nip directed them to an opulent villa, the home of the bank president, whom Nip said she knew very well.

'Now you try,' she murmured.

Blushing, and her heart thumping, Candi pushed her hand to the driver's cock, which was already rigid. A few flicks to the bell end, and he groaned, squirting a heavy wad of sticky hot cream over her fingers. She licked them, finding the taste neutral and not unpleasant.

'That's another myth,' Nip said, laughing, 'that a chap's spunk tastes nasty. Actually, it tastes quite nice, like semolina pudding.'

The taxi driver kissed their hands. '*Obrigado*,' he mumbled, rolling his eyes.

A maid opened the door, and was sent to fetch the bank president from his dinner. He appeared, wiping his lips with a linen napkin, and bowed to Nipringa, with a murmur of 'Milady Vere-Clissitt.' His eyes gleamed, as he scanned the nearly nude bodies of the two girls, still slimed with ochre mud. Nip began to caress his cock, which soon tented his trousers. Murmuring fluently and coquettishly, as she stroked him, she persuaded him of her urgent need for cash, without bothering Daddy, which would be so tiresome. The girls were ushered to the president's study, where he opened a wall safe, stacked with banknotes. Nip dashed off a signature, and took possession of a brick of notes, while demanding the loan of two dresses from the president's young daughters.

The maid fetched two girly costumes, not unlike the punishment uniform at Rodd's, and Nip said they would have to do, but, meanwhile, the president had committed a terrible indiscretion – embezzlement, she was sure – and required punishment for it. The male gurgled with shivering pleasure, as Nip ripped down his trousers, bent him over his desk, and began to lash his bare bottom with his own belt. His cock bobbed stiff, and Candi knelt, to take the huge hard helmet into her mouth, where, on Nip's instruction, she licked and sucked the peehole.

After a beating of thirty lashes, the president groaned, and a hot flood of spunk washed Candi's mouth and throat. She swallowed it, once again pleased to find the taste not disagreeable. The president's wife was calling for him to return to dinner, so the girls had no time to shower. They went to the bathroom, and sponged the mud off each other, before donning the girly costumes: pink pleated tartan skirts, white shoes, blouses, bras and knickers, and fluffy pink ankle socks – all much too tight. Nip borrowed a handbag, rather nice in pink leather, with an Italian designer name. They telephoned for another taxi, which took them to the airport.

Nipringa purchased two first-class tickets for the midnight plane to Rio de Janeiro, and upon checking in, the girls were asked routinely for their ID cards. Candi's heart chilled; she had quite forgotten. Here they were, fugitives of a kind, without papers. Smoothly, Nipringa withdrew two ID cards from inside her panties, and waved the moist, fragrant plastic at the astonished male. They belonged to the bank president's daughters.

'Always palm whatever you can,' whispered Nip, with a saucy wink.

The clerk objected that both girls, despite their girly attire, looked somewhat older, and Nip slightly darker, than the photos in the ID cards; Nip pouted, and said she could explain the laughable misunderstanding. She slipped behind the desk, and pointed at the card, then at her own face, while opening the front of her blouse, to let her naked breasts spill out of their skimpy juvenile bra. Meanwhile, her hand was working at the man's cock.

'So you see, the photo was taken some time ago, before I got my suntan,' she said loudly. 'You naughty boy, I should spank your bottom for doubting me. I'd like to whip you really hard, till your arse is really sore, and crusted with dreadful welts. That's what I do to boys who displease me.'

This seemed to excite the clerk. Goggling at Nip's bared breasts and erect nipples, still flecked with gobs of mud, the man gasped, as she wanked him to come; then he mopped his brow, and blurted that everything was in order. Nip tucked her titties into the tiny pink schoolgirl bra, and led Candi to the departure gate. When they were ensconced in their first-class seats, and sipping champagne, Nip put her hand on Candi's thigh. She whispered that she had told the truth: her greatest pleasure was spanking or whipping male bottoms.

'For a girl, being spanked is nothing,' she declared. 'It's what our bottoms are made for, and I've been spanked and whipped as long as I can remember, for Daddy is a real tyrant, while Mummy believes sparing the rod spoils the child. As a result, I'm definitely unspoiled. Men are a different matter. I learned early that when they spank us, they are really begging *us* to spank *them*. Only they don't know just how painful a girl's whip can be, nor how vengeful her chastisement – the fools! There is nothing sweeter than raising welts on a boy's squirming bare bum, thrashing him to tears and blubbing, with him begging you to stop. And you have no intention of stopping, till his bum is whipped to jelly. Rio reeks of sex, and dishy boys, all gagging for it. They think they want our twats, but what they really crave is our whip on their arse.'

Candi listened, awed at the spurts of come in her tingling twat. Nip's hand slipped up Candi's bare thigh, under her too-tight girl's panties, and into her moist gash. Casually, she began to tweak Candi's stiffening clit. A stewardess poured more champagne, smiling complicitly, as Nip openly masturbated her friend. She flushed, cooing with pleasure, as Nip coolly stroked her

52

bottom, while wanking off Candi; then Nip slipped her hand beneath the stewardess's skirt, and caressed her bare buttocks, moving her fingers under the girl's panties, to stroke her naked cunt. The girl blushed, and murmured thank you, when Nip complimented her on the smoothness of her shaven twat hillock. It did not take long for the girl's belly to quake, her face to redden, and a stream of come to pour into her quivering nylon stocking tops, as, under Nip's expert fingers, she erupted in orgasm. Candi could not resist; sliding her fingers into Nip's juicing twat lips, she massaged the massively hard clit, before gasping in her own climax.

'*Always* travel first class,' murmured the black girl, still toying with Candi's throbbing twat, and squeezing Candi's probing fingers in her own. 'Isn't a girl's greatest pleasure in wanking off? If only boys knew – our interest in *them* is making them cry, and getting them to buy us nice things, while frigging our clits at their pain and shame, and the sight of their wealed bottoms. Now, we've time for some lovely wanks, to get us in the mood for the studs on Copacabana beach.'

4

Punchbag

Thighs and bottom. That is what keeps a girl going and showing. Big, rippling thighs, tanned a succulent brown, leading to a firm, bulging bare cupcake – a girl's cupcake should always be shaved clean – over the pink slice lips, and, round the back, a lovely firm bum peach, with that juicy groove in the middle, that writhes so invitingly when she wiggles her skin globes. Squash the thighs together, especially in the thinnest, briefest, tightest panties or shorts, clinging to the bum and cupcake, and the twin thighs rippling, pressing together, so that any chap watching just can't help but stiffen, or even cream himself, imagining his pego squirming between those hard fleshy pillars. Trap that stiff cock meat, squeeze it with your nutcrackers, watch the helmet bulge helplessly, as you knead the shaft, the thighbacks pressing ever so soft, yet menacing, on his balls; then watch the spurt, lovely creamy stuff, all over your skin and shorts. Mm. Yum. You messy pup, you deserve spanking for that. That's what I should have done with that bastard Darren. Tamed him, made him squirm. But I was the one squirming. Hmph. Never again. Feet, too, of course. A girl's feet must be long and dainty, with toes that look as if they could curl round a fellow's balls and squeeze him to death. Or crush him. Crush his face with her bum, spurting come over his nose and eyes and mouth. How they whimper,

*how they love that. Smelling her, taking big breaths, right
in there, up her secret hole, inhaling her bum perfume like
a fine cigar. Ripe, jutting breasts, meaty but soft and
yielding, the sort you can punch like medicine balls, and
they bounce back for more. But you couldn't walk on your
breasts. Or could you? Wouldn't it be fun to try? You
could be suspended from gym ropes, by your ankles, wrists
too, and try to walk along by waggling your boobs. A
titty-race. What a fun idea. Although perhaps a bit
painful on the nipples, especially big squashy plums like
mine.*

These, and other thoughts, occupied Candace as she
inspected her nude body in the full-length looking glass.
Below, across the bustling Avenida Atlantica,
Copacabana Beach glistened with girls' oiled brown
bodies, flashing the universal pink of their minuscule
thongs and bikini tops. Amongst the girls, prowled
predatory boys, their sleek bodies clad in thongs scarcely bigger than the girls'; soon, smooth ebony Nipringa
and snow-blonde Candi would snare a pair of those
arrogant peacocks, to give them sensuous delights of a
more painful nature than the preening boys bargained
for. For a girl to be dominant, not a spanked, whimpering submissive . . . it made Candi's heart glow, and her
cunt moisten.

She had learned so much in such a short time: from
Miss Simm, from Fiona, and now from Nipringa
Vere-Clissitt, the loveliest, scariest teacher of them all.
Nipringa was there, awaiting her; time for a quick frig,
first. How liberating it was to know that a girl's
constant desire to wank off was healthy and wholesome,
and to be gratified as often as possible. For that, as for
so much else, she had Nip to thank. Virginity was easily
kept in Brazil, where bumming was more normal
practice, and if the pain of a hearty buggery was too
off-putting, then intercrural spunking – the simple
thigh-fuck – was a popular relief for horny studs.

Fucking, Nip explained, was really – or so cocks thought – about humiliation and power, and a good thigh-fuck, without penetration, but spurting juice all over a girl's belly and titties, or even her face, was satisfactorily shaming. Cocks who demanded anal penetration, which was actually the most super fun for a girl, often longed to have their own bums fucked. Candi said she wished she had known that when horrid Darren bummed her and made her suck his spunk through a bendy straw, from her own buggered bumhole. Nipringa often referred to boys scornfully as 'cocks'. Yet, what did Nip want from her? Wanky games, of course, but that was harmless fun; did the svelte black girl have some deeper, sinister motive? As she inserted her fingers into her moistening cunt, and began to masturbate, Candi decided that danger was part of Nip's thrill.

She closed her eyes and imagined a hunky young cock, maybe a bit younger than herself and with the delicious swank of immaturity, nude, his hard, muscled bum gleaming under her fingers, as she caressed his tool to stiffness; his surprise, as cuffs were snapped on his wrists, and Candace lifted her whippy cane over his helpless bare buttocks; his squeals and tears, as she whipped the cock's naked bum flesh to raw red stripes. Her palm rose, over her quivering bottom. Smack! She began to spank herself, just as Darren had spanked her and just as she was going to do, in revenge, on all those tasty male bums.

Smack! Smack! She spanked hard, really hurting, until her bum glowed hot and red and stingy. *It's just the heat, and the constant itch in my cooze. I don't really like the pain of spanks, despite those beasts Darren and Fiona.* Come poured from her tingly wet cunt and she quickly brought herself off. She wiped the come from her thighs, and wrenched herself into her too-tight powder-blue thong bikini.

On her gold lamé stilettos, she tripped gaily through the lobby of the grand old hotel, to be saluted by young flunkeys in bottle-green frock coats. They blushed, as she gave them the look, saying, I know you've a tool ripe for rubbing, and a juicy pair of buttocks begging to be spanked. Today was sure to be the day ...

Nipringa was parked in a prime position. Her nearly nude body, clad only in a minuscule thong, and tiny bikini top that scarcely veiled more than the nipples of her massive black breasts, was stretched on a towel under the broiling sun, overlooking the crashing Atlantic breakers, where a few show-off boys were tumbling from surfboards. Candi flopped onto her own towel beside Nipringa, her head up and already ogling the strutting boy flesh on offer. All those lithe young hunks, waggling their packets in their tiny bikini pouches. She applied sun oil to her teats, belly and legs, getting her fingers right up beside her tiny thong, and slapping her beasts all over, making sure the cocks noticed the ripple of her thighs and titties. Nipringa's bikini was yellow, Candi's blue: the only costumes on the beach, it seemed, that were not a luscious shade of pink. Candi began to worry lest she commit the sin of being unfashionable, and murmured as much to Nipringa.

'Don't worry,' drawled the black girl. 'A bum like yours is always fashionable.' She sat up, tucking an errant breast into its pouch. 'In fact,' she murmured, 'I'm absurdly jealous. I still owe you a spanking, remember.'

Moisture seeped in Candi's cunt. 'If you want,' she whispered. 'I shan't resist.'

Nip laughed. 'You wouldn't take it from a cock, would you? Then why from me?'

'I don't know,' blurted Candi, blushing fiercely. 'I just would, that's all. Perhaps I'm afraid you wouldn't want to wank me any more.'

'Good enough,' said Nipringa, pouting and patting Candi's bikinied cunt hillock for everyone to see. 'Now it's time to trap a cock for crowing.'

'How about that one?' drawled Candi, nodding at a lithe young stud who was preening and pouting, and absolutely full of himself, as well he might be, with a positively superhuman packet bulging in his skimpy thong. 'He looks ripe for spanks.'

'Right, then,' said Nip briskly. 'Do what I do.'

She proceeded to ogle the cock shamelessly, crossing and uncrossing her thighs, and lazily rubbing her bulging cooze, yet giggling and lowering her gaze whenever his eyes met hers. Abruptly, she turned on her belly, and thrust her buttocks high, spreading them and pulling her bikini thong as tightly as possible in her crack, so that her anus was only just covered by the yellow string. Candi did the same, thrusting up her bum, and thrilling at the tight string nuzzling her anus bud, until the boy's shadow darkened the two girls. They turned round, and peered up at his packet, bulging obscenely, and obviously straining to erection. Nip smiled, and asked him if he would mind oiling their bottoms.

'If we did it to each other, people would think we were *bichas*,' she cooed, 'and that would never do, not with a big virile cock like yours turning us to jelly.'

The cock's name was Vasco da Silva. He was eighteen years old and from Paraiba, in the far north. As he kneaded the girls' outspread buttocks, he remarked how brave they were to wear thongs that were not pink: brave or shy. Nipringa said that because of her convent upbringing in England, she was dreadfully shy, and Candi claimed she was timidity itself. Vasco laughed and explained the meaning of the pink thong that was all the rage this season in Rio. Each thong was handcrafted, and individually dyed, precisely the shade of pink of the girl's slit meat. Nip and Candi clapped their hands, and cried that they simply *must* wear pink. By coincidence, Vasco informed them that he shared an apartment in Ipanema with his girlfriend, who specialised in such work. His father owned a vast ranch, but Vasco and Emmaia preferred the freedom of the big city.

'He thinks I should be a gaucho, and Emmaia a housewife,' purred Vasco, making no attempt to conceal the massive bulge in his panties. 'I prefer to be a pleasure-seeker, as you perceive, ladies –' he smirked '– and as for Emmaia, well, you shall judge.'

A taxi took them to a leafy back street near the beach at Ipanema. Emmaia opened the door of the large, airy apartment, which was cool and white, with draped rugs, white leather chairs and uncaged parrots – the casual elegance of the tasteful rich. Emmaia was tall, with rippling, muscled thighs, a narrow slab of bare waist and hard, powerfully jutting bodybuilder's teats; her skin was a sultry olive colour. She wore only a bikini bottom, in a lurid shade of pink, and a white sleeveless T-shirt, cut off just below her braless breasts. Long black tresses were scooped over her head, with a red hibiscus flower perched over the coils. Her smile was dazzling white – a predator's – and her handshake crushing, with her arms knotted in whipcord muscle. Vasco explained that his girlfriend was a kick-boxer.

The girls were shown Emmaia's studio, which doubled as a gym. It was full of paints, dyes and silky cloth, as well as a boxing ring, weights, punchbags, vaulting horses and ceiling rings. Over tea, it was established that Candi and Nip understood the significance of pink, and they agreed that Emmaia would fashion stylish bikinis for them. Smiling, she said that they must both strip. Nude, the girls sat back on an easy sofa, with their legs splayed and cunts showing. Vasco watched, licking his lips, and his crotch bulged with a massive hard cockpole.

'You lustful swine,' purred Emmaia. 'Bend over, and lower your shorts.'

Groaning, Vasco obeyed. He presented his buttocks. Emmaia retreated, took a long run-up, leaped from the floor, and kicked Vasco's arse with both feet. Her bare feet thudded on his buttocks thirty times, while he blushed in shame. Smack! Smack! Her feet landed on the boy's squirming buttocks.

'Please,' he begged, 'not in front of our guests.'

'Especially in front of our guests, you boy pig,' panted Emmaia, kicking the boy in the rump. 'A boy is nothing but a football, for a girl to kick.'

She kicked him for five minutes, while Vasco's face was crimson with embarrassment. After his kicking, Vasco pulled up his shorts, rubbed his bottom, and sat sulking in the corner, underneath the parrot cage.

'A good kicking keeps a boy quiet,' said Emmaia.

Emmaia attended to Nip and Candi. She said that every girl's pink was different, and to expose her true pink, her cooze must be sexually aroused. Therefore, while she took photos of their cunts, she would like the girls to masturbate, and achieve the correct rush of blood and excitation.

Giggling, Candi began to tweak her clit, while Nip masturbated enthusiastically. Nip smiled broadly, as her fingers slopped in her rapidly moistening cooze. Emmaia complimented them on their long clamlike gashes, so pretty, compared to the tight little Brazilian slit, and urged them to hold their quim flaps as wide as possible, while wanking off. After taking numerous split-cunt photos, she pulled down her panties, and parted the lips of her own satin-smooth gash, to show the pink pouch exactly matching her panties. She pulled them up again, and turned, showing them the panties croup, swollen by her buttocks – *two eggs in a hanky*, Candi thought – and shading to a slightly darker pink, almost crimson. Two-tone panties, she murmured, were for the *really fashionable*. The front gusset represented a girl's cunt, masturbated to the brink of orgasm, while her buttock colour represented a different stimulus, perhaps even more exciting.

'I mean the colour assumed when a girl's bare bottom is spanked or caned,' she said, licking her teeth.

Candi and Nip looked at each other, eyes bright with excitement.

'Oops,' Candi blurted, as a drip of her come gushed over the leather sofa.

'We'd certainly want to be really fashionable,' said Nip. 'But a spanking . . . that sounds awfully harsh.'

'As for a caning . . .' added Candi, with a shiver.

'Vasco can attend to your bottoms,' replied Emmaia. 'He is an experienced spanker. Of course, if you don't want to be ultra-fashionable . . .'

'No! We do!'

'Please spank us!'

Vasco ceased sulking, and licked his lips. 'I spank very hard,' he said. 'It will be painful – those lovely bottoms will wriggle – and if they don't blush to my satisfaction, I may use the cane, to firm up the colour.'

'Sounds like naughty fun,' said Nip, with a shrug and her eye on Vasco's bulging erection. 'But I don't think Vasco can spank properly, with his shorts tugging at his cock so tightly. Let him be at his ease, and in the nude to spank us.' She blushed, giggling. 'It will be quite a thrill to be spanked by a naked boy, with his cock stiff.'

Emmaia reached over, and coolly ripped down the boy's shorts, allowing his massive naked cock to spring up like a sapling. Vasco's body gleamed, tanned and hairless; his pubis and balls were shaved satin smooth, which made the erection of his cock supremely menacing. Nip said she would go first, and slid across the sofa, placing her belly across Candi's thighs, with her buttocks thrust up. Vasco took position, lifted his arm, and brought his palm down, with a loud crack, on Nip's bare buttocks. She winced and, as the spanks continued, her bum began to wriggle and clench, and she gasped noisily.

'Oof! You are a good spanker,' she said, panting. 'That hurts like Hades.'

As her spanked bum squirmed, the black girl's come oozed from her wriggling twat, over Candi's bare thighs. The cooze hillock rubbed on Candi's skin, so that Candi's gash too seeped juice. Her thighs slithered in the pool of come on the white leather sofa. Smack! Smack! Emmaia stood with one foot on the sofa arm, and her face pressed to her knee, as she watched Nip's bottom squirm. Her T-shirt was up over her bare breasts, and she pinched her big brown nipples, while wanking herself off inside her pink panties, which were rapidly staining with dark wet come. Her lips bore an angelic smile, and the hibiscus flower in her hair bobbed up and down, as she masturbated.

Vasco's cock jerked up and down, inches from Emmaia's lips, as he vigorously spanked the black girl's buttocks, which were flaring to purple. Long glistening streaks of come from her wanked cunt glistened on Emmaia's rippling thighs. Candi longed to wank off as well, and thrust her thighs together to squeeze her throbbing clitty. After fifty spanks to Nip's bum, it was Candi's turn. Biting her lip, she stretched herself across Nip's thighs, and raised her bottom. Smack! Vasco's palm stroked Candi's naked fesses.

'Oof! That hurts!' she gasped.

'Good,' drawled Emmaia, wanking vigorously. 'There is no love without pain.'

Smack! Smack! Candi's gorge rose, and tears moistened her eyes, for Vasco spanked very hard. She dreaded to think of his slipper, or his cane. The pain stung her wriggling bottom, which she could not help clenching hard, as the spanks rained on her naked flesh, and her face contorted in a grimace. Suddenly, she felt Nip's fingers penetrate her squirming gash, and begin a slow, delicious frig of her gushing pouch and stiff clitty. Pleasure filled her, with an unbearable tickling in her cooze. Smack! Smack!

'Oh! Yes!' she gasped. 'Harder! Spank me harder!'

'Spanking shows what a girl's really made of,' drawled Emmaia. 'The pink on her bum is her true soul.'

'And what are you made of, miss?' said Nip. 'Your bikini is the deepest crimson . . . more than spanks, I'd guess.'

Candi's spanking concluded at the fiftieth smack. She groaned, rose, and rubbed her flaming bottom. Still masturbating, Emmaia grinned fiercely, and grasped Vasco's cock. She stroked his balls, and said she needed much more than hand-spanking, that her bottom was used to the cane.

'Show us then,' said Nip. 'Fair's fair.'

'I am only caned when I am naughty,' Emmaia said, pouting.

'Be naughty, then.'

Emmaia giggled. She stripped off her bikini pants, revealing a lush brown cooze hillock, gleaming shaven smooth. She knelt, taking Vasco's cock between her lips, with her hand cupping his tight balls, and began to caress his peehole and bell end with her tongue.

'He is a terrible boy,' she murmured, her mouth full of her boyfriend's cock meat. She nodded to a lustrous tulipwood cane. 'He has so much spunk, and needs to sperm three times a day at least. Then, I am soundly thrashed on the bare buttocks for my impertinence. I'm no different: I must have four or five wanks a day. He whips me for the crime of wanking off. Life is not fair to us girls.'

The twinkle in her eye, and her slurping pleasure, as she tongued the boy's throbbing cock, belied her words. At her spread cunt flaps, her hand was a blur, wanking fiercely, with come bubbling between her fingers.

'Spanking makes a girl so hot,' said Nip, panting. 'All girls need to wank lots, Emmaia. It is our nature.'

She began to masturbate Candi's twat, and Candi responded by ramming her fingers into the black girl's

63

silky wet pouch, and jabbing her hard wombneck. Emmaia's head bobbed like a pigeon's, with the boy's cock taken all the way to the back of her throat, and her lips smacking his ball sac. The girl squealed, as Vasco wrenched her hair and, snarling, ordered her to spread her cheeks. Trembling, Emmaia crouched, with her big bum up and spread and, still holding her hair, with the hibiscus flower crushed in his palm, Vasco plunged his cock into her anus. It slid in smoothly, and withdrew, soaked with the girl's arse grease, before once more filling her rectum.

'Ahh! No! It hurts!' Emmaia screamed, her body rocking as the boy buggered her, with fierce thrusts of his cock to the root of her arse, so that his balls slapped her anal lips.

The magnificent play of her boxer's muscles jolted her spine and thighs, so that her whole body rippled. Nip dived to Candi's cunt, and clamped her clitty in her teeth, beginning to chew, while sucking and kissing the lips, and making little slurping noises, as she drank Candi's come. Nip cupped her buttocks, and probed her anus with a forefinger, at last ramming two fingers into Candi's rectum, and mashing her colon.

'Oh, don't, it hurts,' Candi moaned, her cunt basin squirming against the black girl's face.

A gold and green parrot flapped onto Candi's bouncing breasts, and began to squawk shrilly, its claws digging at her nipples, while another perched on Nipringa's buttocks, scratching her anus bud. Nip took Candi's clit into her mouth and sucked hard on the distended nubbin, then began to mash it between her lips and teeth. Candi squirmed, gasping and moaning, her hands clutching Nip's hair, reaming the girl's head against her. Shaking and writhing under Vasco's brutal buggery, Emmaia let her head sink to the floor, where she chewed the rug, while masturbating furiously. Come streamed from her cunt, over her pulsing thighs. Candi twisted on top of Nip in a sandwich, and plunged her face between the black girl's scented wet thighs. Her mouth found the swollen clit, which she chewed greedily, sucking and swallowing Nip's come, both tribades slipping and sliding in their pool of cunt juice on the white leather sofa.

Vasco grunted, sweat dripping from his nude body, as he buggered the squirming, sobbing Emmaia. He gasped, and a froth of sperm bubbled at her anal lips, spilling down her come-soaked thighs, as he ejaculated his cream in her colon.

'He's filling me up,' groaned Emmaia. 'It hurts. It's so good, a spunk enema. Oh! I'm coming! Yes . . .'

Candi could no longer hold back, and exploded in orgasm, while the spurt of come from Nip's gash, and the writhing of the black girl's belly, signalled her own spasm. Candi and Nip drank each other's come, sucking the last drops from their throbbing cunts. Nip grabbed Candi's hair, making her squeal, and forced her head between Emmaia's upthrust buttocks. She ordered Candi to suck the boy's spunk from her anus, without swallowing, and deliver it to her own mouth. Candi obeyed, fastening her lips on Emmaia's anus bud, and sucking hard, until her cheeks were bulging with hot creamy sperm, flavoured with the Brazilian girl's acrid arse grease.

'You filthy slut,' snarled Vasco, picking up his cane, and lashing Candi across the buttocks.

She gasped, swallowing the whole mouthful of spunk.

'You bitch!' exclaimed Nip. 'You've swallowed my portion of spunk! Cane the slut till she screams, Vasco.'

Candi was spreadeagled on her back, while Nip sat on Candi's face, with her cunt crushing the girl's nose and mouth, and held her legs up high, in a V shape. Vasco put his foot on Emmaia's neck, pushing her face into the carpet, and, with the swishy tulipwood, began to thrash both bared bottoms, with alternate strokes. Vip! Vip!

'Ooh! You brute!' squealed Emmaia, her flogged brown bottom squirming, as she began to wank off anew.

'You naughty, vicious whore,' hissed Vasco. 'I shall cane your bum till it's one massive crust, purple with bruises, and you won't dare to show your arse in a thong on Copacabana Beach ever again.'

Vip! Vip! His cane thrashed the naked buttocks of his girlfriend.

'Oh! Ahh!' shrieked the twitching brown girl, her fingers frantically wanking her cooze. 'Yes, I'm naughty! Stripe my bum, Vasco!'

Vip! Vip!

'Ooh!'

'Urrgh!' groaned Candi, her voice muffled by Nip's cunt, which was squashing her face.

Both bottoms were soon streaked with livid pink stripes from the cane. Nip's buttocks writhed, squelching, on Candi's face, as Candi's tongue penerated Nip's slit, and began a fervent gamahuching of her sopping cunt and throbbing clitty. Vip! Vip! As the cane strokes rained, stroking Candi on the buttocks and thighs, dangerously near her spread cunt, Nip shifted back and forth, to thrust Candi's tongue from her twat into her anus. Her come drenching Candi's cunt-crushed face, Nip rubbed her breasts with the heels of her hands, tweaking and wrenching her erect nipples, until, when the flogged girls squirmed under their thirtieth cane stroke, she erupted in a savage, moaning climax. Moments later, she pissed long and hard over Candi's face, filling her mouth and nose with pee, which dribbled down Candi's breasts onto the come-soaked leather sofa. Emmaia gasped, as she wanked herself to a come-spraying spasm, then hissed: 'My sofa. You'll pay for that, you slut.'

Nipringa shrieked, as Vasco wrenched her hair, and pushed her face down into the pool of piss and come.

Emmaia and Candi sat on the wriggling black girl, and Vasco lashed her arse with rapid, vicious cane strokes. Vip! Vip!

'Urrgh!' Nip gurgled, her mouth and nose submerged in piss, and her crushed breasts squelching in the steaming acrid lake.

Vasco caned Nip's bare past thirty strokes, with the black girl heaving and squirming. Occasionally she managed to wrench her face from the piss pool and gasp for mercy. Vasco's tool stood rigid again, and he flogged the black girl's bottom with his teeth bared in a rictus of pleasure, while Emmaia masturbated, rubbing her wet cunt on Nip's wriggling kidneys. Sitting on Nip's head, Candi rubbed her crusted bottom, which was smarting horribly, and dreadfully hot to the touch. She desperately wanted to go to the loo, and could no longer hold back. Surely nobody would notice? She peed into Nipringa's hair, and saw her steaming piss flood down the girl's cheeks, into the pool on the sofa. Emmaia's nostrils flared.

'Filthy English bitch,' she hissed. 'Caning isn't enough to teach you a lesson.'

Sobbing and shivering, the whipped black girl was released, to rub her eyes and bottom, while Emmaia explained that Candi required special punishment. First, Vasco mounted Candi, while Nip and Emmaia held her down in a crouch, and the Brazilian boy buggered her pitilessly. Candi wept and squealed in pain, as the giant stiff tool filled her rectum and smashed into her tender colon. When he was near spurt, he wrenched his tool from her anus, and plunged the cockshaft, dripping with sperm and Candi's own arse grease, into her mouth, right to the back of her throat. Shaking with choked sobs, Candi sucked her arse grease from the giant cock, until a fierce jet of sperm filled her throat and mouth, and she gagged, swallowing it, until every last drop had passed her throat.

'Oh! Urrgh!' she spluttered, wiping her mouth.

Nip and Emmaia pinioned her, dragging her to her feet.

'Wait,' she whimpered. 'Where are you taking me? Oh, Nip, I thought we were going to punish boys.'

'I told you I still owed you a beating,' snarled Nipringa.

Vasco slapped her several times across her mouth, and Candi burst into tears. They stumbled into Emmaia's workshop, where Nip bound her wrists with a rope, and Candi's nude body was drawn up towards the ceiling, until she was dangling with her toes above the floor. Her ankles were lashed to heavy rocks, placed wide apart, so that her legs were wrenched rigid and trembling, showing her open cunt and the full expanse of her arse cleft and trembling anus bud. Emmaia stroked her bum weals, and cooed that she had a delightful shade of pink for her new bikini; her camera flashed, as she took pictures of both Nip's and Candi's buttocks. She slipped a tight black hood over Candi's head. A parrot flapped in, and perched, cawing, on top of it.

'Oh, no! Please!' Candi wailed, her voice muffled under the hood.

'Shut up, bitch,' snarled Emmaia. 'Your body is a perfect punchbag.'

Nip asked if they should wear boxing gloves, but Emmaia laughed.

'Bare fists, bare feet,' she said.

Slap! Her left leg shot up, and landed a kick to Candi's titties. Candi squealed. Emmaia followed this with a flurry of punches to the strung girl's belly, and leaped from the floor, legs jacknifed, for a double-foot kick, on Candi's open cunt, landing on the pink gash with a squelching slap.

'*Ohh! Ahh!*' Candi howled, wriggling in her bonds. 'Oh, please, stop.'

Nipringa joined in her punishment, punching her titties, cunt and belly. Candi swayed, shuddering with choked sobs, as the two girls alternated her punishment. After a belly-drubbing from Nipringa's knuckles, Emmaia delivered a flurry of high kicks, to the titties and cunt. While Emmaia battered the girl's titties, Nipringa kicked her from behind, making her buttocks shiver, and sliced her toes up between the outstretched thighs, to jab the defenceless cunt and anus. Vasco, nude and erect, carried a short snake-tongued whip; after the girls' punches, he lashed Candi across the breasts, or flicked the whip directly on her slit, flogging the clitoris and pouch meat with a wet, slapping hiss. Candi's body jerked frantically, as drool bubbled from beneath her hood; after a few minutes of chastisement, a powerful jet of piss steamed from her cunt.

'I can't take it,' she groaned.

'You're both a pair of tarts,' Vasco sneered.

Nipringa glowered, and grabbed him by the balls. 'Watch your mouth,' she panted, squeezing the tender orbs.

Vasco howled, and wrenched her hair. The black girl toppled, releasing his balls from her fist.

'You filthy slut,' he snarled. He forced her to her knees, and slammed his erect cock between her lips. 'Chew on this, bitch,' he sneered.

While Emmaia continued her drubbing of the helpless, squealing Candi, Vasco began to fuck Nip in the throat, just as if her mouth was a cunt. She gagged, as his balls slapped her chin, and his hairless groin slammed against her nose and eyes. The base of her throat bulged with his thrusting glans inside. Candi's body wriggled like a fish on a hook, under Emmaia's merciless kicks and punches; yet come squirted from her battered cooze, and her clitty peeped swollen and throbbing between her whipped cunt folds.

'Urgh ...' Nip groaned, as her head bobbed in the rhythm of the boy's throat-fucking.

'Stop ... please ...'. Candi whimpered. 'I need to come. Please.'

Emmaia's naked cunt glistened with come. She slapped her erect clitty several times with her fist, and brought herself off. Vasco gasped, as his cream spurted in Nip's throat, so powerfully, that bubbles of frothy spunk foamed from her lips, and dripped down her chin onto her jiggling titties. Nipringa rose, sobbing; Emmaia hugged her, and kissed her full on the mouth, sucking the remains of Vasco's sperm from her lips, with her fist between Nip's thighs. A few strokes brought the black girl to orgasm.

Unhooded, and released from her bonds, Candi's hand dropped to her cooze, where she quickly wanked herself to a come. The parrot flapped away, and landed on Emmaia's breast, with its claws clutching her rock-hard nipples.

'Well,' gasped Emmaia, stroking her parrot. 'That was fun. Tell me, Candi, what did you mean "punish boys"?'

Candi explained that the girls' idea had been to find spunky young cocks, and spank them, or shame them, to get revenge for all the wrongs and cruelties boys had inflicted on them.

'But it's all gone horribly wrong,' she said. 'I'm so ashamed ... I got all wet when I was beaten. It excited me.'

Emmaia stroked her chin. 'Sensuous girls always juice when thrashed,' she mused. 'But boys' bums should squirm, too, especially with a rampant spunk like Vasco.'

She grasped Vasco's balls, and squeezed. Whimpering, his knees buckled, and he sank to the sofa.

'Shall we teach him a lesson?' asked Emmaia, licking her teeth.

'Super,' said Candi.

5

Off the Beaten Track

It wasn't at all like her fantasy; for a start, Vasco was already nude, his pink panties discarded, so Candi didn't enjoy the slow, shameful stripping, to reveal the bare buttocks for punishment. But his whimpers of dismay, as Emmaia tied his wrists and ankles to two upright parallel bars, made up for that. Also, his cock was already rigid, despite – or *because of*? – Emmaia's control of his balls, and the fearful prospect of a bare-bum caning. He stood, arms and legs outstretched and helpless to move, with his cock ballooning monstrously at his trembling groin.

Coolly, Candi accepted the cane, flexing the rod and lashing the air with a vicious whistle, while relishing the fear in Vasco's wide eyes. He wasn't shy, not like the boy in her fantasy, but fear thrilled her more than shyness. She moved behind him and stroked his shivering bare buttocks with the tip of her cane, listening to his whimpering sighs. Emmaia and Nip stood with arms folded and lips pursed, like judges at a livestock show.

'I think this arse can take at least forty strokes,' Candi murmured, trying not to let her voice quaver.

'Oh, fifty, I'd say,' replied Nip, and Emmaia agreed.

'He's an arrogant swine,' she cooed. 'We want to see him blub and beg for mercy, don't we? Mercy that he has never shown any girl.'

'Please . . .' Vasco babbled. 'I'm sorry. Don't beat me. I can't stand the pain.'

Emmaia clapped her hands. 'That's exactly *why* you're to be beaten,' she purred.

'I shan't rest until his buttocks are all crusted with weals, and the deepest crimson you can imagine,' said Candi solemnly, her twat moistening, just at the words. 'He'll never want to flog another girl's bottom.'

'Oh, don't go *that* far,' whispered Emmaia, caressing Vasco's balls. 'Just go far enough. We'll have to reduce that disusting erection, of course. Whip him soft, Candi.'

Candi raised her cane, and lashed him across the bare, on mid-fesse. Vip! His bum jerked, and he gasped, as a long pink streak at once marred the smooth purity of the brown arse flesh. Candi licked her lips. Vip! A second stroke took him higher, on the tender top buttock, and he gasped, with a little wailing moan. Vip! The buttocks clenched, and began to squirm, as the strokes etched vivid pink across the boy's bare bumskin. Vip!

'Ooh! Oh, miss, you cane fearfully hard,' he whimpered, his bare arse wriggling.

'Thank you,' Candi said.

Come streamed from her twat, and she wondered if it would be infra dig to wank off, as she caned the boy. Nip and Emmaia both licked their lips, seemingly oblivious to the trickles of come from their bright shaven gashes. Vip! Candi's breasts bounced heavily against her ribcage, as she whirled, to give her strokes the maximum impact.

'Ooh!' the boy squealed, gasping and sobbing. 'Oh! Oh, please stop.'

Vip! Her cane gouged deep crimson ridges in the boy's squirming bare buttocks. His whole body shuddered, the legs jerking rigid at each cane cut, yet the buttocks seeming to absorb the pain, and channel it up his rippling spine, so that he was graceful even in agony, with the stripes on his naked buttocks a thrilling adornment. Vip! Nip and Emmaia could hold back no longer, and, standing to the side, where they could observe both the wriggling flogged buttocks and the tear-streaked face of the victim, both girls masturbated, with slow, squelching frigs of their spread cunts, so that Vasco could see their pleasure in his pain.

Candi's thumb dived to her clitty, and a few tweaks brought her off, to a gasping, thrilling orgasm, that sprayed streams of glistening come all down her rippling thighs. Her caning did not falter. Vip! Glowing in the aftermath of her come, she continued to lash the boy's twitching arse meat, hoping that someone else was keeping the score, although she did not want the flogging to end, ever. A boy, proud and arrogant and haughty, helpless, whimpering and bleating for mercy, as she striped his flesh. Yet that cock was still as stiff as a pole, as if the caning perversely excited him. Vip! Vip! The cane lashed him without mercy.

'*Ahh!* Oh, please stop,' he begged, sobbing.

'Not till your disgusting stiff cock is soft,' Candi hissed.

'I can't help it, miss,' he moaned. 'It's so horrible, yet so unbearably thrilling, to be naked, and whipped by a girl.'

'You filthy perverted beast,' Candi snapped, vigorously wanking her throbbing clit. 'We must get rid of that erection.'

Vip! Vip! She landed vicious cuts to his thighs, sure that boys didn't like that at all.

'*Ahh! Ohh!*' Vasco shrieked, his stiff cock swaying under the girl's lash.

'Stop whingeing like a bloody girl, or I'll whip your balls,' snarled Candi. 'You don't want your balls whipped, I dare say. Now stay quiet, and take your bum-flogging like a man.'

73

'Yes, miss,' moaned Vasco.

'Only one thing for it,' murmured Nipringa.

She sprang up and locked her wrists and ankles around Vasco's neck, and sank her bottom onto his cockpole; Candi saw the tool penetrate her anus, right to his balls. Supported by his body, Nip bounced up and down on his cock, buggering herself. His cock made squishy noises, as it slid in and out of her anus, shiny with the black girl's copious arse grease. Emmaia grasped two ceiling rings, and swung herself up, to land with her belly against Vasco's face. She locked her thighs around his neck, on top of Nip's, and pushed her twat onto his mouth.

'Lick me off, brat,' she ordered.

Vip! As Candi continued to flog the crusted, crimsoned arse, the boy sucked come from Emmaia's juicing twat, while Nip slammed her anus up and down on his stiff tool, her buttocks slapping against his balls and thighs. Come poured from the ebony girl's cunt, dripping down the boy's balls, while Emmaia's come soaked his face. Candi espied a massive wooden dildo, just like Fiona's godemiché. She pulled Nip from the boy's body.

'I say, Candi!' cried Nip.

'Fair's fair,' said Candi.

Nip's anus left the boy's cock with a plopping squelch and a stream of arse grease on his balls, and then Candi rammed the dildo into the boy's anus, plunging it in until it struck his colon. She began to bugger him. Impaled on the gnarled coarse wood, he screamed for mercy. Nip stood and masturbated, tweaking her clit, and letting her cunt juice flow onto the boy's face. After several minutes of buggering him and masturbating hard at the spectacle of the helpless enculed boy, Candi resumed her caning. Vip! Nip seized the dildo embedded in Vasco's arsehole, and mounted him once more. His stiff cock was in her black bum, and she writhed, buggering him with the wooden dildo, and wanking her

74

clit, fucking his tool at the stand, with her squeezing anus, until she came, her belly shuddering, and her cunt gushing come. As Nip's anus squelched his rigid tool, Vasco groaned, and began to spurt, with a froth of white spunk bubbling from Nip's anus lips. Emmaia's cunt juice spurted into her boyfriend's mouth.

'Swallow it all, brat,' she hissed.

Vasco sucked Emmaia's cunt, swallowing all her copious come.

'You dirty beast,' snarled Candi.

Her cane rose, whistled in the air and lashed the boy's helpless bare buttocks. Vip! Vip! The boy's bare bum writhed in agony.

'Oh! No more,' he whined. 'For pity's sake, miss!'

The caning went on, with Candi masturbating to two more orgasms, until Vasco's arse was fully crusted, and Emmaia had come, spurting cunt juice into his mouth, and ordering him to swallow it. At last, panting, Candi let the cane slide down her come-soaked thigh. With a sticky plop, Nip disengaged from Vasco's cock, which flopped half-rigid, glazed with sperm and girl's arse grease. Emmaia leaped to a crouch, and pinioned Nip's cunt, with her face in the cleft of Nip's arse. Holding the black girl's buttocks to her lips, while playing with the clitty, she sucked Vasco's spunk from Nip's anus, and swallowed it noisily.

'Well, I whipped the brat soft,' Candi boasted.

'You!' flared Nipringa. 'It was I who milked his spunk.'

'I beg your pardon, I think I deserve the credit,' said Candi frostily.

Without warning, the black girl leaped on Candi, and began to slap her. Slap! Slap! She smacked Candi's titties, belly and cunt.

'Ouch! Ooh! Nip, stop!' Candi squealed, as the black girl's hands hit her wealed body.

'Saucy cow,' hissed Nipringa.

'Stop! Oh, stop! It's not fair!' Candi howled.

In desperation, she slammed her knee between Nipringa's legs, and the black girl grunted, her eyes glazing, as Candi's knee smashed her clitty against her pubic bone. Candi kneed her again, and again, until, clutching her groin, Nip rolled off her, and writhed in agony on the floor.

'I'm sorry, Nip,' Candi blurted.

'Sorrow is so bourgeois,' drawled Emmaia. 'What the slut needs is remorse.'

She seized Candi's hair, and slung her over the back of the sofa, with her bum up. Fuming, Nipringa rose, to clamp Candi's wrists, while Emmaia knelt, and pinioned her ankles, with her legs and arse cheeks spread wide. Vasco removed from a cabinet a coiled, ugly mass of leather. He flexed it, whipping the air with a jostling noise. Candi gaped; it was a studded leather cat-o'-nine-tails.

'This is a relic of the second voyage of Vasco da Gama,' Vasco said. 'I have the honour to bear his name, and own his whip.'

The vicious leather whip of nine thongs rose above the girl's helpless naked body. Vasco stroked her bottom. Vap! The thongs striped the girl's bare buttocks pink.

'Ahh!' the nude Candi screamed, writhing, as Vasco's cat lashed her helpless bare.

Her sweat-soaked legs jerked rigid, at each stroke of the cat on her arse.

Vap! Vap!

'Ooh! No!' she shrieked.

Her bottom squirmed, as the boy cut into her existing crusts, lacing them to deep, glowing crimson stripes. At each stroke of the whip, her arms and legs wrenched against her captresses, but in vain; the whip lashed her helpless fesses a full dozen savage cuts, while Candi sobbed, wept and squealed, pleading for mercy. Vasco paused, leaped over the sofa, and mashed his own flogged bottom in her face, his anus bud squashing her nose.

'That's *your* mercy,' he growled.

The whipping resumed, with Vasco's bare arse sitting on Candi's face. Candi took two dozen, then another five strokes, until she wailed, and pissed herself. Pee streamed from her dripping cunt, soaking Emmaia's body. Spluttering with rage, Emmaia told Vasco to give her more than a mere whipping. The boy delivered three final lashes to Candi's anus, then threw down the whip, and mounted her scarred bottom.

'Ahh! No!' she screamed.

His rigid cock plunged easily into her anus, and he began to buck furiously.

'Give the slut a real hammering,' said Emmaia.

'Fuck her arse raw,' added Nip.

Candi squealed and wriggled, weeping, as the boy buggered her. The force of his thrusts slammed her belly and teats against the sofa, knocking the breath from her. Smack! Smack! His belly and thighs slapped hard against her buttocks, at each penetration of her rectum, with his balls smacking her cunt lips, which were soaking with come. His buggery smashed her erect clitty against the damp sofa leather, and Candi began to pant in tortured pleasure.

'Ohh! Yes! Ahh! I'm coming!' she squealed.

A flood of come spurted from her gash, and her belly heaved in spasm. Moments later, Vasco's spurt filled her rectum with spunk. It bubbled over her anal lips and trickled down her thighs, to mingle with her rivulets of come. Emmaia ripped a long, bendy drinking straw from an orangeade bottle, and stuck one end in Candi's mouth. She rolled Candi onto her back, while Nip lifted her thighs, and pressed her ankles around her neck, baring her bumhole and buttocks. Emmaia inserted the straw into her anus, and ordered her to suck up all

77

Vasco's cream. Sobbing and choking, Candi obeyed, swallowing the mixture of hot spunk and her own pungent arse grease, while wanking her throbbing clit, until she swallowed the last drop of sperm from her arsehole, and exploded in another orgasm. She collapsed, exhausted, on the come-soaked sofa, while Nip cradled her head between her thighs.

'You did deserve punishment,' Nip murmured.

'I know,' Candi said, snuffling. 'I'm sorry, truly I am.'

'Perhaps we should both chill,' said Nip. 'Find somewhere off the beaten track, take things easy for a while, and, you know, explore our inner womanhood.'

Emmaia reappeared, with two bright-pink bikini panties, one for each of the girls. Both clapped their hands in joy, at the intricate lacing of pinks and crimson, the croup exactly matching the bruises on their bottoms, and the gusset, the pink of their respective pouches. Vasco, too, reappeared, looking sheepish. He, too, wore a girl's pink bikini panties, with the exact stripes of his own crimson chastisement. He held out a bunch of old iron keys.

'We wondered if you would like to holiday in our seaside cottage up north, in Paraiba,' he said. 'We don't use it much; it's the least we can do, to thank you for super fun.'

On the balcony beside the sands, with the Atlantic surf crashing, Candi munched her heart of palm salad, letting the juice dribble into her breasts, over her pink bikini.

'I can't get over Vasco calling this a cottage,' she said.

'More like a palace,' Nip agreed. 'Certainly off the beaten track. It's super, but a bugger to sweep and tidy.'

'We don't really have to wear clothes at all,' said Candi mischievously.

Nip wagged a finger. 'There *are* people around,' she said. 'Yokels are always curious about strangers. If we

78

were nude, we might be tempted to . . . you know, play too much. Haven't we agreed to chill? A few good wanks a day is quite enough to keep a girl fit. Anyway, I like wearing pink. It's rather naughty.'

The girls had agreed on a regime of stress-free leisure, which meant no corporal punishment, and no 'lezzie scenes', as Nip termed their previous caresses. Instead, after meals, they would lower their bikini panties, spread their thighs, and masturbate together, smiling blissfully as they watched their fingers tweaking slopped cunts to leisurely orgasm. When not on their private beach, or shopping in the village market, they were kept busy cleaning the rambling ranch house, or playing gardener in the large grounds, which was stocked with bougainvillea, hibiscus and wild tulipwood trees. They amused themselves by fashioning godemichés and whippy little ladies' canes from the abundant tulipwood, promising to test the canes on each other, when their chill out was completed, but enjoying hearty wanks every night with the huge gnarled dildos, some of them with double shafts, so that Nip and Candi would writhe, bellies rubbing, with the tubes in their cunts, and frigging their clits with fingers enlaced. It wasn't fun and games, just a healthy part of chilling out.

After a few days, the cheerful woman who owned the grocery shop tut-tutted that ladies on holiday should not have to do housework, and offered her daughter to work as their live-in maid, for wages that to the English girls seemed no more than pocket money.

'She is a good worker,' said the grocer, 'but like all Paraiba girls, she is lazy if not supervised. You must spank her bare bottom regularly to keep her alert.'

The barefooted Laura proved to be a bashful, demure eighteen year old, with long black tresses patted in curls, twinkling green eyes, a big, richly swelling bottom over long legs, firm, pert, braless conic breasts, their olive flesh and hard, thrusting nipples generously visible below the straps of her dress. She was ravishing in her cotton shift dress, dazzling with scarlet, yellow and green flowers, which clung to her lithe young body, its sheer line disturbed only by the briefest of panties, a mere string across the full, ripely wobbling bum pears. Coyly, Candi's eyes met Nip's, and they licked their lips, both knowing that Laura's dress must soon come off, and those panties fall, for a bare-bottom spanking.

Yet she was so sweet, well-mannered and industrious, right from the start, that it was hard to foresee any excuse for chastisement. Barefoot, she trilled enchanting melodies, as she washed, scrubbed and swept, and was always tucked up in bed soon after dark, to rise with the sun, and have a delicious breakfast steaming hot for her mistresses. Nip and Candi would leave her to her housework, as they spent lazy afternoons on the beach, until, one day, they returned to the house to the sounds of struggle.

Nip put a finger to her lips, and they tiptoed to the salon, where Laura lay naked on their dining table. Her dress, and bright pink thong, lay on the floor. On top of her was a svelte young boy, also nude, with his huge stiff cock between her pumping thighs, plunging in and out of her distended anus, with his balls smacking her bare buttocks. His body, like Vasco's, was smooth and hairless, the shaven pubis slithering wetly against Laura's own porcelain-bare cunt hillock. The previously demure maid squealed and panted under his fierce buggery, with sweat and come dripping from her writhing cunt basin, and her buttocks slammed the wood with loud slaps, as he impaled her rectum with his tool, right to his balls. Her cooze was filled with one of Candi's carved dildos, with which she slit-fucked herself in the rhythm of the boy's savage buggery, stabbing her womb with the squelching wooden tube, drenched in her pussy juice.

'Uh! Uh! It hurts so! Please don't. I can't take any more. My bum's bursting!' she squealed.

'You're loving it, you cock-hungry slut,' said the buggering boy, panting.

He withdrew his cock almost fully from her anus, his peehole just touching the bud, before plunging inside her rectum again, in savage, slapping thrusts. Laura groaned, her bottom wriggling to meet his thrusts, and the dildo squelching her cunt in a blur of glistening sprayed come.

'Oh! Yes,' she shrilled. 'It's so good. Fuck me harder, Julio, bugger my tripes, spurt your spunk right up my hole, split me with that lovely thick tool . . .'

Nip and Candi hid behind the door, and gaped, their tongues hanging out.

'What a corker,' gasped Nip. 'Look at that huge heavenly tool! And such lovely big bollocks!'

'I've *got* to wank off,' hissed Candi.

'Me, too.'

Their fingers dived beneath the pink bikini gussets, and their gasps of pleasure joined the moans and grunts of the anally rutting girl and boy. Juice poured from Laura's cooze, slopping the burnished rosewood table, and Nip gasped that spoiling the table was one spanking offence, and stealing their godemiché was another.

'As for that dishy boy . . .' she added, masturbating her clit to a come-slopped, heaving orgasm.

'A bum like that deserves the cane,' gasped Candi, as come soaked her wanking fingers, and her belly fluttered in spasm.

They watched, masturbating vigorously, until the boy groaned, and spunk flew from Laura's lips, soaking her buttocks and thighs, and dripping to the dining table.

'Oh! Yes!' she shrieked. 'I'm coming! Ah! Ah! *Ahh!*'

The dildo pumped in and out of her squirming twat, with a spray of come squishing from its shaft, as she rubbed it furiously on her swollen clitty, and writhed, whimpering, in orgasm.

'How gorgeous that was,' the maid panted. 'But you'd better go, my darling. My mistresses are funny ladies – English – they might spank me if they knew I had boyfriends.'

'Boyfriends!' gasped Julio. 'What –'

'Oh! I didn't mean –'

'You slut! I should spank you myself.'

'That won't be necessary, boy,' purred Nipringa, as the girls stepped from their hiding place. 'We shall spank her, and you too. We saw everything. Bumfucking our maid! And with an obscene monster like that –' she pointed to his cock, hanging limp between his thighs, almost to his knees '– you vile pervert!'

'He made me, mistress,' said Laura with a sob. 'I was jelly in his arms. He made me use the dildo on myself, and take a bumming. I couldn't resist. Surely you understand.'

'Quite so,' rapped Nip, 'but you will have to take a spanking, and, of course, we must report this wrongdoing to . . . to the appropriate authorities.'

'Please,' Julio begged, dropping to one knee. 'Not Sergeant Vasconcelos. He hates me, ever since he saw me tupping his sister. I meant no harm, ladies. She was drooling for it – Brazilian blood is hot – but I love Laura. Oh, above all, do not tell her mother. I tupped her too. I tupped the mother of Sergeant Vasconcelos, and also his daughter. He doesn't know. Don't report me to Vasconcelos.'

'Why, that is *exactly* what we propose to do,' said Nip.

'No. I beg you. Punish me, if you must, but do not betray me.'

'We've made canes,' murmured Candi, 'so we might as well test them.'

'My thought exactly,' said Nip. 'The girl can take a spanking, but the boy – why, only the most severe caning will suffice to correct his mischief.'

'The cane?' Julio blurted, staring, as Candi flexed her whippy little school cane.

'On the bare buttocks,' Candi whispered. 'Lashes from this wood on the skin of your naked bum, boy, till you squirm and weep and beg for forgiveness.'

'Oh, no, miss,' he blurted. 'I've been beaten before, but always with my pants on. Please let me put them on to take your whipping. I don't think I could take the lash on the bare.'

'You will have to, boy. I *always* cane naughty boys on the bare. Otherwise they don't weal up with true pink. Naked buttocks it is, and that's final. You have fucked females with disdain. No punishment is too great for you.'

Julio emitted a choked sob. 'Very well,' he mumbled. 'I suppose I have no choice.'

'First, you shall witness your girlfriend spanked,' Nip decreed.

Julio's frown of dismay turned to a leer. 'That will be a pleasure,' he sneered. 'I understand she is everybody's girlfriend.'

'It's a lie,' cried Laura. 'I am faithful. I have never betrayed you, except maybe in the heat of passion, but *you*'ve bummed every girl in Paraiba.'

'Silence,' snarled Nip. 'Your punishments shall be administered at once.'

She lifted her cane, dark breast flesh heaving in her tight pink bikini cups, and Julio's eyes widened, as she whipped the air, with a slashing whistle. Candi gasped, her eyes riveted on the boy's massive cock, for, as the cane whirred, it began to stiffen and rise, until the monstrous tool, glistening with Laura's arse grease, stood stiff and full as an oak tree. Nip ordered Candi to spank the maid's bare bum over her knee, while her boyfriend watched. Candi sat on a bench and patted her thighs to summon the maid for her spanking, while, on Nip's orders, Julio stood with his hands behind his back, and his head bowed. His cock sprang from his shaven loins like a fresh sapling. Laura trembled, as she placed her nude body over Candi's thighs.

'You won't hurt me too much, mistress?' she blurted, her eyes brimming with tears. 'I know I've been a wicked girl, and must be punished, but – oh! the shame – with people watching.'

'Spanking is about pain, as well as shame, Laura, so don't expect it not to hurt,' Candi purred. 'I know what a well-spanked bottom feels like. The burning smart can be quite horrible.'

Smack! She lifted her arm, and brought her palm down hard on the girl's massive bare bum flans, their olive skin shiny and smooth.

'Ooh!' Laura gasped, her bum cleft at once clenching to a thin line.

Smack!

'Ahh!'

Smack!

'Uhh ... uhh ...'

Glowing with pink handprints, the naked arse pears began to squirm. Smack!

'Ooh ...' the maid panted, whistling through her teeth. 'Oh, miss, it *is* horrible.'

Candi told her to try to remain silent, and Laura sobbed that Candi's spanks were harder than any playful chastisement she had received before. Smack! Smack! Smack!

'*Ooh!*'

The girl's bum was well pinked, the spanked buttocks writhing like two glistening fish in a net. Her shaven cunt slithered against Candi's bare thighs, and Candi's own cooze began to moisten, as she gazed at the squirming fleshy orbs reddening under her palm, with a slippery ooze of come on her thigh from the girl's slit. The girl was juicing under spanks. Candi felt the squishy, swollen folds of her gash rubbing her bare thigh, and, poking between the flaps, the hard nubbin of Laura's aroused clitty. Her own nubbin throbbed, stiffening rigid, as her breasts bounced, and she spanked the maid's wriggling bare arse harder and harder. The spanks went to three, then four dozen, with the imprint of Candi's fingers now puffing to cherry-red welts and ridges. Julio gazed, breathing hoarsely, at his girlfriend's torment, with his stiff cock shivering, the hard glans swollen to burst. Laura's wracked, rippling body shuddered with sobs. Behind the boy, Nip had her fingers on the ouside of her bikini panties, rubbing hard, with a big damp stain of come wetting the gusset.

'No sense in waiting,' she gasped. 'I'll whip the boy at once. Get down over the table, you wretch.'

Whimpering, Julio stretched himself across the table, gripping the corners with both hands, his legs wide, and erect cock nuzzling the underside of the tabletop. Nip tapped his balls with her cane handle, until he lifted and spread his buttocks, baring the balls fully, and perching on trembling tiptoes. Nip stroked the taut arse cleft and ball sac with her cane tip, and Julio moaned.

'Please, miss –'

'No use begging for mercy, you scum,' Nip snapped. Vip!

'Ahh!'

Her cane lashed his naked bottom, the cheeks clenching instantly, and the boy letting out a wail of distress. Vip!

'Ooh!'

'Silence, worm,' snarled the black girl. Vip!

'Uhh,' he gasped, his arse flans twitching, as livid stripes streaked the skin.

Vip! Vip! Julio took his beating without wailing, but with unbroken gasps and pants, his bare arse squirming violently, as Nip crusted his bum flesh with dark welts. Beside and below the boy's wriggling nates, Laura's naked fesses glowed fiery crimson, as they writhed under Candi's vigorous spanking. Gasping hoarsely, Laura squealed, moaned and wept noisily, her face streaming with tears, just as a flow of come seeped from her cunt, onto Candi's slippery bare thighs. Vip! Vip! The caning went to over thirty strokes, each of them making the boy's legs jerk rigid, and his back and buttocks ripple in a shuddering dance of agony. His bottom was prettily striped in a tangle of dark crusts and crimson weals, with numerous scorched bruises, where the black girl had caned the backs of his thighs. Above him, Nip's erect nipples and breasts bounced heavily, threatening to burst from their bikini cups, and her slopped panties were dripping come from the gusset. Vip! Vip! Nip delivered two scorching undercuts, right in the arse cleft, and perilously near his twitching balls.

'Ahh! Please, miss, I can't take any more,' he whimpered. 'Please.'

Panting, Nip lowered her cane, wiped her brow, and gazed at Laura's spanked bare pumping up and down under Candi's palm.

'That's what Laura said to you, but you ignored her, as I recall,' Nip sneered. 'Let's see if Laura would like her revenge. Would you, Laura?'

'Yes, please, mistress,' gasped the maid. 'If mademoiselle could just finish this dozen.'

Candi spanked the extra five strokes; Laura's cunt writhed, slapping, on her chastiser's thigh, and, at the last stroke, Laura shrieked, with come pouring from her twat, as she shuddered in orgasm. Eyes glistening, she accepted the double dildo from Nipringa, who helped her strap it around her waist, plunging one prong in her slit, and the other nuzzling Julio's anus.

'No . . . no,' Julio wept. 'Don't make me a *bicha*.'

The fiercely grinning maid thrust violently, and the dildo penetrated his anus to half its length; another thrust, to Julio's squeals of agony, and the gnarled wooden cylinder was sunk completely in his rectum. Laura began to bugger him, with come squirting from her own cunt, as it was fucked by the twin shaft of the godemiché. Candi plunged her fingers to her twat, and began to masturbate beneath her pink thong; Nipringa did the same, while the enculing Laura vigorously wanked her huge stiff clitty, protruding above the shaft of her cunt-dildo. The force of Laura's slamming enculement made Julio's stiff tool tap the wood underneath the table, and Nip suggested Candi do something about the noise.

Candi squatted beneath the table, and, cupping Julio's balls firmly in her palms, slipped her lips around the trembling bell end of his giant cock. Gurgling, she engorged the whole helmet, licking and sucking his peehole, then swooped to take the whole cockshaft in her throat, with her lips pressing his balls. As her head bobbed in powerful sucking fellatio, there was a thump above her. Nip leaped onto the table, and squatted over the buggered boy's face. Taking him by the hair, and holding her cunt flaps open, she pushed his mouth into her wet pink slit.

'Lick me off, worm,' she hissed.

Julio began to slurp at her cooze, taking the bloated clitty between his teeth, and chewing, while Nip writhed in pleasure. She ordered him to drink her come, and his throat bobbed, as he swallowed it. When Nip's belly heaved, and a heavy jet of piss washed the boy's face, she ordered him to drink every drop of her steaming golden fluid. Arse impaled on Laura's merciless dildo, he lapped up her piss and come; his body wracked with sobs, while Nip's fingers tweaked her swollen nipples inside her bra cups. The boy's whimpers turned to grunts and groans. Below the table, Candi wanked herself to a shuddering orgasm, with come seeping from her cunt, just as Julio's cock delivered a copious stream of creamy spunk. As she writhed in climax, Candi swallowed every last drop of the buggered boy's sperm.

'Well,' said a dry, ironic male voice. 'Nice to see you giving instead of taking for a change, Laura. Seems you've apprehended not just trespassers, but escaped slaves.'

'Sergeant Vasconcelos!' gasped Julio. 'I can explain.'

'No need,' drawled the slim, thirtyish policeman, stroking his heavy baton. 'The master's property invaded by hooligans, landless squatters, and they turn out to be fugitives in pink, from his own plantation. You've done well, Julio.'

'Sir, we are English girls,' snapped Nip.

'Tourists,' added Candi. 'You see, we were lent this house by Vasco da Silva and his girlfriend, Emmaia, in Rio de Janeiro.'

'Da Silva? There's no one of that name around here, and anyway, every house, every fishing boat and sand dune and tulipwood tree – *and* cop – is the property of the plantation master. Stupid sluts who escape never think to go far away, or even to lose their slave pink.'

'We are not slaves,' blurted Candi, 'we are English.'

'So are half of them,' shrugged the sergeant. 'Julio, go to the truck and get the heaviest shackles, for they look a spunky pair. I'd bastinado them, and crimson their arses, but the master prefers to take care of that his end. I don't envy them their fate.'

He ripped off their bikinis, and tied both top and panties around their necks, like labels in a livestock show. Nude and sobbing, the girls were bound by handcuffs, left hand to right. Then they had their feet placed in two hobble bars, before shackles were tightened on their thighs and feet, with cruel chains – their ends held by the sergeant – clamping their cunt flaps. He flicked the chains, wrenching their clamped coozes, and the girls shrieked in pain, then shuffled after him, weeping, to the waiting police truck. They were pushed into the back, and made to lie down, for heavy pincers to be fixed to their nipples. The pincers were embedded in the flatbed of the truck, permitting the girls no more movement than sitting up.

'You're the laziest patrolman in the village, Julio,' said the sergeant, 'but we might make something of you yet. There's a promotion to corporal, and I could put in a good word.'

'Oh, Julio!' cried Laura, embracing the naked boy. 'I do love you!'

'Of course, it mustn't interfere with my enjoyment of Laura's arsehole on Sunday afternoons,' said Sergeant Vasconcelos.

Julio and Laura, embracing, with the maid tugging her boy's cock to new stiffness, assured him that nothing could interfere with his promotion to corporal. The sergeant gunned the engine of the truck and, with Nip and Candi lurching in the back, under a hot sun in its cloudless blue sky, they proceeded inland, choking with dust from the primitive track. Behind them, Laura was kneeling, sucking her boyfriend's cock, while he whipped her bottom with a cane.

Vip!

'Ahh!'

'You thoughtless bitch.'

Vip!

'Ahh! God! You're hurting me!'

Laura began to wank her clit. Her cunt gushed come, as she swallowed her boyfriend's sperm, licking her lips as she did so.

'Ohh,' wailed Candi. 'It's all been spoiled. We were supposed to be the ones giving the punishment.'

Nip's fingers were in her wet pink slit. She wanked herself to orgasm, with come pouring down her black bare thighs. She rubbed her come into her mouth, and into her anus, and smiled with joy.

'Looking on the bright side,' said Nip, 'this planta-tion, or whatever it is – a master, like Dr Rodd – well, it can't be worse than school, can it?'

6

Tied to the Tulipwood

'And what is your name again, my dear?' drawled the master, emitting blue smoke plumes from his cheroot, and sipping his iced coffee.

He knew her name; the pretty elfin blonde girl, shivering in the morning sun, was Jacqui Prosset, from Builth Wells. Another girl teenager, seeking that folly of follies, wisdom from travel. This one was utterly luscious, trembling in her thin blue cotton dress, and nude beneath, save for her baby-blue panties. Her mane, braided in lush flaxen pigtails, caressed her upthrust young breasts. The titties were full and jutting high, with big strawberry nipples, clearly visible under the flimsy cotton, while her buttocks promised delight upon delight. They were sculpted full and round, as if by some master craftsman in the fresh, dewy morning of the world, when girls were naked animals, for the pleasure of man. The master wagered that those full arse pears had never even been spanked, or, if so, certainly never quivered naked under the lash of a Brazilian slavemaster. A beautiful maiden in – where? Builth Wells? – must certainly have attracted spanking, and if not on the bare, then on the flimsiest panties, letting the pain sting the nubile flesh, and the naked young nates squirm and writhe in wonderful girl shame. So many girls, so many tender bare bums to quiver under the lash, as the innocent flesh was striped. And every girl's bottom adorably different.

Biting her lip, Jacqui Prosset gave her name. Beside her, two pink-booted monitors, in clinging pink one-piece swimsuits, cuddled their heavy tulipwood canes, and leered at the trembling Welsh girl.

'I didn't mean any harm, sir,' she blurted.

'You said you were homesick,' the master purred.

He spat the stub of his cheroot, so that the glowing tip glanced briefly on her nipple, singeing her dress, and making her wince. He waved another cheroot, and Sarah Wavergreen, the bigger of the two monitors, lit it with a match flicked on the seam of her swimsuit, which was a slightly darker pink than that of her colleague, Emily.

Tears moistened Jacqui's eyes. 'I am a bit homesick, sir,' she whimpered. 'It's not what I expected here.'

'On a plantation, you didn't expect to work?' asked the master. 'You didn't expect to be punished for laziness?'

'But spanking, sir,' she gasped.

'You have not been spanked yet,' he murmured. 'How charming. A girl so young. Why, the buttocks are ripe as pears, but the breasts are hard little buds, beautifully sprouting, thrusting to flower.'

'I'm fully eighteen, sir,' she blurted.

'Then you must have been spanked, even though you look so much younger, so charmingly juvenile. One can see you in a school uniform: a pleated skirt, fluffy socks and a training bra.'

'I am old enough to have been spanked, sir, on occasions, by my dad, mam or brother. Every Welsh girl has.'

'On the bare bottom?'

'No sir, on my panties, or pyjamas, drawn tight. But it's still awfully frightening.'

'Your main crime is wearing that blue dress, against regulations,' he said. 'Pink is the order here. You may take it off. And girl slaves go nude. You must earn the right to wear pink. In fact, you must earn the right to wear any clothing at all.'

Jacqui paled. 'Strip naked, sir? I've only my panties – it's too hot for a bra.'

'Blue panties, I see. They must come off too. You hesitate, maid?'

The master slashed his glowing cigar across Jacqui's breasts, and the girl cried out. A seared gap appeared in the cotton, showing her bare skin. The master clawed the neck of her dress with his long, sharpened, purple fingernails, and casually ripped it from her body.

'Oh!' Jacqui cried, crossing her arms over her breasts, in a vain attempt to shield her nude body from the ogling monitors, and the hot Brazilian sun.

The master pressed his cigar to the gusset of her panties, which sizzled. The girl screamed. Then he ripped off her panties, leaving her nude. He smiled viciously, seeing her massive pubic jungle, the cunt hairs dangling in thick fronds well below her glistening gash flaps and blonde curls crawling thickly over her hips and belly, to obscure her navel. Jacqui started to weep and rubbed her eyes, leaving her naked breasts uncovered.

'Oh! Oh! I don't deserve this!' she wailed.

'But you do,' purred the master. 'You come here dreaming of experience, no? You will have experience beyond your dreams.'

He strutted around her shivering nude body, licking his teeth at the spectacle of the terrified girl's bare buttocks, trembling already, and deliciously goose-fleshed. His fingers delved in her pubic forest and he pulled the hairs at the root, making the girl whimper; then he stroked the naked arse flesh, and she moaned, sobbing and biting her lip. He prised the trembling jellies apart, and tickled the wrinkled crimson anus bud, spread in the bum cleft like a starfish, with its little tender mouth primping, beckoning. The master made no attempt to conceal his rising erection from the two simpering pink-swimsuited monitors.

His fingers slid across the girl's haunches to her flat, trembling belly, and the massive cunt bush, extending from her swollen hillock and fat, drooping gash flaps, almost to her navel.

'A pubic forest as lush and uncontrolled as the Amazon jungle,' the master said. 'You are remarkably, perhaps admirably, hairy at cunt, and have not shaved your quim clean,' he murmured. 'You deserve flogging for it, but I am in a generous mood today – you will retain your forest, and be one of my chosen hairies. It's such a lush growth, and purest blonde. Are all Welsh girls like you, I wonder?'

'You are not going to whip me, sir?' Jacqui gasped. 'Thank you, thank you. I promise I shall be a good girl, and be obedient, and do anything you order.'

The master laughed. So, too, did the monitors. Sarah had her hand cupping Emily Clyde's swimsuited bottom, and was stroking it. The high cut of the girls' swimsuits, covering only an inch of cunt hillock, showed them to be fully shaven. The master stroked Jacqui's cunt bush, putting his finger between her cooze lips and teasing out the big pink clitty, which was throbbing in new erection.

'That, at least, is pink,' he murmured, thrusting his fingers into her slit. 'You are a virgin, I believe?'

Jacqui blushed fiercely. 'Yes sir,' she quavered.

'I approve.'

Three of his fingers were now inside her cunt, squelching in the come that was beginning to seep from the mashed cooze meat. He cupped her buttocks, pressing her cunt basin between his two palms, and inserted a finger into her wriggling anus. She jerked, her pert bare breasts bouncing.

'Ooh, sir, that tickles,' she moaned, her buttocks closing over the probing fingers, and squeezing them.

Come glistened on her quivering thighs, whose muscles rippled, as her cunt oozed juice. The master fastened his teeth on her pubic mane, and pulled hairs from her cunt hillock with his teeth. Jacqui squealed. The master spat the hairs into Jacqui's mouth, and ordered her to swallow them. Groaning, she obeyed.

He snapped his fingers on each of her bulbous nipples, flicking both of the gourds into full stiff erection.

'You'll get more than a tickling from my whip, I'm afraid,' he said.

'Sir! Please, no! I beg you!'

Jacqui began to weep convulsively. The master licked his lips, drawing his breath sharply, for this – a naked girl's terror – was almost the sweetest moment, before the whip leather struck the bare flesh of the helpless, whimpering blonde girl's buttocks.

'You have a choice,' he said. 'You may resist your just chastisement, and be whipped while bound in cruel ropes, followed by whatever extra punishment Sarah and Emily think you deserve for your obstinacy. It could be the bastinado, that is, flogging with rods on your bare feet, or it could be nipple and cunt torture, as only girls know how to inflict. Or, you may wrap your arms around this tulipwood tree, thrust out your naked buttocks for due whipping by your master, and hold yourself up, to take your punishment like a lady. Your bare arse will be stroked due pink, girl.'

Jacqui wiped her eyes of tears. She gazed at the master's uncoiled whip, a sjambok with a forked tongue. Come trickled down her quivering thighs, wetting her bush, with the swollen red gash flaps palpitating beneath the massive carpet of pubic curls. Unconsciously, Jacqui's hands crept to her breasts, and tweaked her turgid nipples. She looked fearfully at Emily and Sarah. Their cunts were swollen beneath the clinging pink swimsuits and juice was spurting unashamedly from their slits, down their massive, rippling tan thighs.

'I will be pink?' whimpered Jacqui.

'Your arse – the very soul of any girl – must shine pink, from a male's whip,' the master confirmed.

Jacqui stumbled beneath the shady branches of the tulipwood tree, and locked her arms around its trunk. She planted her feet in the ochre earth, with her legs spread wide and her naked buttocks upthrust. Come soaked her thighs, dripping to her bare feet.

'I'll – I'll take my whipping, sir,' she blurted. 'I want to be a good girl, and obey.'

'Very well. Now, if you would be kind enough to stretch your arms a little further, you'll find two hand holds. This is a very ancient tree, where miscreant girls have been whipped for the last three hundred years. Up on tiptoes, please, the legs splayed straight – and what lovely legs they are, my girl, a young mare's.'

Gasping, Jacqui obeyed, then cried out, as Emily and Sarah clamped her wrists in a wooden brank, fastened to the tree trunk. A second brank clamped her head, pressing her face against the gnarled wood.

'Bound, sir?' she whimpered.

'It's for the best,' said the master. 'Whipping hurts – you might be tempted to escape.'

He allowed his purple silk robe to fall open, revealing his massive sex organ, fully erect. Unseen by the trussed girl, his cock swayed inches from the crack of her buttocks. His fingers stroked her shaking arse globes, caressing the bare skin, and tickling the spread bum cleft, with his sharp fingernail tweaking the quivering anal pucker.

'Oh, sir, don't,' Jacqui moaned, 'it tickles – it excites me, though I'm so scared. Oh, I don't know what to think.'

'It is a master's job to teach you what to think, girl. Sarah! Find a tree frog, and put it in the girl's cunt. And some dung beetles for it to eat, while he's in there.'

95

Sarah rooted in the branches of the tulipwood trees, and gathered a handful of dung beetles, then pinched a squirming tree frog between her forefinger and index finger. On the master's instructions, she pushed the cargo of beetles up Jacqui's cunt, then opened the girl's flaps, and inserted the tree frog. Jacqui wriggled.

'Oh! Oh!' she cried. 'It tickles so much. I've never had such a thing. Oh, the shame.'

'Wait till you get the giant red earthworms up your arse, you dirty slut,' said Sarah. 'They will tickle you.'

Sarah and Emily licked their lips, and began to finger the wet crotches of their swimsuits, as the master lifted his sjambok. Emily drew the robe from his shoulders, leaving him as naked as his victim. He lifted the sjambok over the blonde girl's quivering bare buttocks.

'You are so young,' he purred, 'so helpless, a nymph caught by a satyr.'

'Please don't hurt me awfully, sir,' she moaned.

'I am afraid I must,' he said.

He must. Of course he must ... those beautiful, firm girl fesses, bare young cupcakes begging to be thrashed ...

The master's mind drifted back to that cruel, hideous Christmas Eve party: himself, a boy, eager for girl flesh; snow carpeting valley, roof, and window pane; the quartet of 'reindeer' girls dressed in wispy red and white wool, with, all too obviously, nothing underneath; his helplessness in controlling the erection of his tool. The gorgeous girls, plying him with punch, and shaking their bottoms, with the fluffy fleece rising more and more over bare thighs, bare buttocks. 'You're stiff, you naughty boy!' 'Wouldn't you like to spank our naughty bottoms, for making you randy?' The titties bared, big pink plum nipples tweaked and rubbed and fingered, till they stood stiff and throbbing as his cock. 'We're hot for you, we must be spanked.' Alison's bum bared, bent over, arse flans wiggling, begging for his palm. The luscious feeling of that first smack on girl's naked bum flesh, the coo of pain, the clench, the little squirm; the passion of his spanks, as he pinked her bare bottom. The young blonde girls, in the springtime of life, their bodies firm and bare and supple, begging to be licked and sucked and eaten up like young fresh peaches. 'Girls love a boy spanking them.' 'A girl's bottom isn't really alive, till it's spanked hot pink.' 'It's such naughty fun.' 'Boy, you must spank all of us, till we squeal.'

Alison's bum spanked, till she was crimson; then Claire's, then Becky's, then Cathryn's, and his cock stiff to bursting, the cream threatening to spurt, as he watched those spanked buttocks wriggle, the lovely downy cunt hairs moistening with juice from those glistening gashes; so pink, so wet. It was no longer a Christmas party game, he knew he had to fuck, and knew that he had the strength to fill all those juicy young bodies with his spunk. His fingers in Alison's twat, probing and poking, and him licking his lips of her fragrant juicy come; she wanted it, no mistake. His cock out, inches from her gushing twat, then four pairs of hands pinioning him, the girlish giggles rising to squeals of delight, as they ripped down his pants, tore off his shirt, made him naked for their pleasure. 'You rude boy!' 'Who do you think we are?' 'He must be punished for his impudence.' 'Let's whip him.' 'Yes, let's.'

The dreadful shiny leather of a riding crop, waving before his eyes. 'You know what this is, boy?' 'Of course I do, Alison, but look, enough of the joke.' Crack! The crop lashing his face. 'It's no joke, worm. You're a beastly, smutty shit, and must be punished for it, like all boys.' 'All you dream of is putting your filthy cock in a girl's twat, any girl's, and any twat.' 'Men! Disgusting.' 'But Alison!' Crack! 'You call me miss, you filthy shit.' 'Please, miss, don't hurt me.' 'Oh, hurt you is what we are very much going to do. It's our Christmas present, a boy's bare bum writhing pink under our cropping.' 'No! Please!' 'Wrong. It's yes, please, worm.' The naked boy, tied and gagged, helpless to do more than wriggle, shuddering, as the crop lashed his bare buttocks. Vap! Vap! 'Ooh! God, it hurts!' 'It's supposed to, you piece of filth.' Vap! Vap! The fire streaking through his whipped bare arse, the shame of his bare bottom wriggling helplessly in front of the cruel girls, giggling at his pain, and his helpless limbs threshing against the cords of his bondage; his tool, throbbing and stiff and trembling with spunk begging to spurt; the more his arse smarted, the harder his erection. 'Disgraceful.' 'A stiffy.' 'We'll whip that out of you, dirty boy.'

Nude, bound with cords at his wrists and ankles, and his cries stifled by Cathryn's bare arse crushing his head; her moans of satisfaction, as she wanked herself to come, with cunt juice washing his face. Then Alison, Claire and Becky all taking turns to whip his buttocks and sit on his face, masturbating their squelching clits over his lips. Cathryn laughed, after her bum had squirmed in heavy orgasm, and a stream of hot acrid piss jetted from her wanked twat, to make him splutter, as he swallowed the steaming golden liquid; always, with the vap of the riding crop searing his naked buttocks. He tried not to squirm – it was unmanly – but could not help it, for no one could fail to squirm under that dreadful, unthinkable pain. And when the girls had flogged his arse raw, to over a hundred lashes, the crusts deep and glowing, and they had all crushed his face with their wet cunts, and pissed on him, his cock bucked and he spurted his come into Cathryn's cool palm.

She licked the creamy sperm. 'That was nice. Wasn't it, worm?' 'Y-yes, miss.' 'Aren't you going to say thank you for your thrashing? A thrashed boy should always thank his mistress for his chastisement.' 'Thank you, miss, all of you. Thank you, thank you.' 'At least we've whipped his stiffy away.' 'Yes, we have.' 'What's to be done?' 'His arse needs treatment. Look at those lovely welts!' 'Mm. I feel fruity, just looking at them.' 'Another wank, girls?' 'Yes, let's.' The girls rubbing their twats, filling their palms with come, and tasting each other's love juice, to cries of 'Merry Christmas!' 'Heavens, you taste good, Alison.' 'So do you, Becky.' 'Aren't boys there just to let us have super wanks, as we laugh at them?' 'Whoever would think otherwise?' 'They are strong enough to give a girl a good spanking, and we all need that, don't we, girls? My bum's absolutely flaming!' 'Gosh, yes!' they choroused.

Cathryn, blonde, big of teat and smile, sneering at the bare boy's whipped shame, pushed her palm in his face, and made him drink her come. He slurped the girl's nectar in grateful ecstasy. When they were finished with him, he was cast out, his buttocks rubbed in snow, and left to hobble home, naked and shamed, with the music of girls' laughter ringing in his ears, his flogged buttocks smarting fire and his face streaming with tears, which turned to icicles as he walked. But he treasured the warm taste of the girl's come in his mouth.

Crack! The master's leather thong slashed the air, and bit into the Welsh girl's shivering bare arse pears, streaking them deep pink.

'Ooh!' Jacqui howled.

Her whipped bottom wriggled and clenched, slamming her golden pubic forest against the tree bole. Crack! He striped her across the left haunch, then – crack! – swiftly, across the right.

'Ah! Oh!' Jacqui shrieked.

Crack! The whip curled between her buttocks, lacerating her bum cleft, stroking the pouting anal pucker and flicking the tip against the pendant wet lips of her quim.

'*Ahh!*' the blonde girl screamed, her breasts scything against the tree bark, as the whiplashes jarred her naked flesh.

Crack! Crack! The whip worked across the squirming arse pears, with Jacqui's long bare legs jerking rigid at each stroke to her bottom. Crack! Crack! The leather took her from underfesse to tender top buttock, streaking her thighs bright pink and lashing her haunches a deep crusted crimson. Crack! Crack!

'Ooh! Ahh! Oh, please, sir, stop!' she wailed, her whole body wriggling as the thong bit. 'I can't stand it! You're hurting me so much! Please, sir, haven't I had enough?'

'Only a dozen lashes?' the master purred. 'I think not, miss.'

Crack! Crack! The whip stroked her across the mid-fesse, etching a lattice of pink stripes on the squirming skin.

'Ooh,' she moaned, as the tears streamed from her eyes.

Crack! He took her once more in the open cleft, the whip flogging her gaping lips, striking the pink slit flesh and stiffened clitty bud. Come sprayed from her twat, as her young body writhed under her master's whip.

'Young girls,' the master said. 'So many. Their tender bare buttocks just made to be flogged.'

'Ahh! Ohh! I can't take any more,' Jacqui said, sobbing. 'I'll do anything for it to stop.'

At each stroke of the sjambok, the master's cock bobbed, stiff as a tree, inches from the young girl's bare buttocks. He flogged her forty cuts, until her naked bottom was a mass of crusted pink weals, darkening to crimson, the ridges of her bum welts deepened by three, four or five expert strokes to the same weal, each of which made her scream. Emily and Sarah masturbated openly, come trickling down their rippling bare thighs from the gussets of their pink swimsuits, as they frigged their twats, bounced their teats and tweaked their hard nipples under the flimsy fabric. Jacqui wept, squealed and moaned, her legs flailing and her breasts slamming

100

cruelly against the tree, with each heavy whipstroke to her writhing bottom. At the fiftieth stroke, the master handed his whip to Emily.

'Remove the tree frog,' he ordered.

Emily opened Jacqui's cunt and permitted the fed tree frog to scamper away.

'You said you'll do anything, my dear girl?' the master purred. 'You will do anything, for you are my slave.'

Without waiting for her answer, he pressed his cock between her buttocks, stroking the bum cleft, so that his balls caressed the livid gashes of the whip's wounds on her thigh backs.

'Ooh,' Jacqui moaned, her spine stiffening, as she felt the cock's helmet nuzzle her winking anus bud. 'Oh, no. Not that.'

The master thrust his loins, and his glans penetrated her anus.

'Ahh!' Jacqui screamed.

He thrust again, and his massive cock vanished halfway up her rectum. Her arse wriggled frantically, squeezing and clenching, to stop the penetration.

'No. The shame. Oh God,' she said, weeping.

The master grunted, as his tool disappeared up her arse, right to his balls.

'It hurts!' Jacqui cried. 'God, how it hurts!'

'Someone else must hurt, to please and excite me,' he said. 'Emily, is it you who will spank Sarah, or Sarah spank you?'

Caressing each other on the swimsuit gusset, the monitors simpered.

'I haven't spanked Emily for ages,' murmured Sarah.

'Nor I Sarah,' said Emily.

'Emily then. You shall spank Sarah to a pleasing pink.'

'Oh, master!' Sarah made a moue, but was not displeased.

'Your flaps open, girl.'

Jacqui groaned, as the master's cock was still inside her rectum. Sarah turned, and unlaced the portion of her swimsuit, baring her buttocks. She bent over Emily's knee. Whap! Whap! Emily's left palm began a vigorous spanking of her colleague's bared bum, which began to clench and wriggle, turning bright pink, as Sarah squealed. Her full, ripe fesses gleamed in the sun, as she was spanked hard.

'Ooh! Ooh! You're hurting me, Emily, you cow!'

'I dare say you'll want to get your own back.'

'Rather! I say, you're making me all fruity, Em. Wank me off, there's a sport.'

'You do want jam on it.'

As Emily spanked Sarah's glowing bare buttocks, she slipped her other hand beneath her victim's smooth-shaven cunt hillock, and began to squelch the dripping cooze flaps, tweaking the girl's clitty, until Sarah moaned, both in the pain of her spanking, and the pleasure of her spanker's masturbation. Emily's fingers tweaked her own clit, through her swimsuit gusset, and she masturbated, as she spanked the quivering bare bum flans of the squirming monitor.

Thwap! Thwap!

'Oh! That's good!' cried Sarah. 'I'm going to come, you bitch.'

'Superb, ladies,' purred the master.

His hips smacking her flogged buttocks and his balls slapping her thighs, drenched with her spurting come, the master began a savage buggery of the helpless young Welsh girl.

'Oh! Oh, God, that hurts!' Jacqui cried. 'You're going to split my bum in two. Have you no pity, sir?'

'None at all,' panted the master. 'With a gorgeous arse like that, maid, you beg to suffer.'

Jacqui's moans and sighs echoed above the crisp smacks of Emily's palm on Sarah's naked bottom. As he was buggering Jacqui, the master's eyes strayed to the pumping nates of the spanked girl. He summoned Emily, who paused in spanking Sarah, and lit another cheroot for him, while he continued his swiving of the Welsh girl, with cruel, powerful thrusts.

'Oh! I've never been touched there!' she said, sobbing.

'I am fucking your colon,' said the master, puffing on his cheroot. 'It is the sweetest, tenderest part of a girl, the soft treasure to which her buttocks are the portal. A girl slave must learn to love her master's sperm washing her innermost tripes.'

'Oh! God!' Jacqui wailed.

'The bitch is spurting come,' said Emily, as she spanked the squirming Sarah. 'She loves it, master.'

'No! I don't!' squealed Jacqui. 'Whipped and bummed! And a bloody frog up my twat! I've never been so shamed or hurt so much.'

Her fucked buttocks writhed, slapping the master's balls, and meeting his thrusts, in the harsh rhythm of his enculement. Juice sprayed from her cunt, wetting the trembling muscles of her rigid thighs, as the master's thrusts slammed her breasts and clitty against the tree bark.

'Oh, no!' Jacqui wailed. 'I need it. I'm going to come. I've never been pleasured like this before. I need to be fucked in the bum. Oh, I've said it. What will people think? I'm a virgin, but it's so good to feel a man's cock in my hole. I need it. God, I need it.'

'We all do,' gasped the spanked Sarah. 'Oh! I'm coming!'

'Me, too,' panted Emily, masturbating hard.

The two monitors groaned in orgasm, as the master grunted, and beads of his spunk bubbled over Jacqui's anal lips.

'Ahh! Ooh! I'm coming!' shrieked the buggered girl. 'Oh, you fucking bastard! It's so good! Fuck me harder, give me all your spunk in my bumhole! Yes! Yes! Ahh! I'm there! Oh, you fucking dirty bastard!'

Creamy sperm bubbled from Jacqui's anus, and come spurted from her cunt, as the master's climax filled her rectum with spunk. With a loud plop, his cock – still erect – squelched from her anus, as his victim sobbed hot tears onto the tulipwood tree. Sarah fastened her spank flaps, and grasped her cane.

'You heard what the bitch said, master. Obscenity and insults.'

'Whip her for it,' drawled the master, donning his purple silk robe.

He stubbed his cheroot, sizzling, in the lake of come and spunk glazing Jacqui's thighs. The monitors, cooing with delight, lifted their canes over Jacqui's naked back. Vip! Vip! Both canes lashed in unison on her pale back flesh, slicing her spine and ribs.

'*Ahh! No!*' Jacqui screamed.

Vip! Vip!

'Oh! Oh!'

Vip! Vip!

'Urrgh! You beasts!'

The nude girl's body jerked and shuddered, as the tulipwood canes flogged her back, and she writhed helplessly against the tree bark. The whipping was pitiless and rapid, the twin canes rising and falling over Jacqui's spine and shoulders, until the fretwork of pink stripes on her back equalled the blotched mass of bruises colouring her buttocks. Her titties rubbed against the gnarled tree bark at each double stroke, as the Welsh girl shrieked and sobbed under the brutal caning.

'Please, don't beat me any more,' she whimpered. 'I've been bummed and caned on my bare bum, with everyone looking on and gloating. I can't imagine any more shame.'

Her whippers chortled.

'You won't need to imagine, at the plantation,' crowed Emily.

'It'll be imagined for you,' said Sarah.

The master lit a match on the bobbing bottom of Emily's swimsuit, and ignited another cheroot. His cock poked stiff from his silken robe, as he watched the elfin girl's pale body turn rich pink under her lashes. The canes striped Jacqui's skin from neck to buttock, bruising her back flesh with deep crimson trenches, while she screamed and wept, squirming in her agony. Come seeped from her cunt.

'It's not fair,' she whimpered. 'You've got me hot and wet, and I need to come again. That frog tickled me so. You brutes.'

'All girls get wet when they're whipped pink,' said Emily, sniffly.

'Don't think you're special,' added Sarah.

'Please. Oh. Wank me off, I beg you,' groaned the flogged girl.

Each masturbating her own quim, her whippers merely laughed.

Vip! Vip!

'Oh! No! I can't hold back!' shrieked Jacqui.

A golden stream of piss burst from her twat, wetting the swimsuited girls' bare feet, and soaking at once into the ochre earth.

'You fucking pig,' snarled Emily.

Their canes began to lash uppercuts, straight on the gash flaps and anus, the pucker still gaping from Jacqui's recent buggery.

When Jacqui had been whipped over a hundred strokes on the bare back, a truck roared to the tulipwood grove, and ground to a halt. From the back of the truck, two dirty nude girls, covered in dust, sweat and grime, were disgorged, to fall, groaning, on the dusty ochre earth. One girl was ebony black; the other golden tan. Both had pink panties knotted round their necks. The master strolled to the gasping newcomers, and flipped them over to inspect their bare bottoms. He puffed excitedly on his cheroot.

'What have we here, Sandoz?' he asked the bare-chested slavedriver, with a whip curled at his wrist. 'New girl slaves. Glorious nates, each slut's buttocks quite superb, and ready for the kiss of my whip. Dear Vasco, sweet Emmaia, for thinking of me.'

He kicked Nip and Candi in their bare cunts, and smiled when they squealed in pain. Then, he tickled the bare soles of their feet, with his whip tongue, till they squirmed and whimpered. Emily and Sarah left off their whipping of Jacqui, and lifted the two newcomers roughly to their feet. The master kneaded their bare teats, making the girls grimace in pain, then probed their cunts, and turned them, to admire their naked, dusty fesses. His fingers penetrated each anus in turn, while Nip and Candi began to sob.

'Superb ... two more luscious English bottoms, for my caress ... the cunt mounds deliciously plump, and the quims showing evidence of healthy frequent masturbation ... a girl who knows how to frig regularly is a girl whose naked arse needs the lash.'

The master caressed their bare buttocks, while the girls stared aghast at the reddened body of the whipped Welsh girl, bound to the tulipwood tree.

'Oh,' Jacqui moaned. 'Bring me off, please, girls. Wank me to come, I need it so badly.'

'Leave the lustful little bitch tied to the tree until sundown,' drawled the master. 'These two sumptuous slaves shall attend me at supper.'

'Oh, you bastard!' shrieked Jacqui. 'What about me? I need to come so badly!'

'She is noisy. Amazing, how a brisk whipping reveals the animal in even the fairest maid. Why, Sandoz will make you come, slut,' said the master. 'He buggers without mercy, and is the only male on my plantation whose cock approaches the size of my own.'

7

Wrenched Pigtails

'I must admit, master, I ... I didn't really know what to think,' said Candi, giggling. She sipped her tea; hummingbirds trilled under a lowering pink sun, above the fragrant blossoming jacaranda trees. 'Seeing that girl punished, and everything. She was so hairy, though. Yuk! I say, Emily does make a nice cup of tea. It is Emily, isn't it?'

'Sarah,' said Sarah drily.

'Oh, yes. Awfully sorry.'

Sarah bared her teeth. 'You might be.'

'Ladies,' said the master, cracking his whip on his thigh. 'Let us enjoy our supper. You, Nipringa, are you enjoying your cup of tea?'

'You know your way to an English girl's heart, sir,' purred Nip.

'I must apologise for your rough treatment, maids. Here in Paraiba – the cowboy country of the wild north – our workers are not as sophisticated as Rio de Janeiro cariocas like Julio and Emmaia. A truck is perhaps not your accustomed mode of travel.'

Candi rubbed her bottom. 'There were a few bruises, sir.'

'None that we cannot handle,' said Nip, smiling.

The girls in their pink swimsuits served hearts of palm salad, tidbits of roasted jaguar and aguti, guavas and mangos and steaming sweet potato. Grease trickled down the English girls' chins, over their bare breasts. Behind them, two mulatto boys, Paulo and Vergilio, nude but for tight pink crotch thongs, swaggered arrogantly, each boy stroking the tongue of his coiled leather whip, and thrusting the massive tubes of cock meat, bulging in his panties, towards the new girl slaves.

'You do not mind being nude?' drawled the master. 'You are, I regret to say, my captives, so I am afraid you have little choice in the matter.'

'Oh, no.'

'Well . . .'

'It was not so much a question,' he continued. 'All new slaves are nude, until they have proved themselves pink.'

'So much more comfortable in this heat,' said Nip, draining her tea. 'I enjoy being nude, it makes me feel so shivery, in the power of such a handsome man.'

She wiggled her toes at the master, while parting her rippling ebony thighs to show her wet pink cunt meat.

'Then you shall enjoy some Brahma beer,' said the master.

'Oh, well . . .'

'Don't mind.'

Candi rubbed her bare breasts, pretending to scratch them, but making her nipples grow stiff, a fact not unobserved by the master's languid eye. She and Nip ate hungrily, and sipped from steins of icy Brazilian beer, served by the barefoot monitors. While the girls ate and drank, the master took their toes into his mouth, and sucked them, making the girls giggle and moan.

'Sir,' said Candi, her mouth full. 'Slaves – I mean, is that what . . .'

'Surely, we shan't be slaves,' said Nip. 'That's for other girls. Of the low class.'

The master released Nip's black toes, and sighed. 'Unfortunately, you were apprehended at illicit trespass on one of my properties,' he said. 'The law is very strict. Enslaved you must be, until I have established your bona fides and purity of heart.'

'But we are English girls!' cried Candi.

'Sadly, in our rough Brazilian northlands, that is not enough. Emily and Sarah, English girls too, may vouch for that, if they please. From slaves, by dint of good service, they have worked their way up to monitors.'

'We have, haven't we, Sal?' said Emily, pouting.

'Certainly, Milly,' said Sarah.

They filled Candi's and Nip's steins.

'There are not many boys on the plantation,' said the master. 'Those, such as Paulo and Vergilio here, are not permitted to pleasure our girl slaves, for that would take their minds off their work in the fields. The boys' job is to *punish* girls.'

'I quite understand,' said Nip, gazing at Paulo's massive cock tube, under his clinging pink pouch.

'The boys apply their arms to the punishment of miscreant girl slaves,' the master continued. 'The whip, on bare bottom, delivered with merciless force, until the poor girl's naked buttocks are striped deep pink, they squirm the lovely bare pears in their agony and her sweet trill of agony begs for mercy. Mercy is a luxury a plantation owner may rarely award. There are other punishments ... you observed the new Welsh girl, a very naughty specimen, left tied to the tulipwood tree. Such a delicious young bottom, so deserving of the whip.'

'That sort – dirty low-class girls – why, they positively need beating,' said Candi.

'Whip their bums raw, I say,' agreed Nip.

'You maids intend to avoid miscreance, I am sure,' the master said.

Candi and Nip shivered, each with her eyes on the other's bare quim, seeing the swollen lips drool cunt juice. The master noticed their excitement.

'It is normal,' he drawled, 'for young girls to be excited by their state of servitude: to be naked, under an all-powerful master's eyes, to know that their bare bottoms shall squirm under his whip, at their slightest disobedience. A girl's longing is to submit.'

Candi and Nip laughed nervously; the master threw up his hands.

'Do not apologise, or try to explain,' he said. 'Those are facts.'

He leaned forwards, and tweaked each of their nipples in turn, with his long purple fingernails. The girls breathed heavily and their nipples stiffened to full erection.

'Do not disappoint me, by trying not to be naughty,' the master purred. 'A girl's soul is made to be naughty, and the divine bare orbs of her bottom to be chastised for it.'

Emily and Sarah poured more beer, and both newcomers began to squirm on their cane-straw seats. The master asked if something was the matter, and Candi blushed, admitting that after all the liquid she had drunk, she was bursting to pee. Nipringa said the same, looking round the clearing for something that looked like a loo. Smiling, the master ordered Nipringa to squat on Candi's thighs, both girls with twats open and facing. In that position, they were to void themselves. Blushing, Nip climbed onto Candi's lap, and both girls clutched each other by the buttocks, with their spread cunt flesh wet and pink, winking, one vulva inches from the other.

'You first or me?' asked Candi, giggling.

Crack! The master's brow furrowed, his whip lashed her breasts, precisely across the nipples, and she squealed.

'Both together,' he hissed.

Sobbing from her teat wound, Candi pissed across her friend's belly. Nip's cunt spurted a huge jet of steaming golden fluid over Candi's rippling thighs, splashing her

110

belly and breasts. Emily leaped forwards, and crammed the two girls' bellies together, so that they were pissing into each other's cunt. Mingled piss spurted from their tight cunt holes, washing their thighs, and splashing on their naked breasts. Fingers pressed together under his chin, the master smiled, while Sarah lit a match on the bottom of her swimsuit, and ignited his cheroot. He smoked, until the girls' pee had ebbed, then poked the cigar down the furrows of the girls' cunts, where it sizzled to extinction. Candi and Nip groaned and shivered.

'Any complaints, maids?' he murmured.

'Well, sir, it's a bit thick –' Candi blurted, ignoring Nip's warning glance.

Crack! The master's thong slashed Candi's piss-soaked breasts. Crack! He whipped her mouth. Candi squealed, and burst into tears.

'Oh! That's rotten! Oh!'

'You are a slave,' hissed the master. 'Nothing done to you is rotten. It is you, abject, squealing girl, who are rotten, and must suffer until you are cured of rottenness. Your bottom must, and shall, squirm under a righteous whip, until it is pink with virtue. Obedience in a girl is everything. A disobedient girl is no girl at all. She must not only obey, for a good girl must not even think of the possibility of disobeying. To kneel before her master, to bare her bottom for his just chastisement, is as natural as the rising of the sun on her naked body, labouring for him in his fields. Do you agree, Miss Nipringa?'

Shivering, with nervous smile, the black girl nodded.

'Then we shall give Miss Candi her first lesson, now, don't you agree, Miss Nipringa?'

Candi stared through her tears at the nude black girl, licking her teeth, as she accepted a whip from Vergilio, whose pink-pantied cock, insolently swelling, brushed against her shoulder.

'Nip! You wouldn't!' she cried.

Nipringa shrugged, smiling. 'You heard the master,' she murmured. 'We are girl slaves, Candi, and who are we to disagree?'

'But it's outrageous –'

'Silence, bitch!'

Nip stood, her bare breasts heaving, and lashed Candi between the lips of her naked cunt.

'Ahh!' Candi shrieked, doubling over in pain, her thighs and belly rippling. 'Oh, God! Nip, I can't believe you whipped my twat! It hurts awfully!'

Nipringa wrenched her by the hair, and pinned her, bare bottom up, over the dinner table. A bottle of Brahma overturned, so that Candi's mane was soaked in beer.

'Better get used to it, slut,' she snarled, raising her whip. 'Was that right, master?'

'Perfectly,' said the master, letting his robe fall open to reveal his massively erect cock, trembling naked, while Emily and Sarah knelt to lick his balls with their tongues, and the smirking mulatto boys pinioned Candi by her wrists and ankles, her legs and arms stretched fully.

She wriggled, helpless, stretched over the table, with her breasts, thighs and twat squelching in oil, butter sauce and salad.

'God! I'm a mess!' she wailed.

'Do your duty, girl slave Nipringa,' the master ordered.

Vap! The twin-thonged whip slashed Candi's bare arse flans.

'Ooh!' she squealed, her nates clenching.

Vap!

'Ahh! Oh! How could you, Nip?'

'Like this, you naughty little bitch.'

Vap!

'Ooh!'

Vap!

'Ahh!'

The black girl's whip sliced an undercut on Candi's writhing twat flaps.

'Ahh!' she screamed, as the double thong flogged her exposed clitty. 'Oh, God, Nip, please stop.'

Nipringa licked her teeth, her bare breasts rising and falling, beaded with sweat. She pouted at the master, fluttering her eyelashes, and twirling her cunt, with her own buttocks swaying, opening and closing, to show him her pink arse pucker. The master nodded that she must continue. He stroked Emily's and Sarah's bare backs, as the girl's tongues caressed his ball sac. Vergilio's and Paulo's cocks were swollen fully stiff, the helmets bursting from their skimpy panties. Vap! The flogging of Candi's helpless bare buttocks continued, past a dozen, then two dozen strokes, until the whipped girl wept uncontrollably, each cut of her friend's thong mashing her titties into the mess of beer and sauce splattering the table. Vap!

'I obey, master,' panted Nip. 'I am your girl slave.'

When Candi's bare arse was mottled deep pink, after fifty cuts of the whip, the master raised a finger, and her whipping ceased. Emily rose, ripped Paulo's panties from his groin, and clasped his stiff cock between her forefinger and index finger. Shaven to gleaming smoothness, and menacing, like naked weapons, his balls and cock glistened pink in the setting sun. Emily moistened the exposed tip of his helmet with her tongue, then applied a fingertip of come from her cunt, and guided the huge cock between Candi's buttocks, pushing the tip into her anus.

'No! Please!' Candi howled.

'Would you rather take tool in your cunt, slut?' hissed Nip. 'Lose your precious virginity?'

'Anything but that,' said Candi, sobbing.

'Anything is what you'll get,' said Nip.

113

Paulo's cock sank to his balls in Candi's rectum, and he began a rapid, fierce buggery, slapping her buttocks with his hips, as he drove into her helpless body. Vergilio stood by Candi's mouth, which was gasping in pain, as she writhed in the agony of her penetration. Simpering, Vergilio thrust his cock between her lips, and began to fuck the back of her throat. His buttocks danced as he fucked the whimpering, choking girl's mouth, and Paulo maintained his ruthless buggery of her anus. Nipringa sat on the master's lap, with his cock between her rippling black thighs, which rubbed the rigid tool meat, as she masturbated him with her legs. His fists mashed her erect nipples, squashing her breasts against her ribs, as she groaned with pleasure.

'Oh, yes, master,' gasped Nip.

Paulo spurted his cream in Candi's rectum, while Vergilio spermed in her throat. Paulo's spunk bubbled from her anus, and Vergilio's from her lips, dribbling down her chin.

'Ooh . . . ooh . . . urrgh,' Candi gasped, in choking sobs.

The master ordered her to swallow Vergilio's sperm, and when she had done that, Sarah sucked Paulo's spunk from her anus with a straw, and stuck the straw into Candi's mouth; Candi was obliged to suck and swallow Paulo's entire load of cream, perfumed by her own arse grease. Nip's pale soles were up, caressing the master's cock; he exploded in orgasm, bathing her bare feet in sperm, which he ordered her to lick from her feet and ankles. Sarah and Emily were openly wanking each other, fingers in each other's exposed twat, with the pink swimsuit gussets pulled up, to bare the creamily shaven cunt hillocks.

'Oh! Yes!'

'Mm!'

Drooling with pleasure, Nipringa bent her head, took her feet into her mouth, and licked up the master's spunk, swallowing it with little moans of pleasure, while fluttering her eyelashes at him. Her reward was a double dildo: one end, with a protruding nubbin-tickler, thrust in her twat; the other plunged into the sobbing Candi's spunk-soaked anus. Nip began to bugger Candi's rectum, while come sprayed from her own twat, and her huge pink clitty stiffened between the black gash flaps, as it was stimulated by the tulipwood tickler.

'Oh, Nip! Don't! How could you?' wailed Candi, writhing under the black girl's enculement.

'I like being a girl slave,' panted the black girl. 'Don't you?'

Nip fucked Candi until she had brought herself off twice, and, after Candi complained that her bum had been fucked raw and hurt like nothing she had ever imagined, Nip slipped her hand under Candi's writhing twat, tweaked her clitty, and brought her friend off at once, in a convulsed, howling orgasm that squirted Candi's come into the mess of beer and sauce that lathered her jerking body. Emily and Sarah cooed, as they mutually masturbated each other to climax, while stroking the bare cocks of the mulatto boys, as part of their own girl wank.

'Have I pleased my master?' simpered Nipringa, thrusting her titties up and licking her erect nipples.

The master laughed, as Sarah and Emily licked his thighs and balls dry of his splashed come. 'A girl slave who pleases?' he snarled. 'A girl slave is not there to please, she is there to suffer. Throw both bitches into the cave, until they start their work at dawn.'

Crack! He lashed his whip across Nip's belly, the tip striking her open wet gash, and sizzling in the wet pink flesh of her ebony slit.

'Ahh!' she squealed.

'Every dawn,' purred the master.

'You really are an awful bitch,' said Candi with a sob. 'My bottom's absolutely aching. I can't believe

115

you whipped me on the twat. And bum-fucked so hard . . .'

'Didn't Paulo? You loved it. That fabulous huge tool bumming you . . .'

'Yes, but that was boy meat, it's different . . . you hurt me more.'

'I'm glad. Anyway, it was the master's orders,' replied Nip. 'And you came so much. Making quite an exhibition of yourself. Quite the little wanker.'

'All girls wank. It's no crime. Don't you wank off every morning? It's not normal, otherwise. A girl who doesn't wank herself to a come at least once a day is nothing but a frigid bitch. But that's not the point. I thought we were friends. Yet, you were so blatantly sucking up to the master.'

'Fat lot of good it's done me,' said Nip, ruefully. 'My, it's hot in here.'

The nude girls squirmed together on a hard floor of ochre earth, in a scooped cavern scarcely big enough to contain them, with a window – no more than a hole – looking out on the swaying jacaranda trees. The hole was curiously unbarred, as if inviting escape to perils unknown. It might admit a lithe young body to wriggle to freedom, but what sort of freedom would she find in the master's demesne? On the floor of their cell, nettles grew amongst the gnarled roots of trees, knobbed sticks poking from the ochre earth. Their bodies were lathered in sweat; they had a jug of water and a stone pisspot, with a long trowel-shaped handle, carved in obscene shapes: scenes of erect cocks and fucked girls' arses. Candi rubbed her breasts, shaking droplets of glistening sweat from her nipples. She fingered the strawberry domes, smiling, as the soft pink flesh hardened. Nip's own breasts glistened with perspiration, oozing from her open black pores, and the brown nipples already stood erect. Her white teeth flashed in the darkness, against her beaded ebony skin.

'Emily and Sarah are so cruel,' said Candi. 'Throwing us in here, kicking us and everything. My twat hurts so. They are really under the master's thrall.'

'Don't you want to be? He's only trying to scare us,' said Nip. 'Make us submit. You see how there are no bars, and we can leave through the hole? Yet we don't. We girls are our own prisoners.'

'Then let's submit,' moaned Candi. 'It is a girl's portion to submit, whatever you think, Nip. The master's eyes, flashing so cruelly, that massive cock . . . how can a girl not submit?'

Toying with her breasts, she took a gulp of water.

'Careful with that. We don't know how long we'll be here.'

'Only till dawn, surely.'

'If you trust the master, as far as you can trust any man.'

Candi tweaked her stiff nipples, letting her hand slide down her sweat-beaded belly to her cunt. 'It's too hot to sleep,' she said, panting.

'Then there's only one thing.'

Nip's toes were in Candi's mouth, and Candi's inside the black girl's. They sucked toes, while their juicing twats pressed together, their buttocks writhing, as the erect nubbins rubbed.

'Oh . . . that's so good,' Candi moaned.

'Isn't it? Are you going to come?'

'You always make me come, you bitch, even when you're fucking my bum.'

'Especially when I'm fucking your bum.'

'Or spanking me.'

'That too. You like it so much.'

'What girl doesn't?'

The two locked and their masturbating gashes squelched wetly. Their buttocks pumped on the raw moist earth, as their come washed their rippling thighs, and drool spilled from their mouths, over their wriggling toes. Nip licked Candi's soles, making her sigh with pleasure.

'That little blondie brat,' Nip cooed, 'tied to the tree, now she deserves spanking. She was well thrashed. Such a luscious little bum.'

'It wasn't so little. Lovely hard pears.'

'You know what I mean. And those girly pigtails dancing, as she was lashed. So wank-making.'

'Ooh! Yes, Nip, fuck my clit with your s. I'm going to come any moment.'

'Ahh . . . me too.'

The girls' enlaced thighs writhed, as their cunts rubbed in a dry fuck, spurting come, as both heaved in orgasm at the same moment. The door of the cave clanged open, and a girl's naked body, its welted bottom and back skin glowing under the moon, tumbled onto the tribadists, who cried out, as the heavy girl meat squashed them. The girl's lush-forested cunt landed on Nipringa's mouth.

'Your new cellmate,' taunted Sarah, her pink swim-suit flashing in the moonlight.

'Miss! There's no room! We can hardly breathe!' cried Candi.

'You've room enough to wank, you smutty sluts,' said Emily, chortling. 'If you don't like your cellmate, you can punish her.'

She slammed the door shut. On top of the naked masturbatresses lay the nude body of the sobbing Welsh girl, Jacqui Prosset. Her flaxen pigtails bobbed, as her breasts heaved with her choked weeping.

'Bloody impudent bitch, coming in here like this, and interrupting us,' hissed Nipringa.

'Damned slut,' snarled Candi. 'A beastly nouveau.'

Nip fastened her teeth around the girl's cunt hillock, getting her tongue inside the slit, and bit hard. Jacqui screamed. Candi pinioned her arms, while Nip, still sucking the girl's clit and pouch, fastened her ankles, twisting them crossways in a painful lock. Jacqui shuddered, wriggling but helpless, and her screams turned to sobs. Her ankles twitched in a frenzied dance.

'You wicked bitches!' she wailed. 'Pleasing the master, while I was left to suffer! I want to please him . . . just me!'

Nip stroked the girl's arse weals, glistening in the moonlight.

'You haven't suffered enough,' she murmured. 'Such a beautiful body, and a huge twat mane for such a little girl.'

'I'm eighteen,' protested the struggling girl.

'Never,' said Nip. 'You don't even look sixteen. You're so breathtakingly lovely, so filthily pure. And you flaunt it, you tease. You remind me of me. But never mind, we'll spank you like an eighteen-year-old.'

'Spank me? You wouldn't,' said Jacqui, sobbing and writhing, as Nip's teeth bit her clit.

'Try us,' hissed the black girl.

Nip and Candi caressed their victim's quivering body: the hard breasts and buttocks, the long, coltish legs, all striped with cruel whip weals. The scarred pink flesh was smeared with pungent cream. Jacqui said that Sarah's and Emily's boss, the slavemistress Serena, had soothed her bruises with zinc ointment. Nip caressed her body, cooing that the girl was too beautiful, too elfinly submissive, to leave unspanked.

'That luscious pink cooze; those hard bum flans and young girl's titties; that sweet, scornful schoolgirl's mouth – just touching her makes me want to wank,' she purred. 'I want to sit on her face and make her sweat as she licks my clit.'

Nipringa stroked her nipples, tweaking the hard brown bulbs into domes of quivering pleasure. Drool oozed from her mouth, trickling down her chin onto her huge black breasts. She licked drops of gleaming saliva from her chin, and bent to suck the drool from her beaded nipples.

119

'The curves of the arse and twat and belly,' she panted. 'The young girl's titties, so proud and cheeky, the legs so lithe, the back sloping into the cleft of that spankable white bum, a lovely mountain valley. Almost too lovely to touch. But we'll do more than touch her.'

'No. Please,' moaned the blonde Welsh maid. 'Haven't I suffered enough? And who are you to talk? You were frigging. You had your cunts together, and were shrimping, toe-licking . . . it's dirty and disgraceful. Nice girls don't do that.'

'Why, you fucking little slut,' snarled Nip. 'You don't wank off? All girls masturbate, especially a sweet little goody-two-shoes like you. That cunt – a beautiful pouting pink orchid – why, it's made to be wanked. Those titties are made to be tweaked; that bumhole to be poked. You've had your finger up yourself while you wank, haven't you? Right up your hole, to the colon, while you tweak that clit, fisting your gash, and pour your come over those succulent thighs. Now you have Sandoz, and the boys, and master, if you're lucky. *Those* tools . . .'

She licked her teeth.

'Well, I do wank, I admit it,' moaned Jacqui.

'And more. You've had plenty of cock up that arsehole. And spanked. Those tender fesses crave spanking.'

'Yes,' wailed Jacqui. 'Sometimes . . . I mean . . . you know. It's normal, surely. I've been bare-spanked by boys. I'll tell you everything, if you want, I promise. I've sucked cocks, and I've been bummed and spanked hard, but I'm a virgin. That's what counts, to be a nice girl.'

'Dirty slut. You've earned more than spanking.'

'And what makes you think *we* are nice girls?' said Candi, frigging her cunt, as she raised her hand over Jacqui's wriggling bare bottom.

Her back draped by flaxen pigtails, the satin pale skin of the blonde's svelte, elfin body glimmered in the moonlight, which illumined the savage pink welts of her whipping. They matched the dripping pink of her cunt, and her wide sensuous lips, bubbling with drool. Her pert young breasts trembled, goose-fleshed and with nipples tautly erect, while her full muscled thighs rippled helplessly, and her long, prehensile toes danced and jerked. Nip dived beneath Jacqui's cunt basin, her nose sniffing the arse grease seeping from Jacqui's anus, and took her whole twat between her lips, biting savagely on the blonde girl's lips and erect clitoris, peeping between the ruby folds. Come from Jacqui's twat oozed into the black girl's mouth, and Nip gurgled, as she swallowed the Welsh blonde's cunt juice.

'Ooh! No!' shrieked Jacqui, as a stream of piss hissed violently from her bitten gash, into Nipringa's throat.

Nipringa gagged, swallowing the acrid golden piss, then bit directly onto Jacqui's stiff clitty. The Welsh girl howled, her cunt spurting more piss into Nip's mouth.

'Oh, God, please!' she wailed. 'Look at me, my naked flesh so ripe for you, ladies. I'm a young girl, nude, and a prisoner, like you. Girl slaves must be friends, surely? I'm no lesbo, but I swear, my body is yours – a fresh and young and virgin and innocent and helpless – and you can do what you want with me. I'll submit, I promise. Girls are born to submit to powerful vixens like you. Wank me off, make me suck your clits or your titties or even your bumholes, but please, no more pain. Don't hurt me, don't spank me, I beg you. You haven't heard the full story. I'll tell you everything about me.'

'You will that,' hissed Nip. 'There's a long night until dawn. That is, if you can speak at all, as we torture you.'

'No! Don't bite my clit! God, it hurts!'

Nipringa wrenched Jacqui's pigtails, pulling the hair to the roots, and Jacqui screamed.

'Spank the fucking bitch, Candi,' the black girl gasped, spluttering with Jacqui's piss and come. 'That's just for starters.'

121

Jacqui was stretched on the ochre floor, now a moist pudding from her own piss and come. Nip had her foot on the small of Jacqui's back, grinding her cooze and titties into the piss-scented mud.

'Oh, don't, please,' moaned the shamed girl.

'When a slut says no, she gets yes,' snapped Nip, baring her teeth.

Smack! Candi's palm slapped the elfin blonde's naked buttocks, and Jacqui gasped. Smack! Smack! The wealed buttocks began to glow with fresh spank welts. Smack! Smack!

'Ouch! It hurts!'

Smack! Smack!

'It's meant to,' snarled Nip, her bare foot on Jacqui's neck, pressing the Welsh girl's face into the piss-mud. 'You deserve it for making such a beastly mess. Spank her harder, Candi.'

Smack! Smack! Candi's palm spanked the blonde maid's wriggling arse plums. At each powerful slap, Jacqui's cunt mound squelched into the mud.

'Ooh! No! Stop!' the spanked girl cried.

'Don't stop, Candi,' drawled Nipringa. 'Pink that croup, or it'll be your bum for spanking.'

8

Bound in Leather

'Don't pink me, please,' Jacqui wailed. 'Look, I can explain. I may seem loose, and accustomed to being spanked, but that was never my fault. I'm a good girl. It's just that – oh, men! I fell under awfully bad influences.'

Breasts and bottom shaking, she began to weep.

'I was at the university in Aberystwyth, studying sociology, and I got into debt. You know how it is. I just couldn't see how I could ever pay the fees. Professor Darmon said he had a job going – a housemaid. Well, that sounded demeaning, but what can a girl do? I took it. He lived all alone, up on the hill, in a big Victorian villa. I arrived for my first day's work, and he was very kind. He sat me down, gave me a cup of tea and talked about my studies and everything. Then he explained my duties. For three afternoons a week, I was to come in for two hours and clean his study. It was a big room, full of books bound in leather, but I thought it would be easy enough. The money was good. He poured me another cup of tea, and said I would have to wear a maid's uniform which he would provide free of charge. Actually, silly me, I thought that was rather intriguing, so I agreed. I thought I might be able to keep the uniform for myself. A good cup of tea does things to a girl, and Professor Darmon said he got his tea directly from a supplier in Madras. It was lovely. I had a third cup, and the professor invited me to change into my maid's uniform, to see if I was suitable, so I did. It was a really nice costume, sort of frilly, and I felt nice in it. And . . . well, that's about it.'

Smack! Smack! Candi spanked the girl's bottom. Jacqui moaned, as her pinking buttocks clenched.

'That's not about it,' Candi hissed. 'There is more. Continue, or I'll spank your big girly arse raw.'

Jacqui whimpered.

'Please . . . you're hurting me . . . don't make me tell . . .'

Smack! Smack! Her bottom trembled.

'All right. I'll tell you. Only, don't spank my bum. As for the cane, I hate it, it's so dreadful. A girl's bottom surely doesn't deserve the cane. And on the bare. I can't tell you how shaming that is.'

'Can't you? So you are used to it. Any decent girl is. What is a girl's bottom worth, if it hasn't tasted a man's cane? The ultimate thrill – perhaps the only one. Go on,' said Nipringa. 'She *is* a tasty piece,' she whispered to Candi.

The black girl caressed her nipples, and, licking her teeth, had her cunt flaps open, with fingers pressing the slimed pink growth of her nubbin, which was standing stiff. She stroked the black pears of her bare arse, caressing her ebony fesses as though they were a lover's lips. Come seeped from the dark folds of her cooze. Jacqui's eyes darted to the cunt lips of the black girl.

'Does it bother you that I like to wank off, at your bare bum and your shame?' sneered Nip.

Jacqui burst into tears. 'You know it does,' she said.

Casually, Nip inserted her finger into Jacqui's anus. The Welsh girl squealed. Nip's finger penetrated her rectum and touched her colon. It thrusted vigorously into the girl's rectum for two minutes, before withdrawing, to leave Jacqui sighing in frustration.

'Oh,' Jacqui moaned. 'Please go on. I didn't mind that a bit.'

Nip licked her finger clean of Jacqui's arse grease. 'You are tasty, but have a lot to learn, young lady,' Nip murmured.

'Tell!' Candi ordered.

Candi watched Nipringa frig herself, and began to touch her own stiffening clitoris. Come glistened on her thighs. Smack! Smack!

'Ouch!' Jacqui's spanked bare bum trembled.

'I'll tell everything,' she said with a sob.

'Do,' panted Nip, masturbating her swollen pink clit, and licking Jacqui's arse grease.

'Professor Darmon made me ... made me strip naked, for my interview,' said Jacqui. 'He admired my growth of hair ... you know, down there ... but he said I must shave it off and be completely clean. So I did shave it. I went into the bathroom there and then, and used three disposable razors to get myself smooth. It was rather a thrill, scraping the razor across my cooze hill, and watching the hairs come off, even though I've always been proud of my big forest. And then I had to show him, very modestly, a quick flash of my twat, and the professor nodded in approval. A girl likes approval.'

'You're pretty hairy now,' said Nip, sniffily. 'Our master seems to respect that, although I don't know why. A decent girl *always* shaves herself.'

'We'll shave her,' said Candi, panting.

'Yes, why not?' said Nip. 'But with what?'

'Our teeth,' Candi said with a leer.

'No! Anything but that,' groaned the tethered Jacqui.

'Tell us your true story, and we might get you a Bic razor,' Nip hissed. 'Or not ...'

'Professor Darmon was a master. After my breaking in, my duties were easy enough, and I learned to like wearing my frilly maid's uniform.'

'And what was that like?'

'Awfully tight.'

'Describe it.'

'Well, no knickers – that was very strange, especially as my skirt was so short. Whenever I had to bend over to dust the leather books with my feather thing, I knew I was showing my bum, and that the professor was looking, and . . . and I didn't mind, somehow. It gave me a thrill to show off my bare bum to a master. He could see my bumhole and cooze and everything, but I waggled the skirt – a lovely pleated thing – up and down over my bottom, so he only got a fleeting look. I suppose I was teasing him. I wore nylon stockings – fishnets – and a very short skirt, and a frilly blouse, with a scalloped bra that shoved my titties up against the cloth of my blouse, so that my nips were quite obvious. I didn't mind that either.'

'You admit you are an exhibitionist, then,' Nipringa said.

Jacqui blushed fiery red. 'Certainly not!' she cried.

'Most girls are,' drawled the black girl. 'But most are too embarrassed to admit it. Go on, slut.'

'But after a few months, he said the conditions of my employment had changed, and he could no longer claim my maid's uniform against his taxes, so I must do the housekeeping in the nude. Apart from my maid's bonnet and very high spiky stiletto heels, which were quite uncomfortable, actually.'

'You did the housekeeping pretty much in the full nude?'

'With the feather duster, of course. The professor insisted on the feather duster. I felt so silly, waving a feather duster, when I was in the nude.'

'Not half so silly as you look now, bitch,' drawled Nipringa, flicking a speck of non-existent dust from Jacqui's left fesse.

She licked her finger, wet from Jacqui's arse grease.

'Ssh,' said Candi. 'There's still more to it.'

'You're very cruel to make me tell everything,' said Jacqui, sobbing. 'I had to make sure the leather bindings of the professor's books were spotlessly clean, and I wasn't exactly perfect at maid's work, so if he found a spine that wasn't gleaming pure, I'd be punished. He said books were sacred, and a mere girl wasn't to look inside.'

'Punished? How?' rasped Nip.

'He would spank me,' blurted Jacqui. 'Spank my bare bottom. There, I've said it.'

'Not everything,' said Candi.

'Must you know?'

'Of course.'

'He bent me over his desk, and I had to put my face in his blotter, and he spanked me three or four dozen on the bare,' said the Welsh girl, sobbing once again. 'Being spanked always made me cry, and my tears went into the blotting paper. I hated it. But he gave me a tip if I was brave. A few coins mean a lot to a student. So I took my spankings. How his palm stung on my bare. Yet I didn't mind, after a while. The warmth and smarting were sort of pleasant, and . . . and I admit that I used to rush to the lav and masturbate after the professor had spanked me. I don't know why, it was just a compulsion. I would rub my hot spanked bottom with my right hand, and tweak my clitty with my left. I wept as I wanked. Yet the shame and pain made me hot and wet. I had to bring myself off. That was all right, until, one day, he found me looking inside his books. They made me blush. They were quite obscene – texts from the eighteenth century, like *Fanny Hill*, only worse, about whipping dens, brothels, spanking parties, and with gravure illustrations. He caught me looking at one of the books, from Paris, with a picture of a nobleman flogging three girls on their bare bums using his riding crop. I don't know what came over me. I was nude, and my stiletto heels hurt so much. My cooze began to juice.

I needed to wank off, so I frigged my clit, looking at that picture. I was going to come, when the professor found me, and got very angry. He said I must be punished with something more painful than spanking. "What could be worse, sir?" I asked. "Why, the riding crop," he answered me. He had it in his hand – a fearful thing of braided leather – and he said, with a horrid smile, that it was whalebone underneath, and would hurt my bare bottom very much. "Not on the bare, with that, sir," I pleaded. "Your bottom is naked, according to your terms of employment, therefore it is seemly and convenient to beat you on the bare buttocks," he said. "Down over the desk with you, hussy." What could I do? I bent over the desk, felt him prise my cheeks apart, so that my bum bud and twat lips were shamefully exposed, and took twelve stingers on the bare, which made me sob and scream and tremble more than any spanking could. I heard him grunt with pleasure as each cut of the crop wealed my bare bum, and when I shrieked and sobbed, and couldn't help my bum squirming, he chuckled, and said I was a good girl. A dozen stingers with a riding crop. At the time, I thought it was the worst thing that could happen to any girl.'

'There's worse,' purred Nipringa.

Jacqui began to sob convulsively. 'I never got my work quite right. There was always occasion to beat me with the crop, and . . . and I couldn't help looking inside those obscene books I was only supposed to dust. Being nude made me hot, I suppose. I looked at some gravures from Amsterdam of a gentleman enculing a young girl with her Dutch skirts up and no knickers, no more than my own age, and I had to wank off again. The professor found me – men always know where to find a girl – and said the punishment must fit the crime. This time, I bent over and took two dozen with the crop, on the bare, and when I was shrieking in pain, and my bum was really raw and squirming like the dickens, I felt the professor's naked cock pressing my bum bud. "No!" I screamed. "It's not just in pictures, girl," he said. "Oh, it hurts!" I shouted, as he penetrated me. It was the first time. I felt so humiliated, so violated. I felt his cock – it was so huge and stiff – stabbing me in my belly and my intimate tripes, and I wept in shame. He fucked me in the arse so brutally – there, I've said it – that my twat juiced. Then I felt even more ashamed that I could relish my own pain so much. Come from my wet pouch was going all over my thighs, even as the professor bumfucked me. He said he was in love with my bum and that I had the nicest, juiciest pair of fesses in all Wales. I didn't mind that. A girl always likes to get a compliment. He said a girl's bottom was the loveliest and best part of her, and the gateway to her soul, and stuff like that. Well, that's how professors talk, isn't it? But as he was poking me up the bum, my twat juiced more and more, and my nubbin got all stiff, and when I felt his hot cream spurting right up my tripes, I just came and came. I felt a right twit, when I was groaning and moaning in this lovely orgasm – the best I've ever had. And my smarting, cropped naked bottom had everything to do with it. The pain of my weals on my bare, and the lovely hot spunk from the professor's big stiff cock, right up my bum: it all sort of melted into a delicious pleasure. He had his hand on my twat hillock as he fucked me, stroking me there, and he said my shaven gourd was just as lovely as my arse melons, that, in fact, a girl's arse and cunt hillock were mirror images. He said my bum was the loveliest bum in the world. Flattery gets a man anywhere, doesn't it?'

Nip stroked her own naked bottom, lovingly, with soft caresses. 'And did he bugger you often?' she sneered.

'Oh! You are truly a cruel questioner.'

'Answer,' said Candi.

'Yes . . . yes, he did. But his cock was so big, like the master's, here, that I couldn't take the pain. That is what makes men our owners: those fearful horrid tools that have us in thrall, and the bigger the cock, the more powerful the master. I admit I loved it, once it was inside me, but before my bumming, he would tease me and tantalise me, stroking his stiff helmet against my pucker without inserting. One time the thought of that monstrous cock up my belly made me lose my water. Of course that earned me a further twelve cuts on the bare. He bound me in cords of the same antique leather as his books. I was bent, bare bum, over his desk for my punishment, as was normal, but with my ankles and wrists strapped to the feet of his desk. I couldn't move. I was helpless, as he flogged and – yes, I must use the awful word – buggered me. Such shame for a girl. Yet he kept saying my bottom was so nice, and begging for stripes and a lovely hot smarting feel. My shaved twat juiced so heavily and I came all the more, for being bound in those leather thongs, while my fesses were smarting so cruelly, and his tool was up me. He made me know who was boss, and that made me come so heavily.'

'But you've let your twat hair grow back, you lazy slut,' snapped Nip. 'What a monstrous forest.'

Nip proudly stroked her own swelling cunt hillock, as smooth as dark chocolate.

'I'm sorry, really I am,' Jacqui blurted. 'I know a clean hillock is better, but it's just that girls at college – in the shower, you know, after netball – they admire a full bush. I suppose it's vanity.'

'Did they do more than admire your bush?' asked Nip, openly masturbating her fully erect pink clit. 'Did they wank you off?'

'Yes . . . why, girls nude in the showers can't help it. You know that, miss. To be honest, the other girls were envious of my job with the professor, and my getting

130

bummed, and probably, they thought, getting better marks in my essays. They would pull my pubic hair, quite painfully, and stick their fingers up my twat and bumhole, to frig me hard, and ask me if that was as good as the professor's cock. They stroked my bottom, fresh with the professor's crop marks. I think they were jealous that he striped my bare. You know how girls are! He ... he flogged me in such pretty patterns. I couldn't help coming, even as the girls were humiliating me so. My juice just flowed. A girl's fingers are so nimble. They know how to please, even as they hurt.'

'Let's shave the arrogant bitch clean,' drawled Nip, panting slightly, with her fingers squelching in her wet pink pouch, sheathed in succulent black cunt meat. 'She's far too fond of frigging and bumming. She's a blasted masturbatress, disgustingly hairy, quite possibly a latent lesbo. In short, she needs a lesson. We'll get that twat mound clean, as a proper girl's should be. Her armpits are so furry, she's like a bloody yak. And there are hairs round her bumhole that should be cleared away.'

'But we've no razor,' said Candi.

'We have our teeth.'

Jacqui squealed, writhing and jerking, as the two girls began to bite her: Nip on the cunt and anus, and Candi on the armpits. They chewed and spat for over twenty minutes, until the sobbing girl's cooze hillock, anal cleft and armpits were smooth patches of blotched bare skin. Nip grasped a clump of nettles, and rubbed them on the bare skin, making Jacqui howl, while Candi, ordering her to stop blubbing like a cissy, lifted the knobbed handle of the pisspot, and inserted it into her rectum. Jacqui gagged with pain, as Candi began to bugger her.

'That'll teach you to weep like a wimp,' Candi hissed.

'Oh! Oh! Ooh!' Jacqui cried, as her bum writhed, and cunt juice seeped from her shaven cooze.

'The bitch is juicing,' said Nip drily. 'Shameless.'

'Don't stop,' Jacqui moaned, as her buttocks squeezed the buggering earthen tool. 'I'm going to come. Oh! Yes! I'm there! You've brought me off! Ooh!'

Come sprayed from her twitching pink twat, as her belly writhed in orgasm. Watching, Nip fingered herself to a come, panting a little, with her bare black breasts heaving, the dark nipples stiff.

'Let's put the slut out the window,' Candi said, panting.

'Are you sure?' asked Nip.

'Of course I'm bloody sure. Look at that bloody bum. Those pears. I'm jealous, damn it. The girl is made for a bloody smacking. She'll fit. Stick her big Welsh tits through the window, and her arse is all ours. God, I love that bum. It's ... it's like mine. I want to wank over it, punish it for making me want to wank.'

Nipringa stroked her stiff brown nipples. Her palm stroked her bottom, tickling herself, as though preparing for a spanking. Her little finger tweaked the exuberant bud of her anus, and she licked her teeth. 'I can't disagree,' she purred. 'But what will happen to her breasts? It could be painful.'

'That's up to those English bitches, Sarah and Emily. I'd like to whip the bums of those whores. Cane them juicy and raw. Lovely welts, lovely squeals, lovely squirms. You know how gorgeous a girl's bare bum looks when it's red and ... you know.'

'I do know,' purred the black girl.

Nip's fingers touched Candi's clit. The pink little nubbin swelled stiff.

'Oh, don't.'

'Do you mean that?'

'Nip ... please ...'

'What do you really mean?'

'Please do. Oh, it feels so nice. Please do me.'

'First things first. I'll do you, after we've punished this filthy slave. A slave gets what she deserves. All girls are submissive, by their natures – slaves, if you like. How can a female beast with tits and bum and belly, all that succulent man-baiting flesh, not be a slave to a cruel master who wants to spank her arse raw – and those titties too? Get real. It's what all girls crave, slavery to a male – if they were honest enough to admit it. We girls are animals to fuck and bum-spank, and that is what we desire. If a man is absent, another girl must do the job, as a teacher.'

'But we can't punish this slave – we're slaves ourselves.'

'Sometimes, a slave is a mistress.'

Squealing, the Welsh girl was pushed through the window. Her big hips jammed the opening. 'My tummy's stuck!' she cried. 'It hurts!'

Candi lifted her hand over the trapped girl's naked buttocks. She wiped sweat from her eyes, and rubbed her breasts of dripping perspiration. 'I'll do more than hurt you,' she hissed.

Smack! Candi spanked the girl's trapped bare bum.

'Ahh!' she squealed, outside, as her legs jerked rigid, and the bare buttocks clenched. 'Oh, don't!'

Smack!

'Ooh!'

Smack!

'Stop, please. My bum's on fire.'

Come oozed from the flogged girl's naked cunt.

'Don't you like it?' hissed Nip.

'How can you say such a thing?'

Smack! Smack!

'Ooh! Ahh!'

Candi sweated, as she laid a pink patchwork on the girl's naked bottom, helpless under her hand. Nipringa watched the Welsh girl's bottom redden, and masturbated coolly and voluptuously, as the fesses jerked under Candi's hand, and the ooze of Jacqui's come became a flow, lathering her quivering bare thighs. Nip

133

balled a fistful of nettles, and rammed the stinging package up Jacqui's cunt, making her howls grow. Outside, they heard the voices of Emily and Sarah.

'What have we here?' drawled Sarah.

'An escapee,' said Emily.

'No! Please!' wailed Jacqui. 'Those beastly bitches are torturing me.'

'You are trying to escape,' said Emily, solemnly. 'You must be punished.'

'Please, no. I can explain,' Jacqui said, sobbing.

'At school in Wiltshire, we knew how to deal with cheeky pups like you. And we know how to deal with you here. There is only one lesson a fractious girl understands.'

Thwap! The whip lashed Jacqui's naked jutting teats, bruising the nipples vivid pink.

'Take that.'

Thwap!

'And that.'

'*Ahh!*' Jacqui screamed. 'Please don't whip me there! Not on my breasts!'

Thwap! Thwap!

'*Ohh! Ahh!*'

Candi smacked the squirming bare arse of the trapped girl, from inside the cave, while the swimsuited guards, their pink costumes gleaming in the moonlight, whipped the breasts of their captive with their sjamboks. The nettles packing Jacqui's cunt emerged, limp and sodden with come, from her writhing wet pouch.

'Such a pervert,' said Nipringa, masturbating her clit, and stroking Candi's naked sweat-beaded bottom. 'She *likes* being punished. Only a genuine pervert enjoys a tit-whipping.'

'Don't you?' asked Candi, as Nipringa's finger probed her anus.

'Why, yes,' purred the black girl. 'And I especially enjoy the tit-whipping of another.'

Outside, in the pale moonlight, Jacqui's naked breasts echoed to the lashes of the guard girls' whips. Thwap! Thwap!

'Ooh! Ahh! Please stop. Don't flog me there, I beg you. My titties hurt awfully.'

'That is the whole point,' drawled Sarah.

'She's a saucy one,' said Emily.

Sarah and Emily chortled, as they flogged the girl on the bare nipples. Double-whipped, her screams echoed through the mud prison cell, even as Candi carefully smacked her writhing arse. Smack! Smack! Her hands laid juicy pink marks on Jaqui's squirming buttocks.

'Take that,' Candi said. 'And that.'

Smack! Smack!

'God, it hurts!' squealed Jacqui. 'I wanted us to be best friends. Nettles up my twat. They sting horribly. You're a right cheeky pair, but I can take that. A spanking I can take too, as it's all in play, isn't it? But these guard bitches are flogging my breasts. It's not fair.'

'Don't you disrespect us,' snarled Emily.

'Whip her belly, the dirty slut deserves it, or her face, if you like,' added Sarah. 'It's all the same to me.'

Thwap! Thwap!

'*Ahh! Ohh! My lips!*'

As the English guard girls in their pink swimsuits whipped Jacqui's face, belly and titties, outside the prison hole, Nipringa began to wank the weeping girl's distended nubbin, while Candi continued to spank her trapped bottom. Between the smacks of Candi's hand, Nip put her tongue into the twitching anal pucker of the flogged girl, and sucked her arse grease, while wanking her own clit and flicking her nipples with her thumb.

'I love a submissive slut,' she drawled, licking her lips. 'Submissive sluts are true girls. Who was the most famous submissive slut of all time? Lucrezia Borgia. She did everything her masters wanted, and lived happy.'

135

Thwap! Thwap!

The naked girl's flogged body shuddered.

'Ahh! God, it hurts,' Jacqui said, sobbing. 'I'm not a submissive, I swear.'

'You'd better learn to become one,' said Nip.

'You're a girl, like us!' cried Candi.

Nip kissed Candi on the lips, while both girls fingered their cunts. The thighs of the black girl and the white girl glistened with spurted come.

'She has a spankable arse,' panted Candi, as Nip tweaked Candi's clit. 'And a juicy bumhole.'

'Better than yours?'

'You cheeky bitch! Let's see, shall we?'

'Let's see now.'

Trapped in an ochre mudhole, bum inside and whipped face and teats without, Jacqui squealed and suddenly pissed, as she was bum-spanked and teat-flogged at the same time. Nipringa had her tongue firmly inside Jacqui's rectum; Sarah clamped Jacqui's face between her thighs, making Jacqui lick the come-wet gusset of her pink swimsuit, while Emily whipped her bare titties. Jacqui's twat seeped come. It was up to Candi to swallow the gush of golden pee from the girl's twitching cooze.

'You bitch!' Candi cried, wiping her lips. 'I didn't need that.'

Smack! Smack! Smack!

Jacqui's bottom wriggled, as Candi's hand coloured the bare flesh pink.

'Ooh! Stop!' she pleaded.

Thwap! Thwap!

Outside the cave, the whips of Emily and Sarah lashed the blonde's helpless bare teats. Cunt juice poured from Jacqui's writhing slit.

'No! No! I'm going to come!' Jacqui wailed. 'You fucking bitches! You've made me so wet! I'm going to . . . ooh! Ahh! *Ooh!*'

136

Come spurted from her cunt, as she came, squealing, spanked on her bare buttocks and lashed on her breasts. Nipringa smiled, panting, as she masturbated to climax, and made Candi groan, as her black fingers tweaked Candi's pink swollen clitty, until Candi too orgasmed. Nipringa took hold of Jacqui's cunt basin, and pulled her roughly back into the hole. The Welsh girl lay in the mud, sobbing, and rubbing the smacks and welts on her naked buttocks and breasts.

'I wanted so much to be friends,' she moaned, drooling. 'But how can we be friends, after all my pain?'

A cruel pink sun crept to the horizon. Emily's face poked into the mudhole. She licked her whip, hot from Jacqui's titties, then, with its tip, rubbed the gusset of her pink swimsuit, stained crimson by a damp tide of her come, where her erect clitoris was plainly visible, straining against the fabric.

'There are no friends, you dirty wanking sluts, when you are slaves of the master,' she drawled.

9

Weighmistress

Candi and Nipringa were weighed by Miss Serena.

'Line up, sluts,' the German mistress ordered. 'Belly to arse.'

Nude, the two English girls pressed against each other. Miss Serena grasped their breasts, squeezing them until the nipples were hard, then placed the teats on a scale. Serena added silver weights, waited until the scale ceased to tremble and jotted the results in her notebook.

'Not bad,' said Miss Serena. 'Both of you girl slaves have a kilo on each bub. The master likes only sluts with proper teat weight. The Welsh bitch was not sufficient, being so young, with little firm titties, but made up for it by her big ripe arse pears.'

'They call this monster the blonde beast from Berlin,' Candi whispered to Nip. 'I'm frightened of her.'

Miss Serena preened herself in her pink swimsuit, with tasselled frills at the crotch, rubbed her ripe arse peach, made sure her massive breasts were firmly contained by the satin fabric, then cracked her whip. The sun was already high, and she was sweating into her pink slavemistress costume. Serena was tall and blonde, and despised equally blonde girls whose bottoms and breasts did not quite match up to hers in size or ripeness. Her Prussian teats weighed two kilos in all, and she was proud of them. As weighmistress of the master, she also had to weigh herself. No boy slaves were admitted whose cocks and balls did not weigh a good six hundred grammes, nor girl slaves whose teats came short of a kilo, unless their arses were big enough to make up the difference. The girls' bare arses were measured, prodded and felt, enabling Serena to calculate the weight of the buttocks.

'Work harder, you dirty, stupid bitches,' Serena snarled, in Portuguese, but with her Berlin accent, the flat vowels of Prussia expressing her contempt for the nude girl slaves toiling in the stables.

With her immaculately shining pink leather boot, she kicked Candi in the anus, the tip of her boot landing with blistering accuracy right in the naked arse cleft. Candi squealed in protest.

'You lazy English slut,' Serena drawled.

'Ahh!' Candi cried, breasts and bum smeared filthy, her nude body slimed up to the neck in dung and muck.

Miss Serena flicked her whip into Candi's arse cleft. Candi's bare buttocks were jolted, and clenched.

'It is all the same, girl slave,' she said. 'Look at your friend Nipringa. She is from the educated class, and does her duty without complaint. Her slave tits are a good twelve hundred grammes.'

Nude, and toiling, Nipringa frowned at the compliment. 'Candi's are nearly as much,' she murmured.

Her remark was rewarded by a cut of Miss Serena's whip across her nipples, which made Nipringa moan.

'Work, don't talk, bitches,' said Miss Serena.

Miss Serena Sonne licked the snake tongue of her whip, and smiled, as her eyes misted over. She remembered her girlhood in Lichtenberg, and the day of her sixteenth birthday, when she had her first bare-bottom spanking.

The director of the gymnasium in Zehlendorf summoned her to his office – her school work was disgracefully sloppy – he suspected she was too fond of boys, and night-time pleasures, when a good German girl should be doing her homework. Serena was a beautiful young lady, and the director could understand the temptation of the West Berlin nightlife, and the boys in the Kurfürstendamm who must be sniffing around Serena's undoubted physical charms, but school was school, and a German schoolgirl must behave, must study. Especially an Ossi, from East Berlin, capital of the former DDR. They must show that despite soft years of communist welfare, they were up to scratch, and understood the value of German hard work and discipline.

Serena was privileged to be at school in Zehlendorf. Sometimes – the director removed his spectacles, breathed on them and polished them – the East Berliners did not quite understand the ways of German democracy, and had to be given lessons in it. In Serena's case, there might have to be a report, and a lot of tiresome paperwork, but there was an easier way to teach her a lesson – a lesson, the director opined, which all girls had to learn at one time or another.

Serena was wearing a pink leather miniskirt, which scarcely covered her pink bikini panties – in fact was not really supposed to – with white calfskin boots, over flame-pink nylon stockings. She trembled a little. Although her costume was normal attire for a Berlin teenager, it perhaps did not meet the austere demands of the senior school where she was privileged to study. The director invited her to raise her miniskirt, if indeed the tight leather skirtlet tube could be raised, lower her bikini panties, and bend over his desk with her buttocks naked, for a bare-bottom thrashing, in the old Prussian style. Serena was too Prussian not to obey an order, and complied at once, although she was quivering at the thought of the pain and shame she was about to receive, but which she knew she richly deserved for her laziness.

There was a curious pleasure in bending over, baring her bottom, and wiggling it, just teasing a bit, for the powerful male who was about to spank her. Serena sensed that she herself, a teenage girl with her bottom shamefully bared, had a certain power over the director. He walked around her, and she could hear his heavy breath. He took a school ruler, a full metre long, from his desk drawer. Serena looked at the heavy wooden ruler, and her buttocks clenched.

'I don't like this,' he said, 'but it is my duty. I propose to give you twenty strokes on your buttocks, with my ruler. When the chastisement is over, you will feel better, I promise.'

'Please, Herr Direktor, get on with it,' Serena said. 'I know I have been a bad girl, and deserve my punishment. I don't like the thought of being whipped on my bare bottom, but I am ready for it.'

'Very well.'

Vap! The ruler descended suddenly on Serena's bare, and she bit her lip to stop herself from crying out at the stinging pain. She felt the director's fingers stroking the smarting welt on her naked fesses.

'I am sorry to stripe a young girl's lovely naked buttocks,' he said, 'but it is necessary.'

'I know, sir,' Serena whimpered, with tears in her eyes.

Vap! The ruler smacked her bare once more, this time at the top of her bottom, where the skin was tender, and the blow more painful. Serena wanted to cry out, but stopped herself. She resolved that she would not give the director the satisfaction of knowing how much the ruler-flogging hurt. Vap! Now the ruler slapped her left haunch, stinging her abominably, and the stroke was followed by another, almost at once, on the right haunch. To her horror, Serena, even as her eyes misted with tears of pain, felt juice ooze from her young girl's cunt. As if being beaten on the naked buttocks, by a man, excited her.

'Oh! Sir!' she gasped. 'Have you whipped other girls?'

'It is often the case,' the director replied. 'A lazy or inefficient girl responds best to the shock of a whipping on her bare fesses. The fesses must always be bare, to teach her the lesson of obedience.'

Vap!

'Uhh ... uhh ...'

Serena's breath was hoarse, and she felt her bare arse wriggling, cheeks clenching in anticipation of each new, cruel lash from the ruler. Vap! The director applied his strokes methodically, to every part of Serena's naked bottom and with plentiful lashes to the haunch. Serena squirmed, weeping. Her naked spine writhed.

'Mm ... uhh ... sir, you are very expert at this. You are a true Prussian.'

'Thank you, Serena. I told you that you would feel better after your chastisement, which must be done with skill. But I see that you are becoming strangely excited, in an immodest fashion. There is juice on your thighs. It comes from your genital parts, specifically, your vulva, whose lips are swollen with immodest lust. You are wet with desire, miss.'

Serena wept. 'I'm sorry, sir, I can't help it.'

'Does beating excite you?'

Vap!

'*Ohh!* God, that hurt! In answer to your question, I don't know, sir.'

'You are not telling the truth. It does excite you. Quite disgusting. I fear your twenty strokes must become forty,' said the director. 'Girls are lustful and deceitful creatures. I must beat girlish nastiness and dishonesty from you.'

Vap! Vap!

'*Ooh!*'

Serena wept, her cunt streaming with copious juice, and her whipped bare buttocks wriggling over the hard Saxon oakwood of the director's desk. Her tender young girl's clitty was stiff, and she rubbed it on the wooden desktop, as her flogged buttocks wriggled at each stroke of the ruler on her bare. Her swollen twat gushed come. Vap! Vap!

'Oh! Sir!'

Vap! Vap!

'Ooh!'

As her whipped bum squirmed, her engorged clitty slammed the desktop. The director lowered his ruler.

'Serena, are you masturbating?'

'No, sir.'

'Don't lie.'

'Well, sir, the beating excites me, I can't deny it.'

'Your juices are fouling my desk, girl! Do you masturbate frequently? It might explain the defects in your schoolwork.'

'Sir, I'm like any girl. We all frig. I do myself – tweak my clit – every night, before I go to sleep.'

'That is normal. Girls are lustful creatures, and incapable of resisting their base physical needs. A maiden's nightly wank, fingers between her legs, under her nightie, is perfectly understandable. But is that all?'

Vap! Vap! Serena's bare arse jerked, as the wooden ruler lashed her pink-striped globes.

'Ooh! Oh, it hurts!'

The caning continued to the prescribed forty. Serena sobbed uncontrollably, her cunt dripping come.

'Answer my question, young lady,' ordered the director. 'Do you masturbate over-frequently?'

'Well, sometimes, I frig in the toilet, in the lunch hour, with Marie-Luise Hammer. I mean, we wank each other off. We squat together on the toilet seat with our panties down, and rub each other's clit until we come. A girl gets so hot for action. Lots of girls go to the toilet and talk about boys, and . . . you know, masturbate.'

'In my school. You vile slut. I'll give you action,' hissed the director.

'Oh! Sir! What are you doing?' shrieked Serena.

'Your punishment continues, bitch,' hissed the director. 'Ossi Lichtenberg sluts like you understand only one thing.'

Serena felt hot stiff flesh at her arse cleft. She looked round, and saw the director's cock, standing stiff.

'A kilo of good Prussian meat,' he sneered.

The director's erect cock penetrated Serena's anus. The stiff cock meat filled her rectum, and his helmet reached her colon. Serena screamed long and loud, her buttocks squirming, as she was enculed for several minutes.

'Oh God, sir! That hurts!' she squealed.

'Silence, slut,' panted the director, as his huge stiff tool squelched in and out of Serena's tender young bumhole. 'Don't tell me you haven't done this many times, in the filthy communist slums of Lichtenberg.'

'Sir, I am a young girl, and a virgin,' Serena said, sobbing.

'Then, under German law, you are still a virgin,' snarled the director, as his spunk filled Serena's anal hole.

His cream bubbled from her squirming anal lips, soaking her thighs, as she wanked herself.

'Oh!' Serena squealed. 'Oh yes!' She rubbed her tender young girl's clit and then erupted in orgasm.

That was then, when Serena was a young Berlin girl of sixteen. Now, a few years later, after having emigrated to Brazil, Serena knew in her heart that whipping a boy or girl on the bare bottom was the best way to Prussian obedience. Everything must be done to measure: the number of strokes; the volume of tears from the flogged youth. She was the master's weighmistress, calculating to the nearest gramme the weight of a young girl's titties, or a boy's cock and balls. Bottoms could not quite be weighed, but must be measured, to the nearest cubic centimetre.

The new slaves – the black girl, Nipringa, her friend, Candi, and young Welsh Jacqui – made quite respectable bottom measurements. Serena liked her work; especially when the brutal Sandoz punished her by spanking her bare bum, then pounding her rectum with his own monstrous two-kilo cock, after her day's work of weighing, measuring and whipping her quota of nude girl and boy slaves.

She did not exactly like Sandoz, in fact would perhaps prefer a mutual wank in the toilet with Marie-Luise Hammer, but Sandoz had the virtue of a lovely brown body, enormous strength, a big cock, and the power of a heavy creamer, with seemingly endless spunk in his big hard balls. Above all, he was disciplined. Perhaps even more disciplined than the master himself. When the master fucked Serena in the arse, he chose not to come. It was an expression of his power, which Serena, of course, respected. But when Sandoz buggered her, he always came, his hot spunk deliciously filling her rectum. He knew how to make a girl feel secure.

'Oh, God. I've had enough of this,' Candi groaned. 'Being weighed like pork sausage.'

'We are girl slaves,' said Nip, 'and here in Paraiba, a mere girl is probably worth less than a pork sausage.'

'Were you pork, I wouldn't eat either of you sluts,' sneered Miss Serena.

'Oh, wouldn't you?' shrilled Candi. 'Don't think I can't make you, you bitch.'

She leaped onto the pink-suited weighmistress, landing a heavy punch to her right breast, which felled the German girl. Candi squatted on Serena's belly, and rained punches on her cunt and breasts. Her fists squelched in the moistening gusset of Serena's pink swimsuit.

'It is an outrage,' groaned Serena.

'We'll have that swimsuit off for a start,' Candi hissed.

145

'No! The master would not allow such a thing. I have earned my pink.'

Candi's nails ripped the nylon from the German girl's breasts. 'Come on, Nip,' she urged. 'In for a penny, in for a pound.'

Nip smiled. 'That bod is too good to miss,' she purred. Her claws ripped the gusset from the squirming Miss Serena's crotch.

'I'm naked!' howled Serena. 'The shame!'

Her knee came up and mashed Candi hard between the thighs, crunching Candi's clitoris.

'Ahh!' Candi screamed, and rubbed her cooze.

'You little slave bitch,' Serena snarled.

The German mistress seized her whip, and lashed Candi savagely on the buttocks, with a flurry of strokes; while Candi sank to the ground, clutching her bruised cunt and sobbing at the lashes, the naked Serena towered over her, and dealt a further flurry of strokes to her breasts. Candi's flogged titties quivered under the merciless whip strokes. Nipringa watched, smiling, with her fingers between her black cunt flaps, manipulating the glistening wet pink of her engorged nubbin.

'Oh! Ooh! Stop!' cried Candi. 'Nip, do something.'

Vap! Vap! The German slavemistress had her foot on Candi's shoulders, pinioning her to the ground. As Candi writhed, helpless, Serena's whip striped Candi's squirming bare bottom, her shoulders and breasts. Her foot flipped Candi like a football. Nip watched, blatantly masturbating her clitty, and stroking her black buttocks, her ebony thighs wet with her come. Vap! Vap!

'Oh! Help me, Nip,' Candi wailed.

Nip's thighs parted, and she pissed on the squirming blonde girl, a long, steaming jet of golden fluid. When her pee had ebbed, Nip flicked her clitty with casual fingers and, in seconds, brought herself off. She bared her teeth and panted a little as she orgasmed; then, her

146

whole body suddenly jackknifing, she leapt into the air, and both her feet slammed Serena between the legs. Serena fell, shrieking. Bare teats flapping, the weighmistress howled for the master, for Emily or Sarah, for Sandoz or the boys, but there was no one. She writhed and gurgled, helpless, while Nipringa sat on her face, with her anus pressed on Miss Serena's nose.

'You realise we'll be flogged for this?' Nip said, with a coy smile.

'Who cares,' Candi panted. 'Let's punish this arrogant slut, while we have the chance.'

'Serena, you filthy bitch, get your tongue up my bumhole,' ordered the black girl.

Nip's buttocks squirmed on the German girl's face.

'Mm. Mm.' Serena gurgled. 'I don't understand.'

'You understand very well,' said Nip. 'You're going to get your tongue right up me, and give my rectum a good cleaning, while Candi sees to reddening your disgusting big bottom. I think it's about time you had a taste of Prussian medicine.'

Miss Serena lay helpless on her back, with Nip squatting on her face, and her legs stretched upright, fully exposing her buttocks and cunt to the sjambok.

'Your sjambok,' said Nip, 'is an excellent African whip, of the finest leather, used equally on cattle or women.'

'No . . . please,' Serena moaned, her voice muffled by the black girl's naked buttocks squashing her face.

'Get your tongue up me, if you know what's good for you,' Nip ordered. 'I want my whole rectum thoroughly cleaned.'

'Mm . . . yes, miss,' moaned the weighmistress.

Her tongue entered Nipringa's anus and, slurping, went through the anal passage, into the rectum.

'Now lick hard, slut,' hissed Nipringa, 'while Candi horsewhips your nasty bare arse, for our shame of being weighed like animals.'

Candi lifted the sjambok.

Vap! The leather thong bit hard into Serena's raised buttocks, on the lower fesse, and caught part of her top thigh.

'Uhh!' Serena gurgled, her tongue deep inside Nip's bumhole.

Vap! The sjambok lashed Serena's squirming bum.

'Ohh!'

Vap! The whip flogged stripes on Serena's thighs.

'Ahh!' the German girl screamed.

'Stop whining, and lick harder, slut,' the ebony nude commanded, her cunt and anus squelching the German girl's trapped face.

'Mm. Mm. It hurts so much,' whimpered Miss Serena. 'A flogging on my bare nates. You don't understand me.'

'We'll do our best to try,' said Nipringa.

Vap! The sjambok lashed Miss Serena's arse, while her tongue delved Nip's bumhole.

'Do I taste good?' panted Nip.

'Mm. Mm. Yes,' Serena gasped.

'My juice?'

'Oh, it's good.'

'Swallow it all.'

'You filthy slut! You have made me want to do that.'

'Then do it.'

Vap! Candi's whip lashed Serena's buttocks.

'Ahh! Oh, God, my arse! It hurts! I can't take any more!'

'But you must,' said Nip.

The black girl rammed her cunt on Serena's nose, juicing heavily into her mouth.

'Oh . . . yes,' groaned Serena.

Her throat pumped, swallowing Nipringa's come. Vap!

'Ooh!'

The German blonde's arse reddened to crimson under Candi's whip. Candi's trembling bare breasts were beaded with sweat dew, and her fingers crept to her cunt, as she flogged the helpless slavemistress with the gleaming leather thong.

'Not the sjambok, please!' squealed Serena. 'It's so cruel.'

'It's your whip, bitch,' Nipringa snarled.

'Not mine. The master's.'

'You are the master's tool.'

Vap! Vap! Candi's whip flashed, and Serena's whipped buttocks writhed, the bare bum flans laced with pink.

'Ohh! Stop!' screamed the German girl.

'You love Jacqui, don't you? You have a passion for the little bitch.'

'It is not love,' Serena said, sobbing.

Vap!

'Ahh! Stop!'

'If it is not love, what is it?'

Vap!

'Ohh!'

Serena's flogged bare bum clenched.

'Speak, bitch.'

Vap! Candi's whip slashed Serena between the cunt flaps. The tip of the sjambok took her on the clitoris.

'Ahh! No!' she shrieked.

Her cunt spurted come.

Vap!

'Ooh!'

'Speak.'

Nip's buttocks squelched on the German girl's mouth. Serena's lips embraced Nip's engorged clit.

'Ooh, oh,' Serena moaned, as she sucked the black girl's cunt. 'You are so powerful.'

A flood of Nip's come drenched her throat. Serena gurgled, as she swallowed the black girl's cunt juice.

'Then speak,' Nip commanded.

'I can't.'

Vap! Vap! Two strokes from the whip lashed Serena's arse cleft, striking her cunt and anus bud.

'Ahh!' she screamed. 'I must piss.'

A hissing flood of stinking golden fluid streamed from her twat.

'You disgust me,' spat Nip, her ebony bottom squirming on the blonde German's face. 'Speak. What is it with this blonde Welsh girl?'

Vap! Candi brought herself off, as she watched Serena's cunt tremble at another stroke of the cattle whip.

'She ... she has the perfect arse,' Serena said, sobbing. 'So big, so round.'

Nostrils flaring, Nipringa parted her buttocks. Her belly fluttered, and she pissed long and copiously into Serena's mouth.

'Swallow it all, you slut,' she hissed.

Gurgling, Miss Serena drank the entire cargo of Nip's liquor.

'Oh!' Serena wailed, gurgling, as she swallowed Nip's piss. 'You'll pay for this.'

As she swallowed the black girl's piss, her fingers were on her clit. Her tongue penetrated Nip's rectum, while she masturbated. She groaned.

'You girl-slave sluts,' she panted, as she wanked herself to climax, with come pouring from her writhing twat, over her beaten pink thighs. 'Oh! Oh! Ahh! Yes! But you've made my perfect arse red. I hate you.'

Nip picked up the sjambok. 'It is I, Nipringa, who have the perfect arse, bitch,' she snarled. 'It is black and smooth as a Tunis grape.'

Vap! She lashed Serena's squirming bare bottom.

'Ahh!' the flogged German girl screamed.

Her twat juiced come over her quivering thighs.

Paulo and Vergilio sauntered into the room. Both were nude, save for black American nylon panties. Their shaven bodies glistened with sweat.

'We could not help overhearing. Such noise girls make! The perfect arse?' drawled Paulo.

'All boys seek it,' said Vergilio. 'The girl with the buttocks like ripe brown pears. Perfect globes of girl flesh to suck, lick and spank.'

'Sandoz knows as little as the master.'

Smiling, both boys removed their panties. The moment the shiny fabric left their flesh, their shaven bare cocks were fully erect. Nipringa squealed, as Vergilio grasped her by the hair, and Paulo sank his teeth into her ebony buttocks, biting hard.

'No! You beasts!' screamed Nip.

Serena smiled, as Vergilio's tool plunged into Nip's anus. Candi held her friend down by the hair.

'Oh! It hurts!' shrieked the black girl.

Masturbating anew, Serena caressed her clit. 'Good,' she purred.

'I will hurt you, slut Serena,' snarled Paulo.

He wrenched her blonde mane, and Serena shrieked. Paulo threw her to the floor, and kicked her bare buttocks several times, making her sob. His foot landed in her cunt, at which her sobs turned to a scream.

'Be still,' he ordered, kicking her.

Wailing, Serena lay twitching on the dirt. Paulo, cock stiff, straddled her bruised body.

'No, you can't! I object!' shrieked Serena, as the boy's erect cock entered her anal passage. Her tooled arse writhed, the ripe bare globes wriggling in agony. 'Ahh! It hurts!' Serena squealed. 'You're so big! You swine. That huge cock. You are a monster. You're right up my hole. Oh! Oh! I hate you. You're right at my sigmoid colon. God, it's so good. I hate you, I hate you. Don't stop fucking me. *Ach, Gott, ich hasse dich, du Schwein. Ich hasse diesen grossen Schwanz, der macht mir so viel verdammt Vergnügen im Arsch.*'

Her pale teats flapped, and the swollen pink lips of her cunt oozed come, as Paulo buggered her. Nip and

151

Serena writhed, sobbing, beside each other, as the boys enculed them. Their bare buttocks jerked up and down, as the naked boys' stiff cocks slammed in and out of their bumholes. Arse grease dripped from their buggered anuses.

'I say, I can't take this,' moaned Nipringa. 'You've such a big cock, Vergilio. Right up my arse. You're almost in my stomach. It hurts so much, and it's not fair.'

'Shut up, bitch,' snarled Vergilio.

He pawed her stiff clitoris, getting his fingers up her pouch all the way to the wombneck, then pulled his fingers from her cunt with a squelching sound, and slapped his fingers on Nip's mouth, making her drink her own cunt juice.

'You're dripping wet, you filthy little slut,' he snarled. 'You want it.'

'No,' Nip moaned. 'Oh, I don't know what I want.'

Smack! As his cock thrust into Nip's anus, his hand landed a hard spank on the ebony girl's squirming buttocks.

'Oh! No! That hurts!' Nip squealed.

'That's what you want, slut,' hissed Vergilio.

He continued to spank her arse, as he buggered her. Nip cried and sobbed, but her cunt flowed with juice. As the boy's huge cock rammed the black girl's tripes, sliding rapidly in and out of her arse-greased anus, tears flowed down her cheeks, but her breath became hoarse.

'Don't stop, you fucking bastard,' Nipringa panted. 'You're going to bring me off. Oh, God yes. Fuck me, you bastard. Fuck my arse hard. Do me. Yes. Yes. Yes! I'm coming! Oh Oh! *Ahh!*'

Nip's buggered ebony buttocks squirmed violently, as come poured from her glistening pink cunt meat, in the throes of her orgasm.

'*Ja sicher!*' Serena, enculed by Paulo, cried. 'I come! You filthy bastard, you are making me come. I am so wet. *Ich bin nass.* Ahh! Ahh! *Ach, ja!*'

Candi masturbated her clitty at the sight of the girls' agony. Come streamed from her twat, to glisten in rivulets on her quivering bare thighs.

The door opened. Sandoz, naked but for a pink loincloth, entered, dragging a sobbing Jacqui by the hair, pulled to her blonde roots.

'Here's Jacqui, the new slave slut, who needs punishment. She's a cheeky whelp, who wants a sound thrashing. Oh! I'm sorry, Miss Serena,' said Sandoz. 'I didn't know you were busy.'

'I . . . I . . . was teaching the slaves a lesson,' panted Serena.

'That bitch Jacqui,' snorted Nip, licking her teeth, as Vergilio's cock plopped from her bumhole. 'I know what to do with a slut like her.'

10

Hot Sweet Potato

Vip! Vip! The tulipwood cane, wielded by Serena, lashed Jacqui's naked buttocks. Vergilio and Paulo, cocks hard, pinioned her with her toes in their mouths.

'Ahh!' Jacqui screamed. 'I didn't know it was going to be like this. Please don't hurt me so much. And those boys licking my toes. It tickles awfully.'

Vip! Vip! The cane whipped her, and a vicious pink weal appeared on the girl's left buttock.

'*Ahh,*' she moaned. 'That's agony. You don't know what you're doing to me. Please stop, I beg you.'

'On the contrary,' said Serena, stroking her crotch, stained moist on her swimsuit, 'I know very well what I am doing to you, my lovely little naked slut.'

Serena's huge breasts shook, as the caning continued, and Jacqui's pale clenching arse pears quickly turned to crimson. Vip! Vip! The wood lashed the girl's helpless bare bum flesh. Each squirming naked buttock was striped in turn, until Jacqui had taken twenty vicious strokes. All the time she jerked, moaning, as the two boys had the toes of both her bare feet in their mouths, licking and sucking.

'Oh! Oh!' Jacqui wailed, as her bare fesses shuddered and squirmed under the German girl's cane. 'Miss Nipringa, help me, please. I can't take the pain. Get her to stop. I've had enough.'

'In your dreams, you blonde cunt,' drawled Nip. 'Candi. Get cooking.'

Candi obeyed. She went to the stove of red-hot coals and, in moments, two piping hot sweet potatoes appeared on a silver plate.

'Ah! No! It hurts!' shrieked Jacqui, as Nipringa pushed one of the sweet potatoes into the Welsh girl's dripping cunt. The tuber filled her squirming pouch.

Serena took the second sweet potato, and parted Jacqui's flogged red buttocks.

'No! No! It's agony!' Jacqui screamed, as the German girl brutally plunged the scalding potato into her anus, thrusting hard, until the hot tuber filled Jacqui's rectum.

Jacqui wept. Her whipped arse squirmed; her two holes steamed with the hot food. 'What have I done to deserve this?' she said, sobbing.

'You are a girl,' said Serena. 'Girls must be punished.'

Paulo's lips plunged to Jacqui's anus, and sucked the food from her bumhole; Vergilio's mouth fastened on her cunt, and sucked the hot potato from Jacqui's dripping wet pouch. Serena, Nip and Candi held the weeping girl down, as the boys feasted. Both boys laughed.

'What a cheap whore,' said Paulo.

'Just another blonde slut,' said Vergilio, 'and a good foodstore. The slut is wet. My potato was beautifully sauced with her cunt juice.'

The boys laughed louder, as they finished eating from the Welsh girl's scalded holes. The eyes of Serena and Nipringa met, and the two girls glowered.

'A girl must be treated as a girl,' said Serena. 'She must regularly be spanked on her bare bottom, and instructed to behave and be obedient to men. But she must never be disrespected. You boys are no more than slaves of the master, and are guilty of disrespect. Down on your knees, boy slaves, and faces in the dirt. Present your arses to heaven.'

'Please, no, mistress,' begged Vergilio.

'In position, boy slaves.'

The two Brazilian boys assumed position. They crouched with their faces pressed to the red earth, and their naked buttocks presented for Miss Serena's cane. Serena took her time, wanking her cunt cleft, her fingers well inside her crotch-stained pink swimsuit, standing over the boys' bare arses, and stroking their buttocks with the tip of her cane. The boys moaned, as her tulipwood stroked their naked arse clefts, tickling their balls and anus puckers.

'I'm going to enjoy this,' she hissed. 'There is nothing better than a cheeky boy slave with his bottom well reddened. But I need a helpmate.'

She gave Nipringa a second four-foot cane of oiled tulipwood. Nipringa bared her teeth in a smile. She raised her cane, kissed it, caressed the oiled wood with her lips, and then lashed, making the cane whistle in the air, an inch from Paulo's bottom. Paulo groaned. Then – vip! – Nipringa brought the wooden rod down on the boy's bare bum.

'Ohh!' he shrieked, his buttocks clenching, and his face sobbing in the dirt, as a livid pink weal striped his bare buttock flesh.

Serena followed suit, and began the lashing of Vergilio, with a thrash in his arse cleft, her cane clipping his anus pucker.

'*Ahh!*' Vergilio screamed, his arse writhing.

The floggings continued, with strokes carefully placed across the boys' squirming fesses. The boys groaned and sobbed, as the tulipwood canes whipped their brown arses, which quickly turned to pink. They shuddered, whimpering, under the floggings. The naked German girl and the naked black girl both dripped in sweat, their massive breasts bobbing, as they disciplined the bottoms of the squirming, whimpering boys.

Vip!

'Ahh,' gasped Paulo.

Vip!

'Ohh,' moaned Vergilio.

The boys writhed, faces in the dirt, as the canes lashed their naked bottoms. Yet both boys had stiff cocks, under the lashing of girls' canes. Their organs stood massively. Candi and Jacqui had their fingers in their wet twats, and were masturbating, their mouths exchanging wet kisses. Their fingers made squelching noises, as they frigged their stiff pink clits.

Vip! Vip!

'Please. No more,' moaned Paulo.

'Enough, mistress!' wailed Vergilio.

'Serena is a mistress, but I am not,' panted Nipringa. 'I am a girl slave. I have no rights. I am subject. So I can do what I want.'

Vip!

'Ahh!'

'I'm so wet and hot. I can't stand it any more,' said Jacqui, panting.

She leaped to crouch underneath Paulo, clasped his rigid cock in her hungry lips, and began to suck.

'I have to have some of that boy meat too,' said Candi. 'I can't resist.'

Candi did the same for Vergilio, taking his entire stiff tool to the back of her throat, and sucking hard. As the boys were flogged on the bare by Nip and Serena, Candi and Jacqui lay squirming in the dirt, their bare bodies filthy with soil, sucking the cocks of the two whipped boys, while they masturbated their clits. Come poured from their cunts into the ochre earth.

'Beating naked boys excites us,' said Nip to Serena.

'I cannot deny it.'

'Then we both need relief.'

Nip placed her hand on Serena's cunt hillocks, then penetrated her pouch.

'*Ach, ja,*' Serena moaned, as Nip frigged her.

Nip's fingers came away with a squelch, and she licked the German girl's cunt juice. 'Mm,' said Nip. 'Don't you want to frig, mistress? Is there nothing nicer than wanking off, when you are flogging a disobedient boy slave?'

'Yes,' said Serena. 'It is permitted. And I love your juicy black cunt, girl slave.' Serena's fingers penetrated Nipringa's cunt. Three fingers filled the ebony pouch. 'You're very wet,' Serena said.

Nip's thumb stabbed Serena's clitoris. 'You are wet, too,' she said. 'Oh! You're right at my wombneck. Don't stop.'

Nipringa got four fingers into Serena's cunt.

'You slave bitch!' Serena gasped. 'That's good.'

Both girls panted, sweating, as they frigged, while continuing to whip the squirming bottoms of the sobbing boys, whose stiff bulging cocks were plunged in the throats of Candi and Jacqui.

'Boys are so disgustingly lustful,' panted Nip. 'They are not nice. Their cocks rise at the slightest view of a girl in a summer skirt. And on Copacabana Beach, when a girl wants to innocently sunbathe in her bikini, there is always some male strutting around with a stiff cock in his thong, and kicking some beastly football at her bum. Males need a lesson.'

'I agree,' gasped Serena.

Vip! Vip! Their canes flogged the squirming boys. The boys' bare buttocks flared to crimson.

'Oh! Don't stop!' gurgled Jacqui, writhing under the pressure of Emilio's cock fucking her throat.

'Oh! Mmph.'

Vip! Nip's cane lashed Paulo. The black girl's bottom wriggled in pleasure, and Paulo's arse squirmed, as the black girl flogged him. As Nip was wanked by Serena, she came, just as Paulo poured his spermload into Jacqui's stomach. Shortly afterwards, Vergilio moaned, as he ejaculated into Candi's throat. Nip's fingers

158

tweaked Serena's clitty, and the German girl yelped in climax, with come pouring down her quivering bare thighs. The entire company were filthy, their naked bodies slimed in ochre mud.

The door opened. Sandoz, still wearing only a loincloth, entered, followed by the master, in a white silk suit and Panama hat, and Emily and Sarah in their pink swimsuits.

'What is this?' said the master, frowning. 'My slaves, dirty as witches? You'll pay for this, you sluts. And none more than you, Serena. Your toes are filthy. I love to suck your toes. I trusted you to keep clean. But you frig a girl slave?'

'I couldn't help it. The black bitch is so beautiful. Please, master, you must still trust me,' said Serena, sobbing.

'You will have to be punished,' said the master. 'To set an example. Remember, you, too, Serena, are a slave, though a respected one.'

'I will do anything to keep my position. I know I have been foolish, and must be punished.'

The master stroked his chin. 'To frig a girl slave is a grave offence. You will be tied naked to the tulipwood tree, and Sandoz will whip you,' he said. 'I think that is appropriate, don't you?'

'Yes, master,' stammered Serena.

'It shall be a full whipping, in front of the slaves, with the leather – shoulders, back, buttocks and thighs. You shall be whipped for an hour. Then Sandoz will take his rod and cane the soles of your feet. After that lesson, you may regain your position of authority as my weighmistress.'

Serena burst into tears. 'Yes, master,' she said. 'I obey. A girl must always obey.'

Candi and Jacqui quivered, hearing the master's dreadful sentence. Nipringa smiled.

'Emily and Sarah,' drawled the master. 'Rope these slaves, and bring them out to watch Serena's punishment. Serena knows she must be punished to remind her that she, too, is a slave. All my women are slaves.'

Candi, Jacqui and Nipringa were roped together naked; the rope was attached to intricately engraved porcelain clamps at their cunts. The girls winced, as Emily and Sarah, smiling, fastened the clamps and bound the girls tightly together. Cunt to bottom, the girls were led out to the tulipwood tree, where Serena was tied to the trunk, her naked body scratched by the harsh bark, and her voice a wail, begging the master for mercy.

'Please, master,' the German girl pleaded. 'I hate pain, though I know my girl's arse must take it. Please spare me too much pain. You know I am your faithful slave.'

'Then you must take a faithful slave's whipping,' said the master.

'Now, you filthy sluts are obliged to witness due punishment,' said Emily, licking the tip of her cane.

'Later, it will be your turn,' said Sarah, with a leer.

Sandoz lifted the rawhide cattle whip.

'Oh, no, please no, not the cattle whip,' begged Serena.

Her arms and legs were wrapped around the tree trunk, roped together, while a heavy belt of Amazon rubber fastened her waist to the tulipwood. It squeezed her waist, leaving a crimson welt.

'Let the girl's punishment begin,' said the master.

Vap! The leather flogged Serena's bare back. Vap! Her naked buttocks took the lash. Vap! Her thighs were stroked. Vap! The whip striped her shivering calves. Her nude body squirmed against the tree bark, as Sandoz expertly covered her flesh in bruises. As he whipped her, Sandoz's loincloth bulged with his erection.

'*Ach! Gott! Das ist furchtbar!*' Serena screamed, as her flogged bare buttocks wriggled.

Sandoz took her to fifty with the cattle whip. Her naked body was a latticework of purple weals.

'No more, please, master,' begged the writhing Serena, her face streaked with tears.

'Another fifty,' drawled the master.

After a hundred whip strokes, Serena's body was raw, and her bare flesh a tapestry of purple and crimson bruises. The German girl cried, tears streaking her cheeks, and falling to glisten on her squirming bare breasts. Throughout her flogging, her cunt seeped come. It trickled down her thighs, to glisten in the sunlight. Smoking his cheroot, the master nodded. Sandoz let his loincloth fall. His huge cock shone massive and naked, standing as a huge menacing pole. Emily and Sarah parted Serena's fesses.

'Ahh! No! It's so shameful,' cried the flogged Serena.

Sandoz's cock penetrated her anus, and began a powerful buggery, his cock tip first penetrating her anus bud, then, with a powerful thrust, filling her rectum. A second thrust got his fully erect cockshaft into her, and his glans touched her colon. Trussed to the tree, Serena writhed.

'You bastard,' she moaned. 'Don't stop. Fuck me, give me your spunk up my bumhole. *Ach, Gott*, you're bursting me. Your cock is splitting my arse. Don't stop.'

The master watched, cigar-smoking, as Sandoz buggered the squirming German girl to orgasm. She writhed against the tree bark, her clit rubbing the hard wood, as she wanked herself off under the male's buggery. Sandoz's spunk oozed, a froth of cream, from Serena's buggered bumhole. The master ordered Nipringa to be released from her cunt clamp and to lick it up. The black girl obeyed, eyes gleaming.

The master drew back, stroked his white kidskin boots, and ran at the tethered girl, raising his leg, to deliver a kick to her buttocks. His boot struck her in the arse cleft. Serena groaned.

'Kick the slave bitch, girls,' he ordered curtly. 'Imagine you are playing football.'

Roped, Candi and Jacqui began to kick Serena's arse with their bare feet. Slap! Slap! Their toes lashed her cleft, while the master watched, drawing on his cigar.

'Not bad. You sluts may one day make the pink,' he said.

Serena wailed, as Nipringa danced a ballet of kicks to her squirming bare arse. The nude black girl jumped, and kicked Serena with both feet. Emily and Sarah joined the dance. Twirling, the English girls delivered savage kicks to Serena's flogged buttocks. Each kick slammed Serena's cunt and titties against the tree bark. Tears streamed from her eyes.

'Oh, master, please tell them to stop,' she pleaded.

The master smiled, as the kicking continued. Abruptly, after ten minutes of humiliance for the German girl, he nodded to Emily and Sarah, and ordered Serena released from her bonds. He took the sobbing naked girl into his arms, and kissed her nipples. Then he turned her round, and licked her bruised arse cleft, his tongue penetrating her anus bud, which Sandoz had so recently buggered. He kissed her striped raw buttocks, then pulled a pink swimsuit over Serena's flogged flesh.

'Thank you, master,' Serena said with a sigh.

'Serena has been corrected. She is once more my treasured weighmistress, wears the pink, and may carry her tulipwood cane to punish miscreants,' the master said. 'Now, it is the turn of the girl slaves to be chastised. They have been duly weighed, they are of good substance, their teats and fesses are sound, but those teats and fesses now must pay for the pain their slavemistress has endured. Then we shall see if they are fit for work. But they must be shamed. Miss Serena, Emily, Sarah, dip these naked slaves in the slime pond, then whip them on the wet bare.'

Nipringa was roped to Jacqui and Candi, and then Sarah hobbled them. The tethered naked English girls were led by Emily and Sarah to a pond of noxious black filth. Down the path of red earth, the hobbled trio had to endure kicks to their arses from the laughing monitors.

'This is worse than school,' wailed Candi.

When they got to the pond, they were kicked in by their bums. Hobbled, they could not avoid falling into the muck. It was not deep. After twenty minutes of laughing, while the hobbled girls wallowed in filth, Emily and Sarah retrieved the girl slaves, dripping wet and stinking. The girls were marched back to the tulipwood tree, and roped to it. The master watched, smoking a cheroot, as the punishment of the slimed girls began. His white silk trousers were open, and Miss Serena, kneeling in her pink swimsuit, had his cock in her mouth, as he observed the flogging of Nipringa, Jacqui and Candi by Emily and Sarah, sparkling in their own pink suits.

'The clean versus the dirty,' drawled the master. 'In my world, the dirty deserve chastisement.'

Vap! Sarah's rawhide whip landed on Nip's dirty buttocks. The black girl groaned. Vap! Emily's whip lashed Candi, and she began to sob. Vap! Jacqui's slimed and filthy buttocks were striped by Emily.

'Ohh!' Jacqui wailed.

'Suffer, you dirty bitch,' hissed Emily.

Vap! Emily flogged Candi and Jacqui, while Sarah applied herself to the squirming ebony girl. Nip's eyes were closed, her teeth bared in a rictus of agony, yet she made no sound, save a hoarse panting breath, as Sarah's whip striped her buttocks. Vap! Vap! The heavy leather lashed the naked girl. Nip's massive black buttocks squirmed. At the twentieth stroke of the rawhide to her arse, Nip whimpered. Tears ran down her cheeks.

'Hurts, then, you slut?' panted Sarah. 'Can't take it?'

'Do your worst, bitch,' Nip replied. 'A slave can't be hurt too much, otherwise she can't do any work.'

'Your work is carving dildos and canes from the tulipwood trees,' snarled Emily. 'Big ones. We sell them in Rio, in Argentina, in America, in Europe, for a lot of money. Some of our best clients are rich folk in London, Paris, Berlin and Rome. If you're cheeky or disobedient, we'll use them on you. In your cunt and in your bumhole.'

'I can take the biggest dildo you have,' spat Nipringa. 'I'm not afraid.'

'Let us put her to the test,' said the master, lighting another cheroot, while Serena sucked his erect cock. 'Emily, fetch the number four.'

Nip was held down by Candi and Jacqui, and her shining black buttocks, beaded with sweat, were parted by the girls' eager fingers. Her anus pucker glistened pink.

'You fucking bitches,' she hissed.

Emily brought a tulipwood dildo, fifteen-inches long and four-inches wide, gleaming brown, and stroked Nip's squirming arsehole with the massive cylinder.

'No!' Nip cried. 'I'm a slave, but I should be treated fairly.'

The master laughed. His naked cock was at the back of Serena's throat. 'There is no fairly here, in my domain,' he said. 'Fuck her arse with the dildo, Emily. I want to watch her pain. It will help make me come.'

'Oh! God, no!' shrieked Nip, as Emily's wooden dildo penetrated her anus. 'It hurts too much.'

'That's precisely what we want,' said the master.

The dildo went all the way to Nip's colon.

'Ahh! Ohh!' the black girl screamed. 'It's too big. I've never taken a cock that big.' Her arse writhed, as Emily brutally buggered her with the giant wooden dildo. Come poured from Nip's cunt. 'Go on,' Nip gasped. 'Don't stop.'

The massive wooden dildo squelched in and out of her squirming bumhole. The dildo was soon anointed with copious arse grease from Nip's anus. Nip's fingers found her wet pouch, and she began to wank herself off.

'I can't take it,' she groaned. 'Oh, don't stop.'

Her fingers squelched on her clitty, as she was brutally buggered by the laughing Emily.

'Oh! Yes! Oh, you bitch! I'm coming!' Nip gasped. 'Ahh . . . ahh . . . yes!'

Her belly convulsed in orgasm, as come gushed from her cunt.

'Now the other sluts,' drawled Sarah. 'May I?'

'Please,' panted Emily, handing her the dildo.

Candi was next for buggery. 'Please, not that,' she pleaded.

'I'm going to do you, you bitch, to teach you a lesson,' hissed Sarah. 'You have no choice.'

The dildo was wet with Nipringa's arse grease. On the master's orders, Jacqui and Nipringa held the naked Candi down, while Sarah plunged the dildo into her anus. Candi squealed. Paulo and Vergilio looked on, stroking their massive cocks, and smiling, while Sarah did her.

'No! Please! God, it hurts!' wailed Candi.

Nip placed her fingers in Candi's slit, and began to tweak her clit. 'You'll like it,' she said softly.

Jacqui looked at the giant wooden tool piercing Candi's rump, and masturbated.

'Yes,' Candi groaned. 'I don't want it to stop. Oh, tweak me, Nip.'

Nip's lips fastened on Candi's engorged clit, and sucked, until the girl squealed to her buggered orgasm. Next, it was Jacqui's turn. Nip and Candi held the Welsh girl down, her arse parted for swiving.

'If I may make a suggestion?' Nip said to Sarah. 'This is a fine and quite painful dildo. With it fastened to your waist by a rubber or leather strap, you could fuck a girl just as a man does. In fact, you would be acting the part of a man.'

165

Emily and Sarah clapped hands. They looked at the master for approval, and he nodded. Serena was sucking his bared cock, her lips moving around the helmet as if licking an ice cream. Moments later, the two monitors appeared with their pink swimsuits undone at the gusset, and giant wooden dildos strapped to their waists by rubber thongs, the organs rising from their cunt basins. The double dildos extended fully into the cunt of the dominant female, and fully into the orifice of her victim.

'No!' Jacqui cried.

Nip and Candi held her down.

Sarah's dildo penetrated the Welsh girl first. The wood slid easily into her greased anus. Jacqui wept, as she was enculed.

'Ooh! It hurts! Oh, you bitch!' she screamed. 'Not up my bum!'

'Yes, up your bum, you little slut,' panted Sarah, as she buggered the squirming blonde maid. 'Where else would you like to have it?'

Sarah's body dripped with sweat, as she fucked the Welsh girl. The wooden dildo made squelching noises as it passed between Sarah's wet cunt, and Jacqui's arse-greased anus.

'Yeah,' groaned Sarah. 'Want me to stop, bitch?'

'No ... oh, it hurts, but it's good,' gasped Jacqui. 'Fuck me, please. Right up the bum. Split me in two. I never thought it would be so good. Oh, you cruel bitch. I'm all wet. I need to wank.'

Emily, crouching, began to lick Sarah's bared bottom, as Sarah fucked the Welsh girl. Jacqui's fingers went to her stiff clit, and she began to wank off. It was not long before she brought herself to a climax. Emily masturbated herself to come, as she licked Sarah's bottom. Jacqui moaned, as her come poured.

Paulo and Vergilio were laughing. They had their hands casually rubbing their half-erect cocks.

'Those boy slaves need a lesson,' snarled Sarah. 'They think we girls are just a spectacle. But they are the spectacle. Master, is it all right to fuck them in the arse?'

'Why, of course,' said the master.

Nip, Candi and Jacqui had to watch as the two boy slaves bent over to take their punishment from Sarah and Emily, with their strap-on dildos. The boys naked brown buttocks shone.

'No. Please,' whimpered Vergilio.

'To be fucked by a girl. It is the worst shame,' said Paulo.

'You are slaves, and must endure the worst shame,' said the master.

The boys writhed, as the girls' dildos plunged into their anuses. Emily and Sarah fucked the boys until they screamed for mercy. The dildos rammed into their arseholes until the boy slaves begged for pardon.

'Master! It hurts!' screamed Paulo.

'It should hurt. You are slaves,' drawled the master. 'There is no pardon.'

The nude boys groaned in the sunset, as the strapped girls fucked them in the arse. They writhed naked, faces in the dirt, as the nude girls rode them. The master watched.

'Emily, Sarah, present your toes,' he commanded.

Emily and Sarah obeyed. While they were bumfucking the squirming boy slaves, they thrust their naked feet in the master's face.

'There is dirt here,' he said, as Serena sucked his cock. 'Dirt must be cleaned, and dirt must be punished.'

He took Emily's feet, one after the other, into his mouth, until they were clean of mud. His tongue licked between her toes. Then it was Sarah's turn. The master licked both girls' feet clean. Then he commanded Nipringa to attend him. Her feet were not especially dirty, although there was plentiful cheese between the ebony toes, but the master licked her toes for ten minutes. He paid special attention to sucking the big toe. He held her feet up, to ensure that he had licked them clean. After that, Jacqui had to submit to the same ordeal, and then Candi. Both girls giggled, and said that it tickled. The master smiled, as Serena sucked his cock, and said that it was supposed to tickle.

'A slave is expected to be dirty,' he said, 'but not a monitor. Sarah and Emily, you must be whipped for your dirty feet.'

The English girls paled. With a plop, they withdrew their dildos from the boys' arseholes.

'No. Don't stop,' groaned Paulo.

'Do me, you lovely whore!' cried Vergilio.

'Boys, whip these girls to obedience,' ordered the master.

He handed the buggered boys fresh tulipwood canes. The boys rubbed their bottoms, while grinning shyly at each other.

'Emily and Sarah, present yourselves,' commanded the master.

'Must we?' asked Emily.

'We must,' said Sarah. 'He is the master.'

Both girls bent over and touched their toes. The master instructed Nipringa to release the spanking flap on their pink swimsuits. With the spanking flap open, the girls' buttocks were bare for the whip. Paulo took Sarah, while Vergilio took Emily. Each boy wielded a four-foot cane. The girls' naked buttocks were spread before them. Vip! Sarah's bare bum writhed under a savage cane lash.

'Ahh!' she shrieked.

Vergilio's caning arm rapidly flogged Emily's naked bottom to pink. Her bare buttocks squirmed helplessly, as the wood striped her.

'No! No! Please!' Emily screamed, as the wood lashed her bare fesses.

The shreds of their swimsuits fluttered in the same rhythm as their flogged bottoms, as the girls squirmed under the whips of the boys.

'You'll have to pay for new pink swimsuits,' said the master. 'It will come out of your slave stipend.'

Vip!

Emily's bum squirmed. 'Oh! Master! Please tell him to stop!' she wailed.

'Not just yet,' said the master.

'Master! Please!' squealed Sarah, whose bare arse was reddening under Paulo's cane. 'This isn't fair.'

'I decide what is fair,' said the master. 'Girl slaves, wank these bitches off.'

As the monitors were whipped, Nip licked Sarah's cunt, while Candi licked Emily's.

'God, yes!' cried Sarah. 'Oh you wicked bitch. Don't stop licking me.'

'Stop it! Stop it!' squealed Emily. 'I mean don't stop it. Oh, I'm going to come. Yes! Yes! I'm there!'

Her belly heaved.

'Oh! You horrid slut! You're making me come!' cried Sarah.

Both the monitors poured come from their cunts, while the girl slaves brought them to orgasm.

'Yes, yes,' groaned the master, fucking Serena's throat, as his spunk bubbled from the German girl's lips, while she masturbated herself to orgasm.

Serena's fingers penetrated her glistening pink slit, right to the wombneck. Her thumb wanked her stiffened clit. Juice trickled down her thighs. She moaned, climaxing, while swallowing the master's copious sperm. Goblets of the master's cream spurted from her glistening red lips. The master smiled, and permitted Miss Serena to lick his cock clean.

'By the way, Miss Serena,' the master added, 'a rich brat from Rio, called Ruggiero, is arriving tomorrow by private aircraft. He thinks he is arriving for a vacation. I shall entrust you to disabuse him of that notion.'

11

Rich Boy Thrashed

The boy, Ruggiero, in his shiny dark-blue, Italian-designer suit, escorted by Emily and Sarah in their pink swimsuits, sauntered into the bedchamber, flicking dust from his lapels. His languid eyelashes fluttered, so as to betray a nervous emotion he wished to conceal. He leered at the scantily clad English girls, and ordered them to bring him a *kaipirinha* cocktail, for it had been a long flight to Paraiba from Rio, on the family Lear jet.

'You are too young to drink cocktails,' snapped Emily. 'I will serve you a glass of mineral water, before your initiation.'

She brought a glass of cold fizzy water, and the boy drank it.

'Pleasure is not what you are here for,' said Sarah.

'I was told it was a special holiday,' the boy stammered, wiping his lips. 'You are servants – you will kindly obey my orders.'

The girls giggled.

'It is a holiday in a way,' said Sarah, flexing her cane. 'It cost your parents a lot of money. And we are certainly your servants.'

'Oh, yes,' murmured Emily. She cracked her cane on the leather of the sofa. 'You have been sent here to learn manners,' she said. 'Old-fashioned English manners. A spoiled rich brat needs discipline. Now, get your clothes off.'

'What?' gasped the young man.

'You heard. Or do you want us to rip them off?'

He smirked. 'I've heard about English girls,' he said. 'I am irresistible to girls. I've fucked every slut on Copacabana Beach, every lovely tan sloe-eye, but you blonde English girls are special. I see now – this is indeed a holiday. You want me naked? You shall swoon. I shall tool you at my pleasure.'

Coolly, he disrobed, and stood nude and grinning before them, his tan body svelte and his massive cock swelling, as he inspected the girls with his arrogant eyes.

'I have had girls like you – not quite as gorgeous as you luscious blonde maidens – but they come to me when I wave my finger. And they come, when I put my manhood inside their juicy little slits. How they come. A big tool is heaven for any slut, and especially when I give her the favour of fucking her bumhole. All girls are the same: they worship cock, they come for cock, and especially like a cock with money.'

'Your money is no good here, Ruggiero, and it's not a holiday in the way you think,' said Sarah. She fingered the delicate curls of his pubic hairs, and her nose twitched. 'Disgusting,' she said. 'Don't they teach you manners in Rio de Janeiro? A girl likes a clean boy. A smooth body is the mark of a gentleman.'

Ruggiero blushed. 'I never thought of such a thing,' he murmured.

'Boys don't think,' snapped Emily. 'That is their problem.'

She had soap and a razor, and grasped the boy by the balls. He groaned.

'Stay down, boy,' Emily commanded.

In a minute, Ruggiero's cock and balls were shaven satin smooth by the English blonde's expert razor. She scraped his cock, balls and arse cleft. Unencumbered by hairs, his cock gleamed, swollen to full bare stiffness.

171

'Most satisfactory! I'd reckon him nearly a kilo,' Emily said, inspecting the boy's shaven cock and ball sac. 'All boys here must have their bits weighed, you see, but that is not our job, it is Miss Serena's. She is the weighmistress.'

'Now,' said Sarah, 'you will please bend over the sofa, with your buttocks raised.'

Emily grasped his balls, and the boy winced. Her palm squeezed the tight orbs, and his cock stiffened further.

'You will *obey*, boy,' she hissed. 'He *is* a treat,' she whispered to Sarah. 'Look at that arse. So juicy. And the cock mound, shaven properly clean, is quite a presentable sight.'

'We are no sluts,' said Sarah coolly, 'and a few strokes of a lady's cane on your bare bottom will perhaps teach you some respect.'

'Cane?' gasped Ruggiero.

'No lady is a slut,' said Sarah. 'But every boy is a dirty little hound, who needs to feel stingers on his bare.'

'I . . . wait . . . I don't understand,' bleated the naked brown-skinned boy.

Whap! Emily caned the air. 'You will understand, very soon,' she murmured.

'There is some mistake,' Ruggiero said.

'No mistake,' hissed Sarah. 'You have been sent here to learn discipline, and that is exactly –' her cane slashed the air '– what you will learn. We have shaved your body clean, so that your tool does not look quite so revolting and hairy, and that is your first, most minor lesson. Others will follow. You have a choice. You can submit, like a good boy, or be sent straight back to your parents in disgrace, as an undisciplined boy. They are friends of the master, and are fed up with an arrogant young man, who thinks money falls from the trees. Needless to say, they will take a dim view of your failure

172

to comply with the master's teaching. You must learn, Ruggiero, and learning involves stiff pain. So, here you are, nude and, if I may say so, with an impressive organ, rather erect. Perhaps the shaving of your pubic forest excited you? No matter, the impertinence of your cock will be caned away.'

'No . . . please,' whimpered Ruggiero.

'It is your choice,' drawled Emily. 'You may submit, and learn what manhood is all about, which is, to obey a lady, or you may be sent home at once, with "failure" marked on your card. If you choose the wiser course, you will bend over, and present your bottom for your justly deserved caning. Otherwise, your parents in Rio will receive a full report. You are an arrogant pretty boy, and arrogant pretty boys must be taken down a peg. If you are obedient, you may go home. If not . . . why, there are boy slaves here, who will never go home, and –' she thrashed the air '– who do not wish to go home. When one knows the master, and his power, and the power of his loyal girl slaves . . . submission is pure joy. Are you ready for joy, Ruggiero? Your first caning in pink?'

'Must I?' gasped Ruggiero. 'Be caned? It is not the pain that frightens me, but the shame. To be whipped by a girl.'

His bare cock stood rock hard.

'There is no "must",' Sarah snapped. 'You have your choice. Though, by the state of that disgustingly stiff cock, I imagine the choice is already made for you. Why is it that a lad always stiffens when a lady proposes to cane his naked bottom? Boys need it.'

Ruggiero took his balls in his palm, stroked his fully stiffened cock, and grinned ruefully. 'You are very wise, you English ladies. You are so lovely; proud bodies in pink swimsuits. Such fat quim hillocks and such gorgeous big titties.'

Emily and Sarah frowned, then smiled.

173

'I have never thought that I should submit to a lady,' Ruggiero drawled, 'or to endure pain from her, but perhaps pain is not unlike love. You see that my manhood speaks for me. I am erect. You will worship me, in due course, as I shall worship you, for no one knows better than I how to pleasure a girl. Very well, I submit.'

'Hurry it up, you whelp,' snarled Emily. 'I can't wait to get some juicy pink weals on that arrogant, proud bottom. God, these blasted boys who think that their cocks give them the right to rule over everything. I mean, look at him. Stands there preening, with that, oh, that huge bare thing, just because he knows he's so gorgeous. That's why we have to cane them.'

Sarah caressed Ruggiero's bare arse. Her lips moved within inches of his quivering naked bum skin. She licked the cleft of his bare arse. Her tongue brushed his anus. Her lips touched the boy's wrinkled pucker for a moment. After a deep breath, she rose, licking her lips.

'Ruggiero, I think it's time for you to take position,' she whispered. 'It will hurt, I can't pretend it won't, but that's what you are here for, and I think you understand that. Now, you will take the English position, won't you? Bottom up, like a gentleman?'

Ruggiero whimpered, as Sarah's fingers caressed his tight ball sac. She squeezed his balls, until he grasped her swimsuited bottom, and Sarah smartly slapped his face, driving his touch from her.

'You do not touch a lady,' she snapped. 'Especially not a lady's private parts. Unless your beastly boy's arse is flogged pink enough to deserve it, and we know you are properly obedient.'

Her index and forefinger stroked the swollen glans of his cock. The boy groaned.

'But now you must be beaten. It will hurt awfully. Beaten with a cane on your naked buttocks. Have you ever thought of anything so terrible? It hurts, Ruggiero,

I can assure you of that. But you will do what Miss Sarah wants. Won't you?'

Sarah pressed his bare balls.

'Yes, miss,' gasped Ruggiero.

Ruggiero sighed, took position over the sofa, and presented his naked buttocks for caning. Sarah instructed him that he was required to maintain full position throughout the caning – that anything less would mean a loss of his honour and manhood – and that he must not question any orders from his girl guardians. He waggled his naked bottom rather cheekily, and flashed his white teeth at the two pink-swimsuited girls, who stood over him, canes drawn, and breasts heaving.

'It's not going to be fun, you brat,' snarled Emily.

Vip! She struck hard. The cane laced a pink stripe on the boy's bare. His fesses clenched, and he groaned. Vip!

'Ahh!'

'No noise, brat,' Emily snarled. 'The master makes us go through a long trial before we become qualified as pink caners, and we mustn't let our subjects make a noise.'

Vip!

'Uhh.'

Ruggiero's breath came as a hoarse panting. His bare buttocks striped pink under the twin canes of Emily and Sarah.

Vip! Vip!

'Ahh . . . ooh.'

The naked boy, stripped of his European designer suit, squirmed, his tan buttocks striping pink with weals. Vip! Vip!

'Oh! God! It hurts! I've never been caned before,' he gasped, as his welted bottom writhed.

'Get used to it,' said Sarah. 'Your cock is stiff, you dirty little bugger.'

'I can't help it,' Ruggiero wailed.

Vip! Vip! His arse writhed, as two vicious cuts from Emily's cane took him in the cleft, right on his bum bud.

'Oh! That's cruel!' he said, sobbing.

'Yes, isn't it?' said Sarah.

Vip! Vip!

The boy's bottom squirmed.

'I'm enjoying this,' Emily whispered, with a shy grin.

Vip! Vip! A pattern of welts emerged, blotching the naked arse pears with deep pink ridges; at every stroke Ruggiero wailed, yet his cock was still throbbingly stiff. Sarah and Emily coolly fingered their come-stained swimsuit gussets, as they watched the boy's bum squirm. Vip! Vip!

'Ooh! Please, stop!'

Vip! Vip!

'Ahh! I can't take it.'

Vip! Vip!

'Ohh! You monstrous girls!'

'It is our job to do this, and yours to take it,' purred Sarah, masturbating, with come squelching from her wet swimsuit gusset, as she licked her lips over the spectacle of the boy's flogged buttocks squirming in her girl's power.

Emily wanked herself off, in between strokes of the cane to the young man's bare.

Vip! Ruggiero squirmed helplessly. 'Oh!' he squealed, sobbing.

Vip! The cane flogged the boy's bare nates. His flogged arse writhed, pinked with welts.

'Oh . . . please,' he begged. 'Stop. It's agony.'

'There is no please,' hissed Sarah. 'And it's supposed to be agony.'

The girls smiled, baring dazzling white teeth, as they wanked off their stiff clits. The cane wood flashed, delivering powerful and expert strokes to the helpless bottom of the subdued boy. Vip! Vip! Vip!

'*Ahh!*' screamed the thrashed male.

The caning continued to thirty vicious strokes, punctuated by Ruggiero's shrieks of pain, until both girls had masturbated themselves to climax, and the boy was weeping uncontrollably, the olive skin of his bottom adorned with a tapestry of pink stripes. Yet his tool still stood high.

'Thirty strokes, and he's blubbing well, yet his filthy meat is still up,' snorted Emily. 'An erection, under caning. We'll have to do something about it. The master would be displeased otherwise.'

'Agreed,' said Sarah. 'These boys. All the bloody same.'

Emily tweaked Ruggiero's helmet. The pink knob writhed under her come-soaked fingers' touch.

'Oh, don't,' he moaned. 'You torment me with such a caress. It's so nice. But, please, don't beat me any more.'

'All boys must be whipped on the bare,' Emily said. 'That is what you are here to learn. That is what boys are for. Those juicy arses, so full of muscle and power, and so gorgeous when in naked submission to a lady. How could a lady not wish to spank them? It is a different kind of caress.'

Emily stroked the beaten male's tight balls, ran her fingers over the ridged crimson welts on Ruggiero's brown bottom, and licked her lips. Ruggiero whimpered in pleasure as the girl's cool fingers caressed his bum welts.

'Oh ... I understand that I needed punishment,' he groaned. 'But you are so cruel. My bottom hurts and stings most dreadfully. To be whipped at all, and then to be whipped on my naked bottom ... you can have no idea how shameful it is for a Brazilian male. We dominate girls, we impress them with our cocks, we don't bend over and ... Oh! You horrid bitches! I didn't mean what I said. Now you've whipped me, I *want* to be spanked. I feel that when you beat my bare bum, your beauty flows into me. Oh, please, give me another lashing. Lash me on the bare. It stung so much, and I wanted it to sting more. I wanted the shame of my bare arse squirming under a cruel lady, and the stinging never to stop. I wanted that beauty.' Ruggiero burst into tears. 'How could I ever have said that?' he said, between sobs.

'You don't ask for an English stinging, you dirty boy, you have to pay for it,' Sarah drawled. 'Boys pay, just as girls wear pink swimsuits. It is in the nature of things. You have to understand.'

'I think he understands arse welts, but there's something else he has to understand,' Emily said.

'May I ... Miss Sarah?' blurted Ruggiero. 'May I please call you by your name?'

'It is my name,' Sarah spat.

'Would you please cane me again? On my bare? It was so lovely ... the terrible smarts ... to feel a lovely lady was punishing me in that way. Making me her slave. And on my naked bottom ... I have never experienced such a terrible delight before. I had a nanny – it was long time ago – and she spanked me, on the bare, when I was a naughty boy, but it wasn't quite the same thing. It wasn't really painful, more a lesson. She took my pants down and spanked me hard, but it was in love. She wanted me to mend my ways. A bare naughty boy with his bum spanked, over a lady's knee, in the campo, why, it was quite amusing to everyone looking on. But today, to be beaten by two magnificent blonde ladies is a strange pleasure. In your eyes, I see a beautiful cruelty. I feel you really need to hurt me, make me squirm, watch me suffer. I love to show off my pinked bare bottom, writhing for a lady's pleasure. I am so ashamed, yet I know my naked buttocks please you, as they have pleased so many girls, while my cock was pumping their lovely juicy cunts. Please – I'll give you anything – do it again. Beat my bare, my ladies.'

Breasts heaving under her pink swimsuit, Sarah reared. 'My ladies. You filthy piece of dirt,' she spat. 'You do not ask a lady, you beg a lady.'

''The cheeky swine,' hissed Emily. 'I think we can do much more than cane this show-off.'

Emily had the naked boy in an armlock, and was caressing his tousled head, while Sarah unfastened the gusset of her swimsuit, and showed her satin-shaven cunt. The blonde Sarah tossed her mane, nose haughtily wrinkled, while she strapped a twin cylinder of tulip-wood around her hips, using a leather whipcord. One portion of the cylinder filled her cooze, while the wooden tube extruding from her twat stood up like Ruggiero's cock, but bigger. Sarah groaned in delight. The boy whimpered and squirmed, but was powerless to prevent Sarah from nuzzling his anus bud with the cruel dildo.

'No . . . wait,' he moaned. 'I didn't mean . . .'

'Nobody cares what you mean, worm,' snarled Sarah, as, with a powerful thrust of her buttocks, she penetrated his anus with the fuck-shaft.

Come seeped from her filled cunt, wetting the wooden tool that fucked the boy's squirming rectum. Sarah smiled, as she bum-fucked the sobbing, helpless boy.

'This is what you do to girls, I suppose – those lovely brown stunners from Copacabana Beach,' she panted. 'Now you're getting a taste of your own medicine.'

'No! Please! Not this!' Ruggiero whined.

'Yes, this,' said Sarah.

'Fucked in the arse. By a girl. I'll never get over the shame. But don't stop. It's so good. Get right inside me, I beg you. Fill me. Fuck my tripes.'

'You're not supposed to get over the shame,' said Emily, pressing her cunt lips to Ruggiero's gasping mouth. 'Lick me off, you cheeky young stud, while Sarah gives you your seeing-to up your cheeky bum, and don't complain, or it will be the worse for you.'

Emily's open pink cooze spurted come over the boy's eager lips and tongue. His bare bottom squirmed, fucked by Sarah, with her double-dildo plugging his anus, as his teeth fastened on Emily's swollen clit.

'That's good,' Emily hissed. 'Perhaps you are not such a bad boy, after all. Mm . . . mm . . . yes.'

'I say he *is* a bad boy,' Sarah said, buggering the lad's arse. 'All boys are bad. That is why they need punishment.'

'The master was a boy once.'

'It's not the same thing. Take that up your hole, you swine. And that.'

'It hurts,' bleated Ruggiero, his lips wet with Emily's come, as Sarah's dildo slammed his colon.

'It is supposed to hurt,' Sarah snapped. 'Without that, a cheeky boy will never learn discipline.'

'Oh, don't stop,' panted Emily, as the boy sucked her stiff pink clitty. 'Yes, take my whole nubbin into your mouth. You know how to do it, you swine. Suck me, swallow my come. Oh, how I hate you. I'm going to climax. Yes! Ooh! I hate you, boy.'

'Wait,' panted Sarah. 'I'm going to spend. Yes . . . yes!'

Emily's fingers grasped Ruggiero's trembling erect cock. She caressed the crimson disc of his swelling glans, and her fingertip sliced his peehole. Writhing under Sarah's buggery, Ruggiero groaned.

'Come for me, boy,' Emily whispered. 'My, you have a lovely bum, and I won't flatter you with talk of your tool. It is a pity we have to make you suffer this way. Or perhaps not. Give me a lovely huge load of spunk from those balls. I know they are longing to spurt into my palm.'

As Sarah buggered the boy, Emily wanked him off, palming his spermload, then rubbing the hot cream into her breasts, and licking her lips. She flicked morsels of spunk from her erect nipples, and swallowed them. Ruggiero was weeping with the pain of his buggery by Sarah, and Emily licked the tears from his cheeks.

'I know it hurts,' she whispered. 'But that is part of being a man.'

180

'The blasted lout has to hurt,' panted Sarah, masturbating her own erect clit, as she enculed the groaning boy.

The boy's brown body wriggled like a snake's, as the English girl fucked him. The other end of the double-dildo was deep in her cunt, at her wombneck, and her juices soaked both ends of the massive shaft, so that Ruggiero's anus was washed in cunt juice from his tormentress.

'God! Yes! That's so good!' cried Sarah. 'You dirty little bastard, I've never fucked such a juicy arse.'

Ruggiero's buttocks slammed against the wood that was fucking him, matching the rhythm of Sarah's hip-thrusts.

'You are very cruel,' he said, panting. 'Please keep on fucking me. I never thought I would ask for such a thing. I fuck girls, and never think of fucking anything else. I have never thought of being fucked – disgraceful! – well, you can imagine. But to be fucked in the arse by a beautiful woman, a blonde English lady . . .'

'I'm not fucking you, you little whore, I'm punishing you,' snarled Sarah. 'Don't you know the difference?'

Ruggiero was silent for a moment, swallowing Emily's copious cunt juice.

'What's the matter with you, boy?' Sarah snapped. 'Cat got your tongue?'

Ruggiero's tongue glistened with Emily's come, which he was swallowing, with a blissful smile. His arse jerked with the pressure of Sarah's buggery, but his lips were busy at the service of Emily's open pink cooze, its cunt meat and stiff pink nubbin dripping with hot twat juice.

'Your juice tastes so sweet. A boy likes this,' he gasped. 'I never thought . . . I've been whipped on my bare arse, and buggered by a girl, and I like it. A girl's cunt on my face, and a girl's tool up my bum . . . a girl's tool . . . it's so new.'

'Of course you like it, my sweet,' drawled Sarah. 'All boys do. That's what makes them boys. They want to be fucked by a girl. But they don't admit it. Why, I know that in Rio they have hermaphrodite girlboys, chicks with dicks, and the men queue up to be fucked by them.'

Her gnarled tulipwood dildo emerged, squelching, from the boy's anus bud. The boy groaned, his bum giving a last squelching squirm, and the English girl smiled, stroking her pink-suited breasts, and tossing her blonde mane. She stroked Ruggiero's bottom. Her fingers caressed the cleft of his bare arse, pinching his anus pucker, and he whimpered with pleasure.

'You are not a bad boy,' she whispered. 'In fact, I think you are quite a good boy. You have a rather nice body, now that we see it without horrid unsightly hair. And such a lovely bottom, and – I blush to say it – a gorgeous arsehole, so sweet and sort of tasty, which is all that really matters in a male. But good boys with gorgeous bodies and lovely bums are the ones who really need punishment.'

'I'll ... I'll take that as a compliment, Miss Sarah,' panted Ruggiero.

'What about *my* compliment?' snapped Emily.

'Your compliment? I bum-fucked him.'

'I sucked his cock.'

'You bitch.'

'I'll whip the smarmy little boy slave this instant. Your favourite bum will be striped pink by my cane. Really hard wood. Sarah, you don't know how to make a boy's arse squirm, not by you. Not even your favourite bum, cute little bugger that he is. In different circumstances, I wouldn't mind if that beautiful big brown tool ... you know ... buggered me. Gave me a proper filling up the bum. You do know.'

'Of course I know. But he's not my favourite.'

'Say you. You've had so many boy bums.'

'I'll stripe the boy anyway. That naked brown bum is too delicious to waste.'

'You won't stripe him any more.'

'Who says I won't?'

Emily snarled. She stood, and ripped off her pink swimsuit. Naked, swivelling her cunt basin, with her pink slit drooling come, she offered herself for combat to her friend. She raised her arms. 'I will, you fucking bitch,' she hissed.

A barefoot kick between the legs floored Sarah. She fought back by biting Emily's cunt. Both blondes were excited by the fight, their coozes visibly oozing come. Sarah's teeth sank into Emily's gash lips, and Emily howled. She ripped Sarah's swimsuit off. The nude Sarah shrieked in dismay.

'Bitch!'

'Cow!'

Ruggiero watched and his cock stiffened, as the two nude blondes wrestled. Sarah rained a hail of punches on Emily's breasts, and clawed her nipples, while, again and again, Emily, squealing in pain, kneed Sarah viciously between the cunt flaps.

'Oh! Ooh! You fucking slag!'

'Slut! Ouch!'

'That hurt!'

'It was meant to.'

The two wrestling girls were bathed in sweat. Ruggiero pushed his erect cock between their pressed breasts. His swollen glans touched their nipples. Both fighting girls panted; suddenly, their lips met in a kiss.

'Oh, Em, I didn't mean to hurt you,' gasped Sarah.

Ruggiero's erect cock slid down Emily's spine.

'We're best friends, aren't we?' Emily moaned. '*Ooh!*' She leaped indignantly, as Ruggiero's stiff cock nuzzled her anus bud. 'What?' she managed to gasp, before the nude boy, gripping her squirming hips, plunged his massively hard tool into her anus. '*Ahh!*' Emily squealed.

With a fierce thrust, Ruggiero's cock penetrated her rectum.

'Oh! No!' Emily screamed. 'It hurts!'

'You'll enjoy this, you fucking slut,' Sarah hissed. 'Don't pretend otherwise.'

The Brazilian boy had the blonde impaled on his massive cock, which squelched in and out of her anus with slow, sticky slurps. His whip-wealed buttocks were clenched tight, and he grunted in pleasure, at each thrust of his cock into the girl's colon.

'Oh, no!' wailed Emily. 'Don't bum-fuck! It hurts so much. That's so big! You'll burst me!'

Under Sarah's nimble fingers, wanking Emily's clit, the enculed girl's cunt sprayed come.

'He's splitting me in two,' said the buggered blonde, sobbing and writhing under the brown cock which impaled her.

'Aren't you the lucky one,' said Sarah, pinioning her friend, and tweaking her stiff clit, beneath the pounding of the boy's hard fierce tool.

'I've spunk for both of you blonde whores,' panted Ruggiero.

'You monster!' wailed Emily. 'I'm going to come. Oh, the shame!'

'You come for the master,' hissed Sarah, frigging her own erect nubbin.

'That's different,' said Emily. 'I mean, no, it isn't really. Oh, this boy's bringing me off. A big hard tool in a girl's bum – what's the difference, as long as it brings her off?'

'Subversive talk, bitch,' said Sarah. 'The master wouldn't like to hear it.'

'Oh! Oh! Yes! *Ahh!*' screamed the buggered blonde, as come spurted from her cunt, and her belly heaved in orgasm.

Ruggiero's cock plopped from Emily's anus, and the boy seized Sarah by the hair. He pushed her face down, and prised her buttocks apart. Her twat was wet, and he oiled his throbbing cock with her cunt juice.

'Wait! Stop!' Sarah shrieked. 'What are you doing? This is an outrage. *Ohh!*'

Her nude body shuddered, as the boy's cock, oiled with her own come and Emily's arse grease, penetrated her rectum. Ruggiero's cock sank into her anal tube, right to his balls, which struck her quivering buttocks with a wet slap, at each powerful thrust of his loins.

'Take that, bitch,' he panted. 'And that. And that.'

'Oh! Yes! Oh, you beast!' gasped Sarah, as her bare buttocks rose to meet the cock of her bugger. 'Oh, that's better than any dildo.'

'I know how to make any slut come,' panted the boy.

His cock slammed her colon.

'Ooh! Ooh! Don't! You're bringing me off, boy slave. It's not fair. It's . . . Ooh! Ahh! Yes! Do me! Split me! God, what a cock! Do my bumhole with that monster! I'm coming!'

Come spurted from Sarah's cunt, as she writhed in orgasm. Ruggiero, panting, withdrew his stiff cock from her anus, and thrust it into her mouth.

'Nngh! Urrgh!' Sarah grunted, as she began to suck the heavy tool, wet with her own arse grease.

Emily wanked herself, while sitting on Sarah's belly and pinching her clit. Ruggiero throat-fucked the groaning Sarah, until his spunk spurted into her mouth, so copiously that a froth of cream drooled down Sarah's chin, even as she swallowed his ejaculation. Emily's tongue licked Ruggiero's anus, as his cock penetrated Sarah's gurgling throat; Emily moaned, as she masturbated to orgasm, her come oiling the writhing belly of the pinioned Sarah. Emily licked up the boy's sperm, which had dribbled from Sarah's mouth to glisten on Sarah's heaving breasts. Sarah's body shuddered, as she swallowed the whole heavy load of the boy's cream.

'Oh, yes,' she moaned, gagging, and then licking her lips. 'I needed that.'

Emily licked every drop of the boy's sperm, where it had spilled onto Sarah's skin. Sarah's nipples were creamy with sperm, and Emily took each nipple plum in her mouth and licked the boy's cream, tonguing the nipple to erection.

'Oh, don't,' moaned Sarah. 'I mean, oh, all right, do.'

Ruggiero watched, as the girls gamahuched, and his cock grew massively hard once more. Emily and Sarah masturbated, and just as their bellies heaved, Ruggiero plunged his cock into Emily's arse.

'Oh! God, you brute!' Emily squealed. 'Yes! Bum me till I split!'

The Brazilian boy enculed her until she came, then withdrew his cock, and obliged Emily to suck him as Sarah had done, until his spunk spurted in her throat, and she swallowed as much as was possible from his massive ejaculation. Meanwhile, Sarah masturbated with the same tulipwood dildo she had used to bum-fuck Ruggiero, and brought herself off to a squirming climax, as she licked the droplets of the boy's copious sperm which had glazed Emily's breasts and belly.

'I say, he's a really beautiful creamer,' gasped Emily.

'A master in the making,' panted Sarah.

'But we must be able to whip that juicy bottom. I mean, look at it. It's so . . .'

'Nice?'

'Spankable.'

'You asked us to cane you again,' drawled Sarah, rubbing her fucked throat and buggered bottom.

Ruggiero blushed. 'I would love it,' he whispered. 'As long as you don't tell anyone.'

Sarah put her arm around Emily's waist, and kissed her on the lips. The two girls' clits met, and rubbed.

'In return,' Sarah panted, as she kissed and wanked her friend, 'you will help us overthrow the bitch Serena, and . . . and the master himself. He services us, but doesn't pay enough. And a girl always wants looking after in that department.'

Ruggiero knelt before the two tribades, and kissed their juicing wanked cunts.

'Anything, miss,' said the boy, on his bended knees.

Emily stroked the boy's buttocks; the bare flesh quivered at her touch. His cock stiffened once more to full hardness, and he blushed.

'I cannot help it,' he whispered.

'I'm not altogether sure you couldn't be the new master,' Emily murmured. 'With that dreadful cock ...'

'It is worse than dreadful,' Sarah said. 'It is obscene.'

'Quite terrifying. Even bigger than the master's.'

'Why, that's treason.'

The two girls continued to masturbate each other, as they made Ruggiero rise from the floor, and knelt to lick his balls. Their knees slithered in the pool of come, oozed by their open twats. Emily took Sarah's nipples between tight fingers, and thrust them at the boy.

'Lick her tits clean of your filthy spunk,' she ordered.

Ruggiero applied his lips to Sarah's breasts, and licked the glaze of his own sperm. Then, he licked Emily's teats dry.

'All girls need a master, you see,' purred Sarah, tonguing Ruggiero's swollen purple glans. 'Agreed, Em?'

Emily took her mouth from its full clasp of the boy's balls. Her nostrils flared, as she sniffed the mixed aroma of his own spunk and the two girls' fucked arse grease.

'Agreed,' said Emily. 'It just depends which one. Isn't it a girl's privilege to choose?'

'Let us overthrow the master, then, and choose a new one,' said Sarah. 'This boy slut will do. His cock is big enough. Mm ...'

Sarah was silent, save for slurps and gasps, as she took the boy's stiff cock to the back of her throat, sucked him to orgasm, and swallowed new spunk.

12

Threefold Flogging

'Line up for your porridge, bitches!' shouted Serena.

'Get in line, sluts' snarled Sarah. 'Arse to cunt. Snouts in order.'

The nude girl slaves – each girl's quim pressed to the next girl's buttocks – shuffled to the cookpot, where they were doled their breakfast of porridge. Emily delivered a whiplash to the buttocks of a girl slave whose twat was not pressed firmly enough into the bum cleft of her neighbour. When served, the girls were permitted to disengage, and squat in the dirt, to eat the porridge with their fingers, from their wooden bowls. On arrival, each girl slave was issued with a wooden bowl, which she must keep by her person at all times. Loss of her wooden bowl was a flogging offence: twenty tulipwood strokes on the bare.

The life of a nude girl slave on the master's plantation was harsh, with constant whippings from Sandoz and the monitors, Emily and Sarah, yet the girls could gossip with each other, rubbing their bare bottoms after the whip strokes of their monitors. Their work was to cull the tulipwood trees for suitable branches, then carve the branches into canes and dildos, which were packed in cartons and shipped to London, Paris or New York. A tulipwood dildo cost the master nothing, except for the porridge he fed his slaves. If the dildo was varnished and lacquered and correctly sculpted, it fetched five hundred euros in the fetish boutiques of the Rue St Denis or five hundred dollars in the luxury sex shops on Fifth Avenue. The girl slaves had to carve girls' faces on the helmets of the massive black dildos, so that the male or female subject who wished to be enculed could enjoy being buggered by a smiling girl's head. Canes were less expensive, yet a batch of polished Paraiba tulipwood canes got a high price from collectors around the world. They had thick knob handles, carved with a girl's face, and her name signed. Those who loved flogging felt that, as they writhed under the lash, it was a sweet brown Brazilian girl delivering a personal chastisement. Thus was the master rich.

'Back to work, sluts,' said Serena. 'At the double.'

Nipringa, calmly finishing her porridge, had her bowl ripped from her fingers by Sarah.

'Your time is not your own, you lazy, idle slut,' hissed Sarah.

Nip's face was forced into the dirt, her arms held down by Emily, and cane strokes delivered by the German girl to her bare black bottom. Vip! Nip's ebony fesses writhed. Vip! A stroke took her in the cleft, lashing her anus bud. Tears sprang from her eyes.

'Aren't you going to squeal, you lazy disobedient slave bitch?' sneered Serena. 'A girl's duty is to obey. When she doesn't, she gets thrashed. It is the way of the world. Take my strokes, and squeal, like the errant maid you are. Eat dirt, you bitch.'

Vip! Vip! Two vicious lashes made Nip squirm. Her eyes were wet with tears, but she made no protest, save a hoarse rasp of her breath.

'Doesn't it hurt?' sneered Serena. 'Don't you want to cry out?'

'No ... no, miss,' sobbed Nip. 'I shan't scream. It hurts awfully, but I can take it. A girl slave must.'

Vip! The flogging from the German girl's wooden cane went to twenty strokes, but Nip took the lashes without a murmur, although she bared her teeth in a rictus of agony. As her naked buttocks were lashed, she filled her mouth with red earth, and swallowed. While the black girl's naked body squirmed in pain, Emily and Sarah masturbated the crotches of their pink swimsuits, until their gussets were stained with come. After the twentieth stroke to Nip's lacerated bare bottom, Serena, gasping, laid aside her cane.

'That is for being a lazy slave,' panted Sarah. 'Eating is a privilege, not a right. Now get carving.'

Nip joined Candi and Jacqui by the tulipwood tree they were culling. Grinning ruefully, she rubbed her flogged bottom. Candi and Jacqui knelt, to kiss the black girl's wealed fesses.

'Oh, you poor thing,' said Jacqui.

'That cruel bitch,' murmured Candi.

Both girls had their tongues on Nip's ebony buttocks, which were lacerated with purple bruises. The welts were swollen to crusted ridges. The girls's wet tongues caressed the raised hard flesh of Nip's welts, and the black girl sighed with pleasure.

'That tickles,' said Nipringa, 'but don't stop. It's much nicer to be licked this way. Your tongues in my weals. I want that. I love a girl's tongue on my whipped bum. My welts soothed by girls' tongues, and their lovely spittle. It's as though I've won a prize of love.'

The tulipwood tree shaded them, and the girls put down their carving tools, while Candi's tongue licked Nip's slit, and Jacqui's tongue probed the ebony girl's anus.

'You are so beautiful, Miss Nipringa,' moaned Jacqui. 'Your skin is so soft and smooth, like satin. Even your welts are beautiful. Such awful ridges. It is wrong for them to flog your lovely black arse.'

'If my welts are beautiful,' said Nip, 'then it is not wrong for them to flog me. Beauty is everything. And flogging a girl's bare arse is an act of beauty. The only way to respect a girl's arse, that is, to respect the girl herself, is to whip her on the bare. Every real girl knows that.'

The blonde girl's tongue penetrated Nip's anus, and reached the rectum. At the same time, Candi's tongue licked Nip's throbbing clitoris. Nip rubbed her erect nipples, as the girls frigged her. Her black breasts bobbed in the shade of the tulipwood tree. All around them, naked girl slaves sweated, perspired fluid pouring down their glistening bare bodies, as they honed the tulipwood branches. Only Nip, Candi and Jacqui were lazing from their work. Each girl had her finger's in another's cunt, masturbating her clit. Nipringa mass-aged her big brown nipples, her bared teeth grinning at the sun, while Candi sucked Nip's engorged nubbin. Jacqui's tongue was deep in the black girl's rectum. The nude girls writhed in their embrace, wanking each other's clits.

'Yes. Go on.'

'Don't stop.'

Come poured from their swollen cunt flaps, as the girls orgasmed under their mutual masturbation. Jacqui had three fingers in Nip's rectum, and was poking hard. Candi had her tongue on Nip's clit.

'Yes,' hissed Nip. 'Yes. Fuck my arse and cunt, you dirty little bitches. You filthy lesbos. I can't resist. Yes!'

Her twat juiced copiously, as she came to climax, and Candi, rubbing her erect nipples, swallowed Nip's spurted come. Jacqui poked Nip's bum until the black girl groaned in agony, then she removed her fingers from Nip's anus with a slurping squelch, and licked Nip's arse grease from her fingertips, with a sly smile and a blushing face.

'Oh, yes!' Nip cried, as oily scented come sprayed from her cunt.

Serena arrived, bearing a cattle whip. 'A disgrace!' Serena cried. 'Master! The other slaves are working obediently, while these slaves are lazy and disobedient. And they are lustful. They have been frigging.'

The master, clad in white silk, sauntered to the scene. 'That won't do,' he said. 'Emily! Sarah! Lazy, lustful slaves must be taught a lesson. A threefold flogging, hobbled at the feet, and strung high by the wrists.'

'Yes, master,' said Emily and Sarah.

Candi, Jacqui and Nipringa groaned, as Emily and Sarah hobbled them in wooden bars at the feet, and handed them to Sandoz, to be taken to the gibbet, for their strung floggings. The girls were hung from their wrists, their bare feet wriggling in their wooden hobbles.

'I'm scared,' Jacqui moaned. 'I feel so ashamed, to be strung up in the nude. And I can't stand the pain. Really, I can't. The whip on my bare bum is awful. And on my back. It's more than I think I can take.'

'We are all strung up,' said Nipringa. 'We must take our lashes. It is a girl's fate to be strung up. You can take it. Every girl can. Every girl must. Girls must bare their bodies, present their naked fesses and bow to a master's whip. That is how they grow to be real women.'

Their full naked bodies were displayed, dangling from the gibbet, the thighs and buttocks quivering, glistening with sweat, awaiting their punishment.

'Cane them fully on their lovely backs and bottoms,' ordered the master. 'That juicy bare girl flesh deserves complete flogging. Sandoz, you will take Nipringa. Emily, you will take Candi. Sarah, you shall take Jacqui. I want no mercy for these gorgeous lazy sluts. It is to be a full bare-body whipping, under the sun. A girl's function is to be naked, and flogged for her impudent beauty. These girls' lungs must be brought to scream, and their nude bodies brought to squirm. Bring the other slaves to watch.'

The three girls groaned, hanging by their wrists from the gibbet, under the hot sun. Their bodies dripped with sweat.

'Oh! This is awful,' moaned Jacqui.

'I want to go home,' wailed Candi.

'Don't you understand?' hissed Nip, struggling in her bonds. 'This is home.'

The other naked girl slaves were lined up by Serena to watch the floggings. They were shy and fearful, but if a girl slave averted her gaze, Serena whipped her a stroke on the buttocks.

'Watch what awaits a girl, bitch,' she hissed.

Vip! Sandoz's cane lashed Nip's bare bottom.

'Ahh,' Nip groaned.

Vip! Emily's cane whipped Candi on the bare arse, and Candi screamed.

Vip! Sarah's cane took the Welsh girl on the buttocks, raising a pink weal, and Jacqui shrieked.

Vip!

'No! Please!'

Vip!

'God, no! It hurts!'

Vip!

'Ahh!'

After a vigorous caning of the girls' buttocks, to thirty searingly harsh strokes, the canes were exchanged for whips, applied to the strung girl slaves' bare backs. Sarah licked her teeth, as she prepared to flog Jacqui. Vap!

'Ahh,' Jacqui groaned, as Sarah's whip striped her shoulders with a huge pink welt.

Nip hung from her wrists, as Sandoz wielded his whip. Vap! His leather striped her back.

'No! God, please, no!' she squealed, writhing. 'Whip my bottom, not my back. My bottom can take anything, but not on the back. Oh! Please.'

'The master decreed you get back-whipped, you dirty sluts,' said Sandoz.

Vap! Jacqui's flogged back writhed, her kidneys squirming.

'Ahh!'

Vap!

'Ohh!' cried Nip, her satin ebony skin pouring with sweat, and wriggling. 'I can't stand it!'

Candi and Jacqui squealed and sobbed, as the whips striped every inch of their backs and buttocks. The girl slaves, forced to watch, let their fingers drop to their shaven cunts, and began to masturbate. Serena, in her pink swimsuit, breathed hoarsely, as the girls' naked bodies writhed under the whip, and her fingers wanked the gusset of her swimsuit. The master drew on his cigar, and smiled.

Nip shuddered, as the cattle whip lashed her naked back. Hanging from her wrists, and helpless in her bonds, she could only squirm, as Sandoz's whip flogged her. The whip was applied to her shoulders, buttocks and thighs.

Vap! The lash bruised her shoulders.

'Ohh!' Nip squealed.

Vap! The lash purpled her arse. Sandoz then whipped her breasts. The leather lashed her erect nipples. The thong played lovingly on the big brown domes of her nipples. Vap! The whip crossed her two nipples at once.

'No!' Nipringa screamed.

Yet her nipples remained erect. And her cunt oozed come. The glistening fluid dribbled down her thighs from her juicing quim, where her clit was erect. Vap! Vap! The whip lashed her quivering thighbacks.

'No!' Nip moaned, her legs shuddering.

It was the pain of the lash on her thighs that seemed to upset Nip so much. Her eyes were wet with tears. 'You fucking bastard,' she whimpered to Sandoz. 'I'll get even with you.'

'Not before I've flogged your dirty black arse to blue,' Sandoz said.

'A nice concept,' said the master. 'But I think purple is more appropriate for a lady of the Indies. Flog these English sluts to crimson, but the black damsel to puce.'

194

'I *am* English,' Nip hissed.

Vap! Vap! The whip lashed Nip's shoulders. Vap! Another stroke took her in mid-back. In an instant, the leather striped her buttocks. Vap! Her flogged buttocks squirmed.

'Ah! No! Please, I can't take it!' the hung black girl screamed.

'But you must,' drawled the master. 'You are my slave.'

Vap! Vap! Sandoz's whip lashed Nip on every inch of her body, as the assembled girl slaves masturbated. Candi and Jacqui screamed, too, as their pale bare bodies dangled, wriggling helplessly, from the gibbet, while Emily and Sarah whipped them up and down. At the fifty-first whip stroke, Nip lost control of her bladder, and pissed over her feet. Her swollen twat released a long, steaming hiss of golden fluid, which streaked her legs. The master knelt, took an Italian olive from a jar, and sucked the olive, while he licked the girl's piss from her toes and calves.

'A good vintage of girl piss,' he said, licking his lips.

'Pissing, miss?' snarled Sandoz. 'That gets you extra punishment.'

'No. Please,' moaned Nipringa. 'You've thrashed me enough, you bastard.'

'There is never enough thrashing for a girl,' the master said. 'A girl's naked fesses are made for whipping. Those beautiful moons are made for nothing else. The whip on the bare flesh. The girl crying. Her twat juicing at the man's whip. Her fingers at her clit, as the leather ridges her arse. And she comes, when a real man whips her. Sandoz, continue this slut's punishment.'

Sandoz rolled down his thong, and revealed his stiff brown cock. 'You're going to see what a bastard I am,' said Sandoz, with a smile.

Vap! The rawhide wielded by the naked erect male lashed Nip's squirming back.

'No . . . no,' she moaned. 'God, I've taken enough.'

Vap! The whip striped her arse.

'Ahh!' Nip squealed.

Emily began to wank her clit, within her pink swimsuit.

'This is nice,' she said to Sarah.

'Yes,' said Sarah. 'That gorgeous black arse. So big, yah?'

Sarah's fingers went inside the gusset of her swimsuit, and began to masturbate her clit. The flogging of the hanging naked black girl continued to a further fifty strokes, while Nipringa wept in her pain. Her body was purple with welts. Sandoz's cock was rigid. With the master's nod of approval, he ordered Nip for his pleasure. Emily and Sarah lowered Nip from the gibbet, onto Sandoz's erect tool. The master waved his smoking cheroot, nodded that the ceremony should finish, and all obeyed. He knelt to kiss Nip's flogged buttocks, his tongue caressing all of her wounds.

'The welts on a girl's whipped bare bottom are the only sight on earth worth having,' he said. He took her toes in his mouth, and began to lick. 'Such lovely feet,' the master said. 'A girl's toes are the best taste on this planet. Especially a black girl's toes.'

He licked Nip's toes for twenty minutes, while Candi and Jacqui bristled. The master licked the pale soles of Nip's ebony feet. He ordered Sarah to light a cigar. Sarah lit another cigar for him. Her approved method of doing this was to insert a cheroot in her anus. The cheroot had to go all the way in. Then, copiously covered in arse grease, the cigar could be lit. The master demanded the very best taste from his cigars.

'Now, it is time,' said the master.

Sandoz clutched Nipringa's belly, then her hips. His cock nuzzled her anus, then penetrated it to the depth of one inch.

'You bastard!' she gasped. 'How can you do this to a

girl? I've been whipped almost to blood, my whole body hurts, and now this?'

'Be quiet, slave bitch,' said the master.

'Oh! God, no!' Nipringa screamed. 'You're too big.'

Sandoz's cock was in her rectum, while Candi and Jacqui held the black girl down. Serena took a fresh dildo from stock, and pushed it into Nip's slit. Nip's cunt juice gushed over the wooden dildo, as Sandoz enculed her.

'My arsehole!' Nip shrieked. 'It hurts so much. Sandoz has much too big a cock. You can't do this to me. Even a slave has rights.'

'No, said the master. 'A slave has no rights. A slave is no more than a juicing cunt and a squirming flogged arse. Look at you, Miss Nipringa. Sandoz is buggering you, and your thighs are wet with come. I must admit that it is appealing come. Pleasantly fragrant.'

'I can't help it,' groaned Nip. He's so big, and a cock at my colon, right up my hole – oh, a girl cannot resist. You bastard males, you know how to treat us. You know what girls want. Oh, yes, Sandoz, fuck me harder. Go on. Split me in two with that horrible cock. Oh, you filthy bastard. Fuck me in the arse. Get right up me. Please.'

Sandoz's dark body was wet with sweat, as he buggered Nipringa. His giant cock slid in and out of her anus, as the black girl cried in pain.

'Oh, God! No! You're right up my hole. God, it hurts. You're in my tripes, with that filthy big cock.'

'That is where you want Sandoz to be, Nipringa,' drawled the master.

'But it hurts so much. He's filling my tripes. He's splitting me in two. He's right at my belly.'

'Do you want him to stop? You only have to say the word.'

'No . . . no . . . not stop,' moaned Nipringa. 'Oh, it hurts so much. It's so good. I'm going to come.'

The black girl's fingers went to her nubbin, and began to masturbate the engorged pink clitoris.

'Bum-fuck me, you filthy bastard,' she hissed to Sandoz, as he thrust his cock into her anus, buggering her so harshly that she cried, with tears cascading down her cheeks. 'But I promise, I'll get even.'

Yet her breath was hoarse, as she wanked herself off under the man's brutal buggery. Come oozed from her cunt, as her buttocks writhed under the assault of the man's massive cock. Nip's fingers were in her pouch, tweaking her erect clit. The man's huge tool, lubricated with Nip's copious arse grease, made a squelching sound, as it slammed in and out of her rectum.

'You fucking shit!' cried Nip, wanking her clit. 'Oh, you're hurting me so much! I'm going to come! Oh, hammer me! Do my arse! Burst me with that horrid fat cockmeat! That big hard cock! A girl is a slave to it! Always was, and always will be! Come on! Come on! Give me your spunk! Split my arse in two! I want your whole load of cream up my hole, you bastard! Give me your spunk in my hole! Give me it!'

Sandoz grunted, as he spurted his sperm into Nip's anus.

As Sandoz climaxed, pouring his cream into her rectum, Nip wanked herself to orgasm. 'Yes. The boycream,' she moaned. 'Ohh. Ahh.'

Her fingers tweaked her clit. She panted, as her come poured down her thighs. Some of Sandoz's cream seeped, frothing, from her anus. She scooped it with her fingers, and licked it up with eager lips. She smiled at Sandoz.

Sandoz smiled back. 'I made you come, slave bitch,' he said. 'You juiced well. I've never seen such lovely shiny girl's come.'

'Thank you for the compliment,' Nip gasped, 'even though you are the cruellest bastard I have ever known. I am happy I made you come. You have good balls, and

198

a tasty cock. A girl cannot resist a big naked cock, finely shaven, and balls well filled with spunk. You gave me a full load, quite a bellyful, to swallow, and your sperm tastes nice. I had a lovely filling of my hole. And the most copious load I can remember for a long time. I've been buggered often, because it's what I like best, and can measure the boy's emission. I love a stiff hot cock up my hole. A girl loves to be buggered by a proper stud. You are special, Sandoz. Your balls are so beautifully big, and I would have loved to suck them, but how can such balls, however big, contain so much gorgeous cream? That is why I must enslave you.'

'I am a real man,' preened Sandoz. 'Not like the master. You, a buggered slave bitch, enslave me? You dream.'

'Sandoz, you treacherous swine,' hissed Serena. 'The master's balls have the best spunk in the world.'

'Let him prove it,' sneered Sandoz.

Serena knelt, and bared her arse. She clutched her naked fesses with her hands, and parted her buttocks wide, to display her anus pucker.

'Master,' pleaded the German girl, 'I beg you for the favour of a buggery. Under the rules of the plantation, a girl slave has the privilege of enculement by her master.'

'You are quite right,' drawled the master. 'Emily, Sarah, divest me.'

The pink-suited monitors took off the master's silken clothes. Nude, he stood, smoking a cigar, with his cock stiff and engorged, before the exposed arse of the German girl. Serena was juicing, her come oozing down her thighs, between her bare toes and into the ochre earth.

'Suck me, Sarah,' the master ordered. 'You and Emily have permission to strip naked. Such beautiful pale bodies must be seen nude and whole.'

'At once, master,' Sarah replied.

Sarah peeled off her pink swimsuit, handed it to Serena, and knelt. Her lips fastened on the swollen helmet of the master's tool. Her hands embraced his bare buttocks. She began to lick his peehole, and suck the corona of the glans. The master smoked casually, while Sarah took his erect cock all the way to the back of her throat.

'Wank yourself off, you slut, as you suck me,' the master ordered. 'You, Emily, will masturbate and lick Sarah's clit and anus as she gamahuches me.'

'Of course, master,' Emily answered.

Emily squatted, and got her tongue into Sarah's cunt, while Sarah sucked the master's stiff bare cock. Her tongue filled Sarah's pouch. Sarah writhed in pleasure. Come poured from her slit, and Emily licked it up, swallowing with a smile. Serena moaned.

'Master, my arse is open for you,' she said.

'These English bitches must wank themselves to orgasm,' the master said. 'Then I may attend to your delightful German bottom. I must say that German girls' arses are amongst the best in the world. Firm, plump and full, and delightfully meaty. A diet of pork. The German girl likes to masturbate herself with a healthy portion of bratwurst. Afterwards, she eats the sausage, sauced with her own come. That is why German girls' cunts are so agile. Yours, Serena, is a prime example.'

'Thank you, master,' said Serena, blushing, with her anus exposed. She began to wank her clit. 'I am wet, just looking at your cock, master,' she panted. 'Please do me the honour of buggering me.'

Emily and Sarah, nude, adopted the 69 position. Upside down, the two English girls sucked each other's dripping cunts. The master stubbed out his cigar in Sarah's wet cunt. The tobacco sizzled to extinction in her cunt juice.

'Oh! Thank you, master,' Sarah gasped, tears misting her eyes.

The master penetrated Serena. His stiff cock nuzzled her anus, and she groaned. Then he entered her to a centimetre, and she howled.

Emily and Sarah licked each other.

'Em.'

'Sal.'

'You've a wicked tongue.'

'You're going to bring me off, you cow.'

'You slag. God, don't stop. That's good.'

The master's cock filled Serena's rectum, and touched her sigmoid colon.

'Oh! God!' Serena screamed, while the master began his buggery. 'You're going to burst me! You're too big, master!'

The master's naked buttocks clenched, as he bum-fucked the German girl. 'Do you want me to stop?' he said.

'No . . . no . . . oh, master, fuck me till I come,' moaned Serena. 'You are my master. Your cock owns me.'

Her arse grease flowed, as his cock squelched in and out of her anus. The master's cock caressed Serena's colon. Serena groaned. Meanwhile, the two English girls licked each other.

'God, Sal, that's good.'

'Lick me, Em,' said Sarah. Her belly heaved, as Emily licked her to orgasm. 'Yes! Oh, yes!' Sarah cried, as she tweaked her own nipples. 'Don't stop, you lovely lesbo,' she moaned. 'Oh, that's good. Suck my clit.'

'I am not a lesbo.'

'Liar, liar, pants on fire.'

'Bitch!'

Emily had Sarah face down, with her bare buttocks pinioned. She took her cane, and with the wood, caressed Sarah's bare. Sarah shivered.

'Don't be too hard on me,' she moaned.

'You dissed me,' Emily murmured, 'so you get a spanking.'

Vip! Emily's cane lashed Sarah's bare buttocks.

'Ohh,' Sarah groaned.

'You know I am only doing this to you because I love you,' said Emily.

Her tongue licked Sarah's arse cleft. Her nose sniffed Sarah's anus. Then her cane lashed once more. Vip!

'God! You filthy cruel slut!' screamed Sarah.

Vip! Vip! Emily's cane whipped Sarah's helpless buttocks. Sarah's bottom writhed.

'I want that arse of yours pink,' hissed Emily. 'Then I'll know you're mine.'

Vip! Vip! The pitiless cane flogged her again. Sarah's pinking fesses squirmed.

'Make me yours,' said Sarah, sobbing. 'Pink my arse, you horrid bitch. Oh, I hate you.'

Emily took the weeping Sarah to a hundred strokes on the bare bottom, while the master bum-fucked Serena. When Sarah's flogging was over, Emily and Sarah embraced.

'Does my bottom look nice and pink?' Sarah asked.

'Oh, yes. Beautiful. But you are such a bitch. Oh, let me kiss you.' Sarah knelt, and kissed Emily's nipples. 'You really hurt me with your cane,' she murmured. 'My bum is stinging awfully.'

'I meant to hurt you,' said Emily. 'Didn't you like it?'

Sarah went down, and licked Emily's toes. 'Yes, I did like it,' she whispered.

She sucked Emily's toes, on both feet.

'That tickles,' Emily said.

Sarah's tongue went up Emily's calves, then her thighs. Sarah licked Emily's bare buttocks, and Emily sighed. Sarah licked the body of the girl who had whipped her. When her tongue began to lick Emily's juicing cunt, Emily groaned. Her arms embraced Sarah. Then her tongue began to lick Sarah's clitty. Come spurted from their cunts, as their tongues tweaked their engorged nubbins.

'Yes!'

'Yes!'

'Oh, I'm going to come!'

'Yes! Ahh! Me too!

'Ohh! Don't stop! Lick me!'

Come flowed from their shaven twats, as the two nude girls orgasmed together. Buttocks heaving, while buggering Serena, the master smiled, watching Emily and Sarah.

'Good,' he murmured.

Sperm flowed from the master's cock into Serena's anus. His hot cream bubbled from her anal lips, down her squirming thighs, to her feet. Emily and Sarah, wiping come from their twats, squatted to lick the master's sperm from Serena's bare feet.

'The best spunk,' panted Sarah.

Emily took Serena's toes in her mouth, and began to lick them dry. 'No better spunk than the master's,' she said.

'Thank you, master,' Serena groaned. 'Oh, thank you.'

Sarah parted Serena's thighs. 'You filthy slut,' she snarled. 'Take this caress, and be proud of it.'

While Emily licked Serena's toes, Sarah's lips fastened on the German's squirming clit. Her fingers tickled Serena's anus, then penetrated.

'Don't you like that?' Sarah murmured, masturbating her own clit.

She had three fingers in Serena's rectum. With her other hand, she grasped Serena's bare titties, squeezing the nipples. Her fingers fucked Serena's arse, wiping the colon.

'*Ach!* You are hurting me!' squealed Serena. '*Das macht schade.*'

'Do you want me to stop?' said Sarah.

'No! Go on!' cried Serena. 'Do me! You filthy shit bitch, I love it! *Ach, ja, du Sklavenhund! Fick mich im Arsch, bis zu Orgasmus!*'

203

13

The Master Overthrown

'If you want to be fucked in the arse, you gross German bitch, then you shall be,' Sarah said coolly, with her three fingers inside Serena's rectum. 'Emily, would you do me a favour, and please fetch a number-four strap-on double-dildo?'

Emily simpered, and obeyed Sarah's request. She brought a shining dark tulipwood double-dildo, with a rubber waist thong. 'This one was made only yesterday,' she said.

'It's always nice to break in a new godemiché,' Sarah drawled. 'Strap me with the dildo, please, and make it good and tight.'

Emily knelt, and fastened the waistband around Sarah's hips, then inserted the female portion of the dildo into Sarah's cunt. It slid into her wet pouch, filling her, and Sarah groaned and smiled. She had Serena pinioned, with her fingers up her arse, but now she released the German girl. Serena turned, to see the giant thirty-centimetre long and ten-centimetre wide dildo, sticking up like a giant wooden cock from Sarah's cunt basin.

'No! Not a number four!' she gasped.

'You begged to be fucked in the arse,' snarled Sarah, 'and you're going to be. You're getting the full number four, right up your hole, and into that tight rectum.'

Emily wrenched Serena's hair by the roots, holding her down, while Sarah penetrated the girl's arse with the giant dildo. Sweat poured from Sarah's face and breasts, as she struggled to get the engine into Serena's bumhole. With a squelch, Serena's anus sucked in the tulipwood, and Sarah began to bum-fuck her. Held by the hair, wrenched to its roots, Serena could only sob and squirm, her naked buttocks writhing, as she was bum-fucked by Sarah.

'*Ach, Gott!*' shrieked the German girl. 'It hurts so!'

The cunt portion of the double-dildo slid in and out of Sarah's pouch, with Sarah's copious come oiling the wood. Sarah's naked breasts bounced, lathered in sweat, and Emily's lips went to Sarah's nipples, to lick her breasts dry.

'You are splitting me!' shrieked Serena. 'My arse is in agony! Master! Please tell the bitch to stop!'

'No, I rather like the spectacle,' purred the master. 'You have such a lovely big arse, Serena, so you can take a lovely big dildo up your hole. The number four is my pride and joy. I designed it myself. Please continue to fuck her, Sarah.'

Sarah buggered the squirming blonde, who was weeping in huge gulping sobs, at the pain of the giant dildo in her arse.

'Master,' said Nipringa. 'May I speak?'

'Crouch, with your face on the ground, and present your bare arse, slave,' said the master. 'That is the only way a slave may address her master.'

Nip crouched, face in the dirt, and bare buttocks spread.

'Proceed, slut,' said the master.

'Master, yesterday, at my slavework, I took a liberty – I made a new invention, and sculpted a number five. It is bigger and harder than any of your other productions. It is a double-ended device, a cunt and anus dildo combined. May I have permission to test it in Jacqui's holes?'

'A number five? Why, yes,' said the master, stroking his chin. 'If you have done well, you might be awarded the pink. You may rise, and test it on Jacqui.'

'No!' wailed Jacqui, as Candi held her down by the hair, with her arms twisted behind her back.

Nipringa strapped onto her waist the giant two-cylinder godemiché. Licking her lips, she parted the blonde girl's buttocks. The black wood sprouted from her cunt basin.

'I'm a boy today,' hissed Nipringa. 'I'm a black boy with a big cock, the biggest, hardest cock you've ever felt, and I'm going to fuck your cunt, and your tiny little girl's arse until you faint.'

With her strapped-on black wood, she penetrated Jacqui's bare-shaven anus bud.

'No. Please. Not in my bum,' Jacqui moaned.

The gleaming dark-wood dildo slid into the blonde's wet cunt. It penetrated her squirming anus, to the squelching of Jaqui's arse grease, filled her rectum, and went right to her sigmoid colon, as Nip began a brutal bum-fucking.

'No! No!' the Welsh blonde shrieked.

'Yes,' said the ebony girl, dripping sweat and come, as she rode the squirming pale body of Jacqui.

Nip's teeth were bared, as she fucked the blonde girl's cunt and arsehole with the massive dildo. Her own cunt dripped with juice, as the other end of the dildo filled her pouch. With Nip's heavy body in control of the blonde, Candi released Jacqui's arms, which flailed helplessly.

'Oh! No!' Jacqui shrieked. 'You're bursting my bum! You're hurting me so! And to be fucked in my cunt by a horrid wooden thing! I've never known such shame!'

Yet her twat juiced. As she was buggered by Nip, Jacqui began to wank off. While her buttocks squirmed under the black girl's fierce buggery, her fingers went to her clit, and began to tweak the engorged nubbin in her

206

pink pouch. The master approached, ordered Nip to withdraw, and Nip obeyed, removing the number-five dildo with a sucking plop from Jacqui's holes. The master extinguished his cigar in the juice that was pouring from Jacqui's cunt. The brown cylinder sizzled in her squirming come-filled twat.

'Ahh ... no ... you bastard,' Jacqui groaned.

'I trust that did not hurt too much,' said the master.

'You are cruel, sir,' Jacqui said. 'You and Nip. This buggery hurts so. And stubbing your cheroot in my wet cunt is more pain than a girl should bear. The horrid sizzle of the ember. I cannot help being wet. I am a girl.'

'Let us see if we can lighten your pain,' said the master.

He wore only a pink G-string. At his instruction, Sarah removed it, leaving him nude, with a huge erect cock. Jacqui was turned belly down and, while Nip strapped on a number four and buggered her from the top, the master's cock slid into the sobbing blonde girl's juicing cunt, filling her. His cock squelched her wet pouch, beginning with a slow slide, then quickening the pace of his bucking, until he was fiercely fucking the girl's cunt, and his glans slammed her wombneck.

'Master! I was a virgin!' screamed Jacqui.

'Not any more, I fear,' said the master. 'Now you are used goods.'

'Ahh!' Jacqui cried. 'It's too big! I never dreamed a man's cock could swell so large! And the dildo in my twat and bum! No girl should be filled so much!'

'Yes, she should,' hissed Nipringa, her own cunt flowing, as she buggered the Welsh blonde. 'It is what girls are made for. To be filled. You don't want to be a virgin. You want to be fucked by big cocks. That's what all girls want, and it is all we want.'

'And what about boys?' sobbed Jacqui, as she writhed under her double fucking. 'Why shouldn't they be fucked? What about the master? Shouldn't his arse be filled? Doesn't Sarah want to fuck him in the bum?'

'What an interesting, if disloyal concept,' said the master, as he fucked Jacqui's cunt, with her come dripping over his huge engorged cock, which was slamming her, 'and one which has earned you a full-body flogging, you sweet little girl. But one which, I fear, may never come to fruition.'

'Don't be too sure of it,' whispered Nipringa.

Her wooden number-four dildo fucked Jacqui's arse until the blonde girl wept in agony. Meanwhile, the master's cock thrust in Jacqui's juicing pouch. Nipringa gasped, as the cunt portion of the dildo brought her to climax. Her come spurted over the bodies of Jacqui and the master.

'Ohh!' shrieked Jacqui. 'I've never felt anything like this before! Oh, master, fuck me in the cunt, make me come! I'm so wet and your cock is so big! I don't know what's happening to me! Yes! Burst me with that cock! Oh, I'm coming! I never came before without wanking off! I wank off every morning, because I need to come, but I had only my fingers, and now I have a huge tool in my twat . . . oh, please, don't stop! Fuck me, fuck me! Yes! I'm almost there! Ahh! Ohh! I am your slave!'

Jacqui's belly fluttered, as her cunt spurted come, and she climaxed. The master smiled, grunted and sighed, as his sperm spurted into Jacqui's juicing twat.

'Satisfactory,' he said. 'But the dear little girl slave has earned another full-body flogging for her insolence. Suggesting that I, the master, should be fucked in the arse by Sarah, like a common girl slut. Emily, Sarah!'

'Yes, master,' said the pink-suited monitors.

'Take this cheeky slut out at once, and string her by the hair.'

'Ahh!' Jacqui screamed, as the laughing English monitors, strutting in their pink swimsuits, wrenched her by her hair.

Emily knotted the girl's long blonde tresses to the gibbet, and strung her. Jacqui's naked body hung from

208

the gibbet, free, but for the knot that held her long blonde hair to the gallows. Her hands flapped, her bare breasts bobbed and her legs wriggled, but the blonde girl was helpless, awaiting the whip.

'No. No,' she wept, as her body dangled. 'You can't do this to me. Surely I've been punished enough.'

'No girl has ever been punished enough,' said the master. 'You have earned a full body flogging, and that is what you shall get. Hung by your hair, as a filthy slut deserves. Look at these bare feet. They are disgusting. Someone must lick them clean. We cannot flog a girl slave who has dirty feet.'

The master knelt, before the hanging body of the Welsh girl, and applied his lips to her dirty toes. He took the full toes of her left foot into his mouth, and sucked until the ochre dirt came off. He took her right foot into his mouth, and sucked the toes for five minutes, until they were clean. Jacqui gasped.

'Oh, that tickles,' she said. 'But it's nice. Oh, master, please don't flog me bare. It is so shameful to be suspended by my hair alone. It hurts so. And I'm so frightened of the whip on my bare. Please, oh, please, don't flog me. I've been whipped so much, and it hurts so badly, and I was a virgin, and a good girl, and I don't think I deserve it.'

The master's tongue licked her shaven twat. The hillock of her mound writhed. Come flowed from her twat.

'Oh,' Jacqui moaned. 'Oh . . .'

'This is your answer, you filthy slave,' he rasped. 'A good girl must be enslaved and punished.'

His tongue penetrated her slit, and began to suck her cunt juice. Emily and Sarah held Jacqui's buttocks, as the master greedily swallowed her come.

'No. Please,' groaned Jacqui. 'Oh. Yes. Oh, I'm coming. You're bringing me off. Oh. Yes. Don't stop, sir.'

Her cunt spurted come, which the master devoured, swallowing it with sighs of ecstasy. His tongue was merciless on Jacqui's clitty.

'Ahh!' Jacqui screamed. 'Oh! It's so good! I'm almost there!'

The master's fingers entered Jacqui's anus. First, one finger – the blonde girl groaned – then two, and finally three. Jacqui shrieked, as she was finger-bummed by the master.

'Yes …. yes . . . come on.'

The master bit her clitty, with his cigar-stained teeth. '*Ahh!*' Jacqui shrilled.

Then he took her whole cunt mouth between his lips, and sucked her. His tongue entered her anus, and tickled the tender place.

'Yes. Yes. Don't stop,' Jacqui moaned. Come poured from her licked cunt. 'Master! I love you!' Jacqui cried. 'I am your slave!'

'Love is not an option in Paraiba,' the master said.

The master withdrew from her, and wiped his lips of Jacqui's copious come. His tongue was coated with her arse grease. He put a finger to his tongue, and wiped Jacqui's arse grease into his nose, breathing deeply.

'That's lovely,' murmured the master. 'That's the best girl's arse grease I've ever tasted or smelled. However, it is not for a slave to love her master. A slave must hate her master. Don't you understand, girl slave? Unless you hate me, I am not your master. Emily and Sarah hate me.'

He gestured to the pouting Emily and Sarah.

'Yes, master,' simpered Emily. 'Sarah and I hate you with our guts. That is why we obey you.'

'This bitch is well strung,' the master said. 'She hangs well. Her hair is long and firm. Whip her naked bottom, and her bare back, till she screams. Whip her breasts. I want scars on those luscious fruity nipples. Then she will properly hate me. And then I may get to tolerate her.'

Emily and Sarah raised their rawhide whips. Sarah took the girl from behind. Whap! Her first whipstroke lashed Jacqui's naked buttocks, and the blonde nymphet groaned. Vap! Emily took her from the front, with a stroke across her nipples. While Sarah flogged her bottom and shoulders, Emily whipped her belly and breasts, and Jacqui screamed and wept, tears streaming down her cheeks. Her flogged body wriggled helplessly from the gibbet.

'No! Please, no!' she begged.

Vap! Vap! Her flesh glowed crimson.

'You wanted to be a slave, didn't you?' said Nipringa.

'No! Well . . .'

Vap! Vap!

'So that you could earn the pink?'

'I don't know . . . *Ahh!*'

Emily's whip took the girl right between the thighs. The leather thong landed in her pink wet pouch, and whipped her clitty.

'Ah! God! No!' Jacqui howled. 'It's agony!'

Yet her cunt did not stop juicing. She oozed come, moistening her wriggling thighs, as she was flogged.

'You don't earn the master's pink, unless you can take the whip in the pink,' hissed Emily. 'We all have. You must, girl-slave bitch.'

The master's cock sprang hard. He snapped his fingers at Nip. The nude black girl, glistening with sweat, squatted at his order, fingering her cunt, as her lips fastened around the engorged glans of the master's cock. Come dripped from Nip's cunt into the ochre earth, as she took the master's cock to the back of her throat, and began to fellate him.

Vap! The twin rawhides striped Jacqui's dangling body, on back and front. Her breasts were welted crimson.

'Ahh!' the blonde screamed. 'Oh, God, stop!'

While Nip sucked the master's helmet, the crouching Candi's lips were on his balls. Sandoz stood nude and erect, grinning. The master ordered him to fuck Nip-ringa in the arse, and Sandoz complied. While Nip sucked the master's cock, she groaned, as Sandoz's massive tool penetrated her rectum. Arse grease squelched from her anus, as Sandoz buggered her. She groaned, but could not speak, as the master's cock was fucking her throat at the same time as Sandoz was fucking her arse. Her eyes were full of tears and hatred. Emily and Sarah laughed, as they whipped the helpless Welsh blonde.

'She squirms well,' said Sarah.

'And stripes well, too, on the titties,' said Emily. 'Good crimson. I could do this all day.'

'Then let's do it all day. I could whip this luscious nude bitch forever. Make her squirm, make her squeal, make her wriggle, make her beg for mercy. Which she shan't have.'

'But only if the master pleases,' said Emily. 'His black slut seems to please him with her mouth. And Sandoz is doing his duty, giving her proper punishment from the rear. Look at that huge cock poking the girl's anus. And that little blonde Candi licking the master's balls.'

Vap! Vap! Two whip strokes lashed Jacqui's body: one stroke on the buttocks, and one on the back.

'Ahh!' she screamed.

'But I want to lick the master's balls,' Emily said, licking the tip of her whip, which had just delivered a crimson welt to Jacqui's back. 'I'm jealous of those slave sluts.'

The flogging of the suspended Jacqui continued to a hundred strokes on her naked body from the whips of Sarah and Emily. Jacqui screamed and wept, wriggling from her bound hair, as her girl flesh was flogged. The back, buttocks and breasts were fully welted. Emily and Sarah laughed, as they whipped the helpless teenager. At the hundredth stroke, the master signalled that the blonde's flogging could stop. Candi had her tongue deep inside the master's anus. At that moment, Nip sucked the master's cock until his sperm washed her throat, and she swallowed every drop.

Emily and Sarah freed Jacqui from the gibbet. The flogged girl groaned as she was released.

'How could you girls do this to another girl?' she asked, sobbing.

'With pleasure,' hissed Sarah. 'Kneel, and kiss the whip, slut.'

Sobbing, Jacqui knelt, and kissed the whips that had flogged her nude body raw.

Emily and Sarah buttoned the master into his white silk trousers. Then Ruggiero swaggered in. He wore only a pink girl's thong, and carried a tulipwood cane, a metre in length.

'That's mine!' Emily cried. 'You beastly slave, you've stolen one of my thongs.'

'It's so hot. A fellow doesn't want to wear much more than a thong. I envy you slaves, being nude, under this sweltering sun. A girl slave's property? I can help myself to whatever I want from girls,' sneered Ruggiero.

'Not my girls,' snarled the master.

Under his pink thong, Ruggiero's massive cock was swollen to erection. 'Who is really the master here?' asked Ruggiero. 'Who wears the pink? And who has the biggest cock? I think it is myself. The master is too fond of whipping and buggering nice little teenage girls. Perhaps we should give the master a taste of his own medicine. Perhaps he really desires to be whipped and buggered himself.'

'You insolent cur,' snarled the master.

Sarah licked her lips. 'Yes, let's see if Ruggiero's right,' she said. 'Girls, seize the master.'

'You filthy disloyal bitches,' the master hissed, as the girls held him down, with his arms twisted behind his back in a half-nelson, and stripped him naked. 'Sandoz! Tame these cunts.'

Sandoz shrugged. 'What can I do?' he said. 'I am only one against many. Ruggiero seems the man of the moment. Power is a fickle goddess.'

Nipringa strapped the number-five double-dildo to Jacqui's hips. She parted the master's buttocks, while Candi sat on the master's face. Ruggiero lit a cigar, and ordered the Welsh blonde to bugger the master.

'No!' the master cried. 'Emily! Sarah! Do something! This is an outrage!'

'What can we do?' drawled Sarah. 'It seems that Ruggiero is the new master – well, he is rather masterful – and girls must always obey a master.'

The two English girls wanked off, as they watched Nip's number-five dildo, strapped to Jacqui's loins, plunge between the squirming buttocks of the master, who was held down by Nip and Candi. The tulip-wood godemiché penetrated his anus, filling his rectum, and he began to shriek, as the Welsh girl buggered him.

'Take that, you swine,' panted Jacqui. 'Who's the master now?'

'How dare you, bitch,' groaned the master, squirming under the blonde girl's buggery. 'It hurts. You have no right to hurt me, you miserable girl slave. I'll get even with you. You will suffer punishment undreamed of.'

'Your cock is stiff, master, as this miserable girl slave buggers you,' drawled Nipringa. 'I fancy she might bugger you to a spurt. And it might be the last spurt you are permitted to have, for now you are going to be enslaved. The oppressed become the oppressors. Ruggiero, will you kindly fuck me in my arse to show that you are the new master?'

'Gladly, slave bitch,' said Ruggiero, stripping off his pink thong to reveal his giant cock.

His helmet gleamed purple. He parted Nip's sweat-beaded ebony fesses, and drove the glans into her anus. Nip squealed in pleasure. The full shaft of the cock penetrated her, right to his balls, which caressed Nip's greased bum. He began a savage bum-fuck.

'Oh! That is so good,' gasped Nipringa. 'You are the master now.'

'Oh ... oh,' groaned the former master, as Jacqui bummed him. 'Oh, what are you doing? I'm going to come. Don't stop. Fuck me up the arse, you Welsh whore. Do me. Yes.' Sperm spurted from his cock. 'Oh! I'm coming! You bitch!'

'Emily, Sarah,' said Nipringa. 'Take this worm away in ropes, and give him a welcome flogging on his bare arse. He is our new slave, and Ruggiero is our new master.'

'No! Please!' cried the former master, as Emily and Sarah pinioned him by his balls, and led him to a flogging stool. They roped him by his hands and legs, while he sobbed.

'There is no please,' said Nipringa, licking her teeth.

She picked up a cane, and began to flog the former master on his naked buttocks. His cock was stiff, as the cane lashed his bare. Vip! Vip!

'Ahh! Please, no!' the bound naked male shrieked.

The cane striped pink with every stroke on the man's buttock-flesh and, at each stroke, he cried out in anguish.

Vip!

'No! Ah! Please, stop!'

Vip!

'Mercy! Mercy!'

He wept, as his bare arse wriggled.

'There is no mercy for a male whore, who likes being buggered by girls,' Nipringa said. 'When you've been righteously flogged, you'll be thrown in the cave, and then sent to perform your duty of carving the tulip-wood, along with the girl slaves. Ruggiero is our new master. And I am our new weighmistress. Understood?'

'Yes,' said Emily.

'Absolutely,' said Sarah.

'Wait!' cried Serena. 'I am the master's weigh-mistress!'

'Not any more,' said Nip. 'Candi, would you kindly cane this bitch until she maintains a proper silence?'

'Cane the German bitch, Candi,' Ruggiero drawled. 'She is only a slave. A slave has no right to make noise.'

Serena's face was pushed by Jacqui into the red dirt. She sobbed, as her arse was bared for the cane. Candi lifted the tulipwood, and lashed Serena's bare arse. Vap! The heavy wood made a fearful slashing noise, as it sliced the German girl's ripe buttock pears.

'Ahh!' Serena screamed, as her bum pinked.

Vap!

'Oh. No. The pain,' Serena snuffled, shuddering, as her bare breasts squirmed in the dirt.

Vap!

'Stop! No!' shrieked the former master, as Nipringa flogged his writhing buttocks.

Ruggiero took a cheroot and lit it with a matchstick, which he lit by striking it on the toes of Serena's left foot. He gave the match to Nip, and told her to extinguish it. Nip extinguished the match on the former master's balls, which made the man howl. She pushed the blackened stick into his arsehole and continued to flog him.

'You bitch, you slut,' said the former master, sobbing.

Vip! Nip's cane lashed the male's bum, which squirmed helplessly, as the welts formed.

Vip!

'Ohh! No!' he squealed.

Vip!

'Ahh!' the former master screamed, as his arse purpled.

His buttocks writhed under Nip's flogging. She whipped him to fifty strokes, while he sobbed and wriggled and screamed. The girls laughed.

216

'I think I am going to enjoy being master,' said Ruggiero, puffing contentedly on his cigar. 'Especially being master of you, Nipringa, you ebony bitch. Enough of this fool. Stick him and Serena in the cave, until it is time for their morning's work. We have more important things to do. Kneel and suck my cock, Nipringa. If you pleasure me, then you earn the pink. So suck well.'

'Gladly, master,' said Nipringa.

Laughing, Emily and Sarah frogmarched the beaten former master and the sobbing Serena to the cave. Nip knelt and got her lips around Ruggiero's massive erect cock. She caressed his buttocks, as her tongue flicked his peehole.

'Yes,' he groaned.

Her lips and tongue pressed the corona of his glans, and he began an incessant moan, as his cock stiffened to rigidity. Candi began to lick his balls, while Jacqui bit his nipples.

'You wicked bitches!' he cried. 'Oh ... yes! Don't stop! Oh, you evil witches!'

His sperm spurted into Nipringa's mouth, and she swallowed every drop, while Candi had his balls fully in her mouth, and Jacqui had her tongue in his anus.

Ruggiero lay down, panting, as Candi licked his cock and balls clean, and Jacqui licked his anus.

'A girl's tongue up my arse?' Ruggiero snapped. 'Girls are truly depraved creatures, and must be disciplined. Spank me, you dirty girl slaves. Crimson my arse. I order you to spank me with tulipwood canes. Sarah and Emily accustomed me to this pleasure of feeling pain from a girl's lashing. So do it to me. It makes me feel a true man to take a thrashing from a girl.'

He stretched his nude body in the red dirt, before his naked girl slaves.

Candi lifted her cane. 'Are you sure, master?' she asked.

'Yes, he is sure,' drawled Nipringa, lifting her own cane.

'It is an order,' said Ruggiero. 'I am master.'

Jacqui took a rawhide cattle whip. 'I'm going to enjoy this,' she said with a giggle.

Nipringa lashed the first stroke to the master Ruggiero's naked bottom. Vip! She laid the lash carefully on the lower fesses, near his balls, so that he squirmed in fear, lest the rod slash the orbs. Candi followed, with two quick cane strokes to the boy's haunches, which raised instant crimson, and made him wince.

'Yes,' he groaned. 'Oh, yes.'

Jacqui followed with a stroke of the rawhide across his bare back. The whip cracked on his naked skin.

'Ahh!' he screamed. 'Yes! Don't stop, you bitches! Flog me! Pink my bare arse! I am your master, and you must obey!'

'I shall certainly obey, master,' hissed Jacqui.

Vap! Vap! Vap! Her whip cracked three times across his shoulders. The master Ruggiero writhed. Each stroke drove the naked boy's erect cock deeper into the dirt.

Vip! Nip's cane lashed his buttocks, at the tender top, beneath the spinal nubbin.

'Ohh,' he moaned.

Vip! Vip! Candi lashed him on the backs of his thighs.

'*Ahh!*' he shrieked.

Vip! Vip! Nip stroked his naked fesses.

'Ohh! Ahh!'

His whipped buttocks squirmed, with his erect cock writhing in the ochre earth. Nip squatted, thighs apart, and pissed. A golden stream of fluid steamed from her twat over the master's head.

'Oh, you cruel bitches,' Ruggiero gasped.

The flogging of the new master continued, until his body was purple with bruises. Candi and Nip used their canes, while Jacqui used the rawhide on his back, which was rapidly striped in a latticework. The girls took turns

218

to piss on his face, while the master Ruggiero sobbed in protest. Candi threw a bucket of water over him to cleanse him. Nip pushed his head into the earth.

'Eat, master,' she whispered.

'No ... what ...?'

'It is good for you.'

Nipringa took a handful of earth, stuffed it in her mouth, and began to chew, then swallowed, with a beatific smile. 'Eat clay,' she said, her mouth full. 'It does you good.'

Ruggiero took a mouthful, chewed and swallowed.

Vip! Nip's cane lashed his bottom. 'Eat more, you brat,' she drawled.

The master gobbled up the red earth.

Vip! Vip! The canes of Candi and Nip whipped his bare, as he ate dirt. His arse squirmed.

'You've eaten earth,' snarled Nip, 'now fuck it.'

Vip! Vip! Nip and Candi's canes striped Ruggiero's buttocks, and Jacqui's rawhide lashed his shoulders, as his cock ploughed the ochre earth. Each girl had her hand on her juicing twat. They wanked their clits, as they saw the new master's massive tool fuck the dirt.

Vip!

'Ahh!'

Vip!

'Ohh! You bitches. I'm coming. Don't stop. Oh, yes, yes!'

While the girl slaves wanked themselves to orgasm, Ruggiero ejaculated into the mud. Nipringa, panting from her come, took the new master by the hair.

'That hurts!' he squealed.

Nip took a handful of spunked earth, and ate, licking her lips, as each morsel of dirt went down, then pushed Ruggiero's face into the mud where he had spurted. 'Tasty spunk,' she said. 'Now you eat some.'

His face in the dirt, Ruggiero ate mud, spermed with his own cream, while Nip and Candi delivered a further thirty cane strokes to his bottom. He wept and wriggled as he was flogged, but his cock rapidly stiffened. The naked Jacqui embraced him in the dirt, and began to suck his cock.

'I hate you,' she said, sucking his glans. 'Every girl slave must hate her master. But I love your cock. It's so big. Every girl loves a big cock above all else.'

The boy and the girl, covered in slime, writhed in the dirt. Jacqui got Ruggiero's whole stiff cockshaft to the back of her throat, while he licked the mud from her buttocks.

'Dirty. Let me whip that off,' said Nipringa.

Vip! As Jacqui sucked Ruggiero, Nip's cane lashed Jacqui's bare bum.

'Ahh!' Jacqui screamed, biting Ruggiero's cock.

'Yes!' shrieked Ruggiero. 'Oh, you cruel bitch! Yes! I'm coming!'

Ruggiero came in Jacqui's mouth, and, caned by Nip, Jacqui wanked herself off, as she swallowed every drop of the new master's spermload.

'You have all earned the pink,' Ruggiero gasped.

The girls knelt before him, and licked his balls. 'Thank you, master,' they said.

14

Girls in Pink Swimsuits

'Darren only ever bummed me, you, know, in the hole,' said Candi, sobbing. 'I was a proper virgin before. He spanked me on the bare, when I was stroppy, and made me cry, but he never put his cock in my twat. I mean, I understood that if a girl was stroppy, she got a spanking on the bare. Then she had to suck her bloke off. I liked sucking Darren off. He had such a lovely cock, I could lick it forever. I used to swallow all his spunk. It was lovely and hot and creamy. But he only fucked me in my bumhole. He respected my virginity. One night, he took me to dinner, in a really posh restaurant, and we had oysters and champagne – really good champagne, I can't remember the name of it, but it was French, and beautifully chilled – and then we went back to his flat. Then he stripped me. It was slow and beautiful. He kissed me on the lips, and said I was the loveliest girl in the world. Well, I melted. His lips were so tasty. Then he took my blouse off. He unhooked my bra, and kissed my nipples. He didn't just kiss them, he chewed them, until I was practically coming. He kissed me all over. He rolled my panties down, and kissed my navel and my twat and my thighs and my bumhole. Then he took my nylons off, and licked my toes. No one ever kissed my bumhole or licked my toes before. It tickled so much, and his tongue was so beautiful between my bum cheeks. I was so wet. He put his cock into my bum. It hurt at first, but after he started bum-fucking me, and I got into the rhythm, it was pure pleasure to have my bum filled by a man. I felt I was his slave, and it was the loveliest feeling on earth. Isn't it the best thing, when a girl feels she is totally in the power of a strong man? He filled me up with his cock until I thought I was going to burst, and while he was doing me, he tweaked my clit with his thumb, and made me come like a fountain. I was making a bit of a noise, as I came, while he gave me his whole load of hot spunk up my bumhole. It was lovely. Darren was a gentleman.'

'In fact, the most wicked pleasure is to rob a juicy boy of *his* virginity.' Nipringa said. 'Especially by fucking him up the arse. When a girl fucks a boy up the arse, with a wooden dildo, that is the loss of a boy's true virginity.'

On Ruggiero's orders, Nipringa handed out pink swimsuits to the girl slaves. Candi cheered up, with a smile, and Jacqui cooed, as they found Serena's swimsuits fitted them.

'Lovely.'

'Super.'

'Cripes, she has a big bum.'

'Well, so have you.'

'There's a brown scorchmark on my gusset.'

'And on mine.'

'That Serena's arse needs a sound whipping. Her bum's too big for her own good. And she leaks dung. It's digusting for a grown-up girl's bumhole to leak dung. She's a big blonde maiden. She should know how to cope.'

'A big bum is a girl's best virtue,' said Ruggiero. 'In fact, it has been argued by sages that a girl has no virtue whatever, other than the size and beauty of her buttocks. I tend to accept that view. Although there are philosophers who think that teat size is also important.

Now that I am master, you slave sluts are entitled to the pink, and may wield the cane on the field slaves. You shall attend faithfully to your duties, otherwise your pink shall come off, and my cane shall visit your own bare arses. Those arses, by the way, are always available to my tool. If I order any of my monitors to squat, and present her fesses, she must do so.'

'Yes, master,' said Nip.

'Respect, master,' said Candi.

'I am your slave, master,' said Jacqui.

Emily and Sarah glowered.

'I suppose we must accept our new colleagues,' Emily said.

'It is the master's wish,' Sarah replied. 'Our new master.'

'The old master must be suffering, sweating in the cave, with Serena,' Emily said. 'However, it's the way of the world, isn't it? What goes up, must come down. Serena leaving scorchmarks in her underwear! The nerve of the bitch. I wonder which of us will be the first to squat for Master Ruggiero.'

Ruggiero ordered Sarah to insert a cigar into her anus, lubricate it in her rectum, then light it for him and transfer it from her lips to his. She obeyed at once. Smoking the cigar, perfumed with the girl's arse grease, he snapped his fingers.

'You. Nipringa. Bend over and present your buttocks. I want to poke you in the arse.'

'Yes, master,' said Nipringa.

She crouched, bum presented.

'Candi, you will please divest me,' said the master.

Candi stripped the master Ruggiero, and he advanced, with erect cock, on the satin-bare black bottom of Nipringa. The master's cock sprouted to a huge erection. His helmet gleamed purple, nuzzling Nip's anus bud. His whole erect shaft pushed at Nip's anus.

'Ahh, it hurts,' she groaned, as his swollen purple glans slid into her anal channel.

Her buggered bottom writhed. He thrust, and got his stiff cock into her rectum.

'Ohh! Ooh!' the naked girl shrieked.

'Shut up, and take your medicine, slave bitch,' snarled Ruggiero. 'I am your master now.'

'Ohh,' Nip groaned, as the master's cock fully penetrated her, right to the colon. He chewed his cigar, as he buggered the black girl.

'I am the master now,' he said, laughing.

He enculed Nip for over five minutes, without spurting and without making her come, even though her bum was writhing under the pain of his buggery, and her cunt was juicing heavily. As Ruggiero's massive stiff cock squelched in and out of her bumhole, come from her wet twat spilled down Nip's thighs. Yet she did not come to climax. The girl slaves watched, as the master Ruggiero bum-fucked the ebony girl, yet she did not orgasm. The girls began to giggle.

'Can't bring her off.'

'Not big enough.'

'Isn't my cock big enough for you, slut?' he rasped.

Nip's arsehole squelched with grease. 'Yes, master,' she gasped. 'But . . . if you'll permit . . .'

With a plop, she ripped her buttocks from Ruggiero's cock, which was left trembling, stiff and glazed with Nip's arse grease. Ruggiero moaned.

'I want to spurt my spunk in your arsehole, you bitch,' he wailed.

'Girls,' Nipringa ordered. 'Hold Ruggiero down.'

Candi, Emily, Sarah and Jacqui held the groaning boy.

'Sandoz,' Nip commanded. 'You will assist me in giving the new master his operation. That will make him a true master.'

'Gladly, miss,' said Sandoz. Sandoz produced a gleaming cut-throat razor. 'This will only hurt a little bit, master,' he said.

224

Ruggiero shrieked, as Sandoz made a tiny incision in the shaft of the boy's cock. The master moaned, as tiny brass nuggets were thrust by Sandoz into his foreskin and into the shaft of his cock. With a few deft needle threads, Sandoz sewed up the incision. The cock became hard and lumpy, twice as heavy as before. Nip applied her lips to Ruggiero's glans, and his cock swelled to twice its normal size. Nip tweaked his balls, and the brass nuggets rang.

'They are called Chinese bells,' said Nip.

'Now, Master Ruggiero, with a loaded cock, you will be able to pleasure any girl. Please return to my bottom. I am your ox.'

'That's funny,' said Ruggiero. 'When I was a boy, I had a nursemaid called Adriana, a delicious black girl, twenty years old, from San Salvador. We took a bath together, and she washed me all over. This continued until I was sixteen. One day, when I was of age, I became stiff, and she asked me if I masturbated. I was too ashamed to admit the truth, that I masturbated twice or three times a day, thinking of her nude black body. She took my cock between her muscled thighs, and rubbed me. "Tell me the truth," she ordered. I said that I wanked off, thinking of her naked body. "Well," she said, "there is nothing to be ashamed of. In future, you will wank off on my naked body, won't you, Ruggiero? It's healthy and good, and pleases a lady." She frigged me to sperm. That's what she said, "I am your ox." After that, Adriana would strip for the bath, and open her thighs, and I would masturbate, spurting my spunk on her bare black belly. Then she would bathe me, as always. One day, we were in the bath, and Adriana began to frig herself. She saw my pole stiff, and put her lips around it. She sucked, and I spurted my sperm into her mouth, while she wanked herself to come. She swallowed all my sperm. Then we had a good time, embracing in the soapy bath water. Adriana was wanking off as I kissed her breasts – she had gorgeous big brown nipples – and she said she was naughty for swallowing my spunk, and needed to be spanked for it. So I turned her over in the bathtub, and began to spank her bare wet bottom. She wriggled and squealed, and began to wank herself off under the water. After I had spanked her fifty smacks, she brought herself off, with rather loud cries, as she fingered her clit. Her foot caught my cock, between the toes of her left foot, and she began to tug my tool. I could not escape. Her big toe frigged me until I spurted new cream all over her feet, while she wanked herself to a new orgasm. Then, she brought her toes to her mouth, out of the water, and licked my sperm off her feet, with a delicious glint in her eye.' He waggled his loaded cock at the girls. 'Look at me now,' he said, as his Chinese bells rang.

'You are still a boy,' said Nip. 'No male ever really grows up.'

Ruggiero's erect tool entered the black girl's anus. His bells clinked, inside his massive loaded cock.

'Oh! God! It's so big,' Nip gasped. 'Fuck my arse, master, please.'

Ruggiero thrust his engorged cock into the black girl's rectum.

'Ahh,' she groaned. 'Yes.'

Candi and Jacqui began to masturbate each other's clits, as they watched Nip buggered, to the sound of the tinkling of Chinese bells.

'It hurts me, but it's so good,' gasped Nip. 'Your cock is so wadded. Fuck me in the arse, master. I beg you, fuck me till I come. Allow me the privilege of dripping my arse grease over your stiff tool. Jingle your bells inside me, master.'

The boy's buttocks began to thrust brutally. Panting, Ruggiero fucked Nip in the arse, his huge cock, bulging with bells, squelching fully into her rectum, then the tip of his loaded cock slamming her colon, until she screamed in pain.

'God!' she cried. 'I didn't know the bells would be so hard!'

'I am going to do all of you,' panted Ruggiero. 'You filthy masturbating sluts. Nipringa, wank off as I bum you.'

Moaning, Nip brought her fingers to her juicing cunt, and began to masturbate her clit, while the master, on top, buggered her. He thrust her face into the dirt.

'Eat, bitch,' he snarled.

As she wanked off under buggery, Nipringa took a mouthful of ochre earth, chewed, and swallowed.

'Another,' said the master. 'If you bitches can eat dirt, then I won't waste money feeding you.'

Nip ate dirt until her stomach bulged, while the master's cock plunged into her tripes. As she ate the clay, her twat spurted come over her wanking fingers.

'Yes,' she groaned, her mouth full of earth. 'Mm ... ahh. Ahh.'

Her belly writhed in orgasm, as her nude body was squashed into the dirt. Candi and Jacqui wanked each other to climax. Ruggiero withdrew his stiff cock from Nip's anus.

'You are next, my ripe bitches,' he said to Candi and Jacqui. 'I'll bugger you, but first, I'll punish you for masturbating without permission. Strip nude and crouch, faces in the dirt, and present your arses for chastisement.'

Whimpering, the two girls obeyed, after carefully folding their come-stained pink swimsuits.

'Now eat dirt, while I flog you,' sneered Ruggiero. 'Take big mouthfuls, chew well, and swallow. It is good for you.'

He lifted his cane. Vip! Vip! Two stingers lashed the bare bottoms of the mud-chewing slaves. Their bare buttocks clenched at the vicious cane strokes, and began to squirm, as Ruggiero, cock stiff and jingling with his Chinese bells, took their bare-arse caning to thirty

227

strokes. Vip! Vip! The cane lashed the quivering naked buttocks of the two moaning girls, while Emily and Sarah smirked, each masturbating her cunt, under her pink swimsuit. The flogged girls wept, faces pressed to the dirt, as they pissed themselves: Jacqui at the twelfth stroke, and Candi at the fifteenth.

'Eat dirt, you filthy slaves!' Ruggiero snarled.

Jacqui and Candi crammed their mouths with the ochre earth.

Vip!

'Ohh!'

Vip!

'Ahh!'

Vip! Vip! Two strokes took them in their arse clefts, lashing their anus buds and lips.

'*Ahh!*' the girls screamed.

Emily and Sarah wanked off, giggling, wetting their pink swimsuits with massive stains of come from their juicing coozes.

Sandoz laughed. 'You cheeky wanking bitches,' he said.

'What?'

'How dare you!'

He wrenched Emily and Sarah by the hair, and made them kneel.

'Oh! What are you doing?' cried Emily.

'This is an outrage!' squealed Sarah.

Sandoz's cock was stiff. He took a tulipwood cane, and began to lash the pink-suited bottoms of the two squirming English girls, while holding them by their blonde manes.

'You masturbate without permission, like the other sluts,' he sneered.

Vip! Vip! The cane seared rips in the swimsuit bottoms of the girls. Ruggiero looked at Sandoz, and nodded his approval. Sandoz ripped off the straps at the tops of the girls' shredded suits. The girls' big breasts spilled out, and Sandoz began to cane Emily and Sarah on their naked teats.

'Oh! God! No!' Emily howled.

'Please, not my breasts!' shrieked Sarah.

Vip! Vip! The dry crack of Sandoz's cane striped the squirming girls' breasts, purpling their nipples.

When their breasts were bruised raw, and their faces glazed with tears, the nude Sandoz ordered Sarah to take his cock in her mouth, while Emily was to lick his anus, and make sure to get her tongue in all the way. Nipringa knelt too, beaming, and began to lick Sandoz's balls. Sarah moaned, as she took Sandoz's massive swollen glans between her lips, and began to lick his peehole. He laughed and, with a thrust of his buttocks, plunged his cock to the back of her throat, right to his balls, which Nip was eagerly licking.

'Uhh,' Sarah gurgled, as she sucked his full shaft.

Emily crouched, panting, and wanking herself off, as her tongue entered Sandoz's anus, and penetrated him to his rectum. Sandoz sighed his approval. Emily's cunt oozed come. Nip began to finger her clitty and, as Sarah's throat sucked the male's giant cock, she also began to masturbate Sarah's stiff clitty. Both girls dripped come from their swollen twats. Wet pink meat gleamed between the black flaps of Nipringa's cunt.

Meanwhile, Jacqui and Candi squealed, as the master's cane striped them on the bare. Vip! Vip! The tulipwood rod lashed the naked girl flesh, leaving deep crusted welts, ridged purple, on both Candi's and Jacqui's bottoms.

'Oh! Master! Enough!' Jacqui squealed. 'Bum me, but don't whip me any more.'

The master threw aside his cane. Bells jingling, he thrust his cock brutally into Jacqui's upthrust anus. His balls slammed against her bruised thighs and buttocks, as he began a savage buggery. Jacqui squirmed and squealed.

'Hold the bitch down,' the master ordered Candi.

'Yes, master,' said Candi.

Candi twisted Jacqui's arms behind her back, and held her pinioned, while the master tooled her anus, his belled cock fully thrust to her colon. Jacqui wailed, as the massive tool slammed her. Come oozed from her cunt.

'Wank the bitch off,' the master ordered Candi.

Candi put her fingers into the Welsh girl's pouch, and tweaked her swollen clitty.

'Uhh ... uhh,' Jacqui moaned. 'Don't stop. Bugger me, split my bum in two, wank me off, yes.'

Her belly writhed, as her twat spurted come, and she climaxed. The master did not come, but withdrew his cock from her greased anus, with a tinkling of bells.

'Now it's your turn,' Ruggiero said to Candi. 'Turn your arse up, slut.'

'Yes, master,' Candi whimpered. 'Fuck my bum, but please don't hurt me.'

She crouched in the mud, with her bare buttocks spread high.

'Hurt you is exactly what I intend,' said Ruggiero. 'You'll feel the full weight of my Chinese bells. Anus open, buttocks spread. That is an order.'

'Yes, master,' Candi said.

Ruggiero knelt, and licked the mud from her toes. 'I can only fuck a clean girl slave,' he said, slurping, as he sucked Candi's feet.

'Oh, master. That tickles,' Candi moaned. 'It's nice.'

Ruggiero rose, cock erect, and penetrated Candi's upthrust anus. He began to fuck Candi vigorously in the arse. His cock filled her rectum, and the girl groaned.

'Get underneath the slut and lick her clit,' he ordered Jacqui. 'Get your nose right in her cunt.'

Sandoz's hips jerked, as he fucked Sarah in the throat. Emily's tongue was fully stretched into his anus, while Nipringa licked his balls.

'Who'll be the first to spurt with these whores, master?' he said. 'I'll give a prize of a tulipwood tree to any slut who can make me come, and I'll bet you two trunks of tulipwood that you spurt first, with that luscious little bitch.'

Ruggiero glowered. 'You're on,' he said. 'Let's fuck these sluts, and see who has control.'

'Please, master,' Candi wailed. 'Give me your sperm up my hole.'

The master bared his stiff cock, stroking his glans, and thrust savagely into her anus.

'Ahh!' Candi screamed.

Sandoz took his cock from Sarah's throat and Sarah moaned, licking her lips around his swollen balls.

'But I want to swallow your spunk,' she gasped.

Sandoz slapped Sarah away, with a vicious smack to her mouth, and took Emily by the hair. Sarah fell to the ground, sobbing. Nipringa parted Emily's buttocks for Sandoz's cock to enter her anus. Emily squealed in agony, as the giant cock filled her rectum. The master and Sandoz, both buggering a squirming nude girl, smiled at each other.

'Who lasts longest. Bet?' said Sandoz. 'Whoever comes first, has to wear a girl's pink swimsuit for a week.'

'Bet,' panted Ruggiero.

They began to slide their cocks in and out of the girls' dripping arseholes, very slowly, as the girls groaned under the bum-fucking.

'I wanted Sandoz's spunk,' said the mud-slimed Sarah with a sob. 'You filthy bitch, Nipringa.'

She leaped at the black girl, and delivered a savage punch to her breasts. Nipringa groaned in pain; her eyes flashed, her thigh rose, and her toes kicked Sarah between the cunt flaps.

'Ahh!' Sarah screamed.

She fell. Nip straddled her, sat on her face and spanked her writhing bottom. Sarah whimpered, as Nip pissed in her mouth. The two nude girl slaves wrestled in the dirt. So copious was Nip's piss that Sarah was able to slip her face from under the golden stream, and grab Nip's feet. Sarah toppled Nip, who slipped in the lake of her own piss, and kneed her in the groin, then sat on her face, and began a vicious spanking of her bottom. Nip groaned, writhing, with her face pressed in the dirt, as Sarah's palm lashed her bare arse. Thwap! Thwap!

'You're hurting me,' moaned Nipringa, her mud-slimed bottom squirming under spanks.

'It's meant to hurt, you dirty slut,' hissed Sarah. 'I was being mouth-fucked by Sandoz, I wanted his spunk, and now that bitch Emily is going to get it.'

Nipringa twisted her flanks, rose, and fastened her teeth on Sarah's nipples. She bit savagely. Sarah screamed, as the black girl's teeth chewed her erect nipple buds.

'No. No! Please!' she cried, as her bare body shuddered in pain.

Nipringa wrenched Sarah's blonde mane, grasped a tulipwood stick, and pushed Sarah's face into the dirt. Vip! The first stroke took Sarah in the cleft of her buttocks, striking her cunt lips and anus bud, and the flogged girl howled.

'No! No! I'm a good girl! I don't deserve it.'

'Yes, you do,' hissed Nipringa. 'Good girls are the ones who deserve it.'

Vip! Her cane began to whip the squirming Sarah on the full expanse of her buttocks, raising crimson ridges, which turned to purple, as Nip applied the cane over and over again to the same weals. Vip! Vip!

'Ohh!' Sarah screamed, her buttocks writhing helplessly under the black girl's whipping.

Vip! Vip!

'Ooh! Ahh! Please stop! My bum is stinging! Oh, how can you be such a cruel bitch?'

'Because I am a cruel bitch,' purred Nipringa.

Sarah's pale bottom, after ten minutes of flogging by Nipringa, was crusted with deep purple welts. The master, fucking Candi in the bum, and Sandoz, buggering Emily, looked on with smiles, as Nipringa whipped the screaming naked Sarah.

'Excuse me,' said an English girl's voice. 'Am I in the right place? I'm awfully sorry to interrupt anything, but I was told about this pleasure ranch in Paraiba, and I had to see for myself. I say. Goodness. May I join in the fun?'

Candi looked up, and saw, through eyes wet with tears, the face of Fiona Dondelay. Fiona wore a fluttering pink silk party frock, strapped to her shoulders, with the skirtlet halfway up her bare thighs. She had no underwear, and her teats and shaven cunt were clearly visible through the flimsy silk. Simpering, she lifted her skirt, baring her cunt basin, and from her twat, she took some wet banknotes, and tipped the taxi driver, who licked his lips, drooling, and eyed her body, before she waved him away. Fiona smoothed her skirtlet over her bare tan thighs. Her eyes met Candi's.

'Well, if it isn't Candace Crupper, my little slave from Rodd's Academy,' Fiona drawled. 'This will be fun.' Then she saw the naked male buggering Emily, and her jaw dropped. 'Why, Dr Rodd,' she gasped.

'My name here is Sandoz,' he snarled. 'Get that frock off, bitch, and present your arse for a caning. The impudence in presuming to come here.'

'I thought ... if I paid, well, it is like a vacation resort,' Fiona stammered.

'The only vacation you get here is hard work and slavery,' snarled Dr Rodd. 'Get naked, or I'll rip that frock to shreds.'

Trembling. Fiona let her pink frock slide from her naked body. She folded it carefully, and placed it on the table.

'Now crouch,' ordered Sandoz/Dr Rodd, 'and show me that big white arse.'

'Really,' gasped Fiona. 'You can't do this. I mean, really. And my bum isn't white. I sunbathe in the nude, and have an all-over tan. I'm really quite golden.'

Ruggiero, buggering Candi, slapped Fiona on the mouth. 'Obey, you insolent bitch,' he hissed. 'Or you'll be shut up in the hole, with Serena and her boyfriend.'

Whimpering, Fiona crouched naked in the dirt, with her bottom upthrust for punishment. 'I didn't come here for this,' she snivelled. 'I came here for pleasure.'

'This is your pleasure, you beastly mot,' said Nipringa. 'This is all of our pleasures.'

'It's your pleasure,' groaned Sarah, flogged by Nip. 'Oh, you cruel bitch.'

Dr Rodd/Sandoz put his fingers inside the buggered Emily's twat, and began to rub her clit, as he buggered her. Her twat juiced come, flowing down her quivering thighs. Continuing to plough her colon, he wanked her, until she gasped in orgasm, then withdrew his stiff cock, dripping with her arse grease. He took a cane, and stood, cock stiff, over Fiona's bare bottom.

'You always were an arrogant slut,' he said. 'Now you may eat dirt. Take a mouthful of good red earth, and swallow.'

Fiona gobbled the dirt.

'Urrgh,' she gurgled.

'Swallow, slut,' ordered Dr Rodd.

Fiona made choking noises, as she swallowed the clay, but then her mouth went back for some more. 'Mm . . .' she moaned, munching the dirt.

Vip! The tulipwood laid a pink stripe on her bare buttocks.

'Ahh!' Fiona squealed.

Vip! The cane lashed her top buttock.

'Oh! No! That hurts so!'

234

Vip! Vip! Two strokes striped her thighbacks.

'Ahh!' Fiona screamed.

Vip! Vip! A further two cane lashes whipped her haunches, which crimsoned at once.

'No!' Fiona cried, squirming under cane, as Nipringa held her down by the hair.

'You were fond of caning schoolgirls,' Nip said, while the male caned the weeping nude girl, 'and now you are getting some of your own medicine. Your big bare arse is going to be a tapestry of welts, Fiona. Criss-crossed with purple. You won't want to sit down for a week.'

Vip!

'Ahh!' Fiona screamed, as Dr Rodd lashed her a vicious cane stroke between her bare thighs, taking her on the cunt and anus bud.

Nipringa, having finished her punishment of the sobbing Sarah, sat on Fiona's head, masturbating her clitty, and allowing her cunt juice to flow into Fiona's blonde mane, as the weeping girl shrieked under her bare-bum flogging. Vip! Vip! The cane took Fiona on every portion of the buttocks, until her arse was a cauldron of pink, crimson and purple welts.

'Yes! Give it to the bitch!' cried Candi, buggered by Ruggiero, whose Chinese bells jingled in her squirming bumhole. 'I was her slave at school, and now she can be mine! Make the slut suffer! Cane that bottom till she can't stand it any more! Make the bitch squirm! Oh! Master! Fuck my arse till I come, I beg you! Make *me* squirm under your tool!'

Nipringa twisted Fiona's hair into a strand, and began to masturbate with it, using the wet fronds to tickle her clitty.

After sixty strokes of the cane, Fiona wept uncontrollably. Her cunt juiced. Sandoz/Dr Rodd inserted his stiff cock into Fiona's anus.

'No. Not there,' groaned the flogged maiden. 'It hurts so abominably.'

Dr Rodd laughed, and pushed his stiff cock into her rectum.

'Oh! God! No!' squealed Fiona.

He began to thrust, and his swollen cocktip slammed her colon.

'It hurts up my bum!' cried Fiona.

Her cunt spurted copious come. It trickled down her arse cleft and thighs. Dr Rodd, known as Sandoz in Paraiba, spanked her bottom with his leathery palm, as he bum-fucked her. The enculed girl squealed, yet gasped with pleasure, as the teacher's massive tool filled her rectum.

'Oh! Yes! Do it to me!' she cried. 'Fuck my bum, sir! Split me in two! Give me all your hot creamy spunk up my bumhole!'

Fiona screamed, as Dr Rodd buggered her. Her bum squirmed under his thrusting cock, which slammed her rectum, and emerged, dripping with her arse grease, before penetrating the weeping girl's anus once more. At the same time, Nipringa had her face under the girl's squirming cunt basin, and was sucking her clitty. As she was buggered, Fiona juiced heavily, and Nipringa smiled, with a tiger's leer, while she swallowed all of Fiona's come. Meanwhile, Candi groaned under her buggery from the master's jingling Chinese bells, hammering her rectum.

'I've never known such pain,' Candi said, sobbing. 'But don't stop, master. I am your slave. Please spurt your spunk in my bumhole. It is your bumhole, your possession.'

Her cunt juiced heavily, dripping onto the ochre earth.

The master laughed. 'You bitches always want spunk. When you get a master's spunk, you have power over him. Better, what you get is pain and shame, as all girls deserve.'

'Oh, Master Ruggiero!' cried Candi. 'Please spunk in my hole!'

Ruggiero ripped his tool from Candi's arse, and thrust the engorged organ into her wet cunt. Pushing her face into the ground, he began to fuck her from the rear, in doggy fashion. His belly slapped against her buttocks, as his massive loaded cock jangled in and out of her cunt.

'Ahh! Yes!' Candi gasped. 'Fuck me, master, fuck my cunt. It's never been so wet before.'

Ruggiero's stiff tool plunged into Candi's willing open cunt. His cockmeat filled her pink wet pouch.

There was a growl of a motor-car engine. A Benz with Rio licence plates drew up, and a tall blonde girl, bare-legged, dressed in a powder-blue miniskirt and skimpy blue silk halter top, that scarcely covered her huge breasts, stepped out. Her long blonde mane waved in the breeze, and caressed the nipples, clearly visible under the silk top. She was smoking a cigar, held in the corner of her mouth.

'How interesting,' she said, in a nasal Berlin accent. 'May I join your scene? I see that nudity is acceptable here, so you will not object if I strip off.'

Coolly, she took off her skirt and top. She wore no panties. The newcomer strutted nude, her tan body completely shaven, with a gleaming cunt hillock, and began to masturbate, watching Dr Rodd bum-fucking Fiona. Her fingers squelched in her dripping cunt, as she masturbated, smiling.

'I am looking for Fräulein Serena Sonne,' she said. 'I am Marie-Luise Hammer. Fräulein Serena owes me money. She is bonded to me, and I intend to take her as my slave. Where is the girl?'

'She is in prison,' said Ruggiero. 'She is a miscreant, and is in the cave, sweating. But she is my slave.'

Marie-Luise's nostrils flared. 'You defy me?' she hissed. 'I will not have any mere male defy me.'

She seized a cane, and, as Ruggiero fucked Candi's cunt, began to cane him on the bare buttocks. Ruggiero squirmed, groaning.

'Yes!' cried Ruggiero. 'Go on! I'm coming! Yes!'

'Give me your spunk, master,' begged Candi.

Ruggiero whimpered, as the German girl flogged him on the bare arse, and he spurted into Candi's cunt, filling her with his spunk.

The nude Marie-Luise, breasts quivering, turned to Dr Rodd, fucking Fiona. 'You are another arrogant male,' she said.

Vip! Her cane lashed the male's bare arse.

'Ah!' he squealed.

Vip!

'Ohh!'

Vip!

'God! I'm coming! Ahh . . . yes!'

Fiona wanked herself to orgasm, come pouring from her lips, as Dr Rodd's spunk filled her anus.

'This is interesting,' said Marie-Luise. She picked up the number-five dildo, and quickly strapped it to her waist. 'I want this luscious black girl,' she said. 'Bend over, slut.'

Nipringa obeyed, licking her lips. The German girl began fucking her in both cunt and arse, with the prong of the dildo fucking her own cooze. Come trickled down the German girl's golden thighs, as Nip wanked her own clit.

'*Ach, ja,*' Marie-Luise groaned, as she came to orgasm, her cunt pouring come down her thighs.

Nip grunted, as she wanked herself to a climax. Marie-Luise withdrew her strap-on dildo from Nip's body.

'Now it is your turn,' she snarled at Dr Rodd.

Nip held Dr Rodd down, twisting his arms behind his back. Squealing, he opened his buttocks, and Marie-Luise began to bugger him with the sculpted dildo. The wood entered his anus.

'Oh! God, no, it hurts!' he cried.

'It is what males deserve,' hissed the German girl.

Her buttocks thrust, filling the male's rectum with tulipwood. Dr Rodd's cock stood rigid, as he was buggered by the girl.

'Ohh ... ohh,' he moaned.

A bead of spunk appeared at his peehole, and then he jetted his full cream into the ochre earth.

Ruggiero crouched, buttocks presented, before Marie-Luise. 'Please,' he whined.

'You will bring me my slave Serena,' Marie-Luise commanded.

'Of course. Just do me, I beg you. Please fuck me in the arse, miss.'

The German girl mounted the boy, got the dildo into his anus, and began to bugger him. Her breasts bounced, as her cunt basin slammed over Ruggiero's arse.

'Yes,' Ruggiero groaned, writhing under buggery. 'It's so good. You're bursting me, miss. Go on, go on.'

Like Dr Rodd, Ruggiero spurted under the girl's buggery.

'Now bring me the bitch Serena,' panted Marie-Luise Hammer.

Ruggiero went to the cave, and brought back Serena, and the former master, who sat glumly in the dirt, while the two German girls embraced.

'You ran away, my love,' said Marie-Luise, 'and I had to come all the way to Brazil to find you.'

'Please forgive me,' moaned Serena.

'After you've taken pink,' ordered Marie-Luise. 'Bend over, with your face in the dirt.'

Serena obeyed. Marie-Luise lifted her cane. Vip! Vip! The wood lashed Serena's naked buttocks in brisk fire, and Serena sobbed. Her flogged bum squirmed, as Marie-Luise whipped her to 34 strokes, blatantly masturbating her engorged clitty as she flogged. When Marie-Luise threw down her cane, she crouched between Serena's thighs, and licked her cunt, while Nip sat on Serena's face, pissing in her hair, until Serena squealed in orgasm under Marie-Luise's tonguing.

'Why do you girls let males have control?' snapped Marie-Luise, licking her lips of Serena's come.

'Yes, girls,' said Candi. 'We wear the pink. We are buggered and whipped and shamed. But we can fuck, with the tulipwood dildos. Why shouldn't the men wear the pink?'

Ruggiero laughed. 'A man, wear pink?' he guffawed.

'Why not?' murmured Nip.

In an instant, the males were pinioned by naked females, and forced to don pink girls' swimsuits.

'Now you look much nicer,' said Marie-Luise, with her arm around Nip's waist, while Candi and Jacqui exchanged kisses and wanks. Their fingers caressed their juicing cunts.

'We are the mistresses,' Nipringa said, 'and you males are our slaves. Here are the canes for our naked bottoms. You will use them without fail, whenever we are naughty, for naughty girls must be punished on the bare.'

'Yes, mistress,' chorused the males, preening in their pink swimsuits.